QUETZAL

DAVID S. WELLHAUSER

GNOSTIC DEMENTIA PRESS

Copyright, 2020 by David S. Wellhauser.
All rights reserved.
Gnostic Dementia Press,
Guelph, Ontario, Canada
ISBN: 9798691618871
https://www.davidswellhauser.com/

CONTENTS

JOIN MY INFERNO CLUB

Join my 'Inferno Club' to get news, an Advance Reader Copy of a new release, and future book ideas.

It's completely free to sign up and you will never be spammed by me, you can opt out easily at any time.

Follow the link below to join the party!

http://eepurl.com/dynHzH

1

───────

NIGHT BIRDS

"THE GRATE'S been left off again," Zavala said, stepping around the steel mesh cover.

"Komodo's hungry." Zhenli placed a hand over the manhole's lip. A pungent, baked smell twisted from Bornler's exposed sewer. Komodo was more than a sewer system, if the rumors were true. Zavala pushed against the alley wall: moldering, peeling posters from the previous summer still visible beneath the decay. The alley was papered with these down to the stage door of Chin's Review. Many sons of the rich still came here for the entertainment they could not risk in the other districts.

"You should keep out of that," Zavala's voice cracking, but not with the years. These hung heavy on him. That morning, checking out of the shelter, six blocks over, Zavala caught sight of himself in the polished chrome behind the reception desk. Even the shower and shave had not saved him from the truth. The lines on his face were deep and the whites of his eyes jaundiced. Through these ran thick, red veins. Zavala had wanted to stick out his tongue, but that would have exposed more truth.

For the betters, truth was fine. Not having to live against the fact of Bornler gave them a cushion from Zavala's facts they would not have wanted any part of. That's not what the ruined old man thought, but it was an approximate translation of his despair. Truth was the province of those free of hunger and violence. Zavala wondered if they believed in none of the gods or the God filtering down from the northern empires because they might end up paying for their crimes. If retribution waited for them, their lives would be different.

Deeper concerns for the godless sorts troubled Zavala when he was sober or opioid free. The old faiths would return them until they got it right. Contempt and villainy were the opposite of getting it right. Back they would be, and out here in Bornler with the other failures. Were they right; was it this and nothing else? Maybe. Probably. When Zavala thought about this, when he had the time and energy to drag up his year at the provincial college before the cloud appeared on campus, taking him along when it left. Deep decades ago that was — and he had not been much of a student. If Zavala had been any kind of scholar, he would have gone to one of the three capital universities.

One reason he came to the capital had been to see about night classes. This was not the reason he told himself when a surge of honesty took him. On those occasions, it was because he could not face his father. The opioids only became a real problem after... "There's nothing down..." Not finishing, Zhenli pulled back and rolled away from the manhole.

"What?" edging further from the Komodo.

"Something moved," a hand to his face. Zavala and Zhenli had been together, in the beginning for the alliteration, in the years that had passed since... Had it been years? Zavala was uncertain. Three springs he could remember; beyond his memories did not go.

Long-term memories remained solid, but the memories since arriving in the capital were fluid. Memory had not ceased playing its part, but this was no longer certain. If the memories had been narrative asides, they would have been less of a problem. How, though, does an aside feed an empty belly? How does an aside staple a sphincter torn from a night's shelter under the overpass? If memory and life were only stories, there would not have been a problem.

Memories were more... "The Komodo's waking." Zhenli rose to his knees.

"Does it smell?" Zavala stepped to the hole. Chin's stage door banged against the wall.

"Get off me," a woman screamed. Zavala and Zhenli pushed back behind an overflowing dumpster. In back of this, the metal had rotted away. Through this, rats, cats, and cockroaches gained access. One of the latter ran over Zhenli's foot. Snapping this, the cockroach flicked from the toe, arching over the heads of the young man and woman. He, little over twenty, trotted a few steps behind her: all dyed, poofed hair with black roots where it parted at the center. A plastic overcoat covered a halter with a wide belt over a tight mini and torn leggings. He saw the insect pass above and between them.

"What..." stopping at an argument coming from the roof of the building opposite Chin's; hearing the same exchange, the woman wheeled, catching sight of Zavala and Zhenli. Screaming, she staggered back on stilettos, spilling into the street, knocking over two empty bins.

"Petr..." voice ending in a woof of air.

"Mala?" Petr turned from the roof where the shouts had exploded into rage. Running to the fallen young woman, he passed the dumpster, not seeing Zavala and Zhenli. "Are you okay?" taking Mala's hand.

A scream came from the sky. Mala and Petr froze. Zavala and Zhenli sensed what was happening. Stepping from the dumpster to catch the end of the night bird's song as it fluttered to a hard landing on the stage manager's Asian import. The windows exploded, and the roof crumpled. That end of the alley was dark, so they could not see the breed of night bird it had been, but there were only two kinds in Bornler. The betters not having the coin for the actress then the more common birds Zavala and Zhenli came across every few weeks. Before they could tell which it was, Mala was screaming, pulling Petr after her.

"We should..." not resisting.

"Come on. You want no part of that...I don't...let's get..." Not finishing, she yanked Petr so hard he stumbled into her. The pair tipped one over the other onto the street. It was late, too late for there to be any foot traffic on the side street. Chin's Review faced one of the few trafficked roads of Bornler, but drivers knew to keep from the lesser arteries. When the young couple picked themselves up, they left the night bird to Zavala and Zhenli. If they dared not step into the Komodo, desperation had long left carrion squeamishness behind.

Zavala had to teach Zhenli this when the alliteration gag still had legs, but with hunger came courage. Desperation would have been a better choice, but once passed, the first couple of night birds was all it had taken, and Zhenli was as determined and cruel as Zavala. Perhaps more brutal, but that only got the pair in and out faster. Even now, Zhenli ran for the night bird. Zavala had been wary enough to warn him of the Komodo trap, and Zhenli skittered around this. It was uncertain if the missing manhole cover was a trap, but these had been so in the past. Whoever disappeared into the Komodo was not seen again.

Before Zavala could reach the bird, Zhenli was strangling it. Several steps back, Zavala waited for the sharp crack of bone. On instinct, he turned and looked up: leaning over was the outline, against the full moon, of a head and shoulders. "We've been spotted." Zavala pointed.

"There's nothing there," looking from roof to Zavala.

"Get what you can..."

"This one's rich," waving a billfold and a necklace over his shoulders. Next, he took the bird's belt, platform shoes, and heart-shaped glasses with pink lenses.

"Come on," tugging Zhenli by the arm, he allowed himself to be pulled from the alley.

"Pollock," Reina shouted over the bass. She called twice more, holding out the Malacca Flip. Setting the long-stemmed martini glass on the sodden table, the mint leaf slipped beneath the foam of the cherry-colored cocktail. Flopping down in the thin cushioned naugahyde sofa, Reina jostled Pollock in the shoulder. "What are you..." Glancing beneath the table she looked away, rolling her eyes. "You could have taken her to the non-binary," installed two years before, but often used for run-off from the ladies' room and sex. Once the moral panic had subsided, and people became accustomed to the collective void, eyebrows remained in place.

Juan, Zemmoa's owner, had polled users about building one large restroom. Most assumed it did not matter where anyone pissed or shat — after all, women with cups had been joining the men out back since Juan had taken over the space, re-christening it Zemmoa. Before Zemmoa, it had been a warehouse; before that a factory; before that a drug lab; before that the building had been empty for fifteen years. At one point, condemned for multiple code violations, rumor had it money changed hands. There had been issues following the condemnation and resurrection, but these sorted themselves after a slapdash renovation.

Injuries and two disappearances followed the restoration, but more money changed hands, and the police looked the other way. The Safety Commission had bridled and called for an inquiry, tabling this after the commissioner's accident. The problems stopped with the warehouse conversion. Once Juan had taken over, rumored to be fronting for one of the larger Cartels, injuries and disappearances ceased. The problems out back, where a hardcore group of clubbers drank, fucked, and voided, was dealt with by a high-pressure hose and reusable hazmats. Many in the city would do anything for a payday: hosing down *the latrine*, dubbed not a month into its designation, was far from the worst job on offer in Bornler.

The men's and ladies' rooms were still in use; many of Zemmoa's customers continued to prefer binary options. Juan assumed taking the progressive position preferable to living it.

"Come out, Anbessa." The coppery-red head with a wide streak of purple, running from front to back, continued bobbing. Pollock Merino's eyes possessed the distant, loopy expression she had known so well when the two of them experimented with courtship. It was the first non-polyamorous relationship either had in five years. Reina had been faithful for about two months before a night of clubbing, drink, and drugs had ended in an orgy back of Zemmoa, beyond the latrine and run-off. What counted for beyond was a tall cedar fence separating Zemmoa from a bankrupt parking garage. The second and third floors of the three story structure were used for squatting, but the first floor had been designated for impromptu orgies. Impromptu was questionable for it had been supplied with mattresses, sofas, and a variety of inflatables. Dotting the floor were used condoms and abandoned sex toys.

It was not the orgy that had ended Reina and Pollock, but where it happened. Even though she presented him with a doctor's certificate declaring her free of STDs, Pollock remained unconvinced, since these could be purchased from several pharmacies that had sprung up around Zemmoa to service the clubbers when forethought failed. With the zemmoans, as the regulars had come to be called, this was the norm.

Pollock groaned as he finished and Anbessa crawled from beneath the table adjusting her skirt and brushing her knees clean of cigarette butts, empty wrappers, and club grit. From her purse, Anbessa pulled a wet-wipe and scrubbed a sticky patch on her right knee.

Having managed the worst of this, she dropped the wipe into an empty traveler. Leaning over the cup, Anbessa puckered and let fly with Pollock's plug. Hitting the inside of the cup with a muted smack, the traveler teetered and righted itself. Anbessa, taking a napkin from her purse, ran this over her tongue before stuffing it in the cup then placed the traveler on the empty table next to them. Reina watched as she touched up her lipstick. How many times in Zemmoa had she done the same: at tables, the non-binary, the latrine, and next door? With care, she placed her fingers to her eyes and pressed, attempting to relieve the eye strain.

Pulling back her hair into a loose ponytail, Reina watched Anbessa take Pollock's hand, the grip absentminded as they scanned those moving by the table. Pollock was good for half a dozen orgasms before the end of the night and maybe three more in a singing room. He was one of the more energetic lovers Reina had outside of professionals. The only drawback was his compact penis. Pollack, always the gifted amateur, worked around the natural disability with inventive positions and vaginal metaphysics. For this reason, Reina's infidelity was not physical in origin. There was a malaise at the center of the relationship she could not identify, nor did she trust the answers of traditionalists and reactionaries — no matter the stripe.

If Catholicism and Islam had been morally harsh, the latter reaching for the surgical prophylactic, the feminista Wiccans, founded on the back of a Late Empire nudist flagellant, were little better...if morally elastic. Wicca had no problem embracing progressive ethics but shied from the open practice. Reactionaries came in many varieties: from those campaigning against the practices to those embracing the theory, if not the fact. As always, there was what was said and what was done. The gap, the French deified within impenetrable tomes of textual obfuscation, was frustrating. If the reactionaries said one thing while keeping the rent boy on the side, the progressives said the other without following through. Beta males and females filled the latter's ranks.

Low testosterone drove the wedge between her and Pollock. For all his glorification of the sex act, there was little male in him. There were no displays of aggression, dominance, assertiveness, protectiveness, hierarchy, and all the small gestures of toxicity women and the binary challenged were no longer to accept. Privately, they all hungered to be dominated, loved, and protected. There were limits to this. No one wanted to be burqaed, raped, or abused, but there was something to be said for the alpha version of sex and family. This was all theory. Reina did not know how she would react if courted by an alpha. Secretly, Reina doubted she would ever learn.

Looking about the tables and dance floor, there were no alphas in sight, not that they would not have been welcomed. The non-binary, most particularly, longed for the ragged edges of toxicity but were frustrated by toxic binarism. Zemmoan men were not toxic, which was what they were not to be. Zemmoan men were polite, kind, retiring, feminist, submissive, female led, and uninteresting. Pollock was a good lover, but he was a low testosterone feminista with nothing Reina longed for. That was why she had betrayed him, why she had returned to promiscuity and polyamorous conservatism.

"Where have you been?" Pollack asked, not finding anyone of interest at hand. Still holding Anbessa's hand, he reached for the Malacca Flip.

"Next door," loudly enough that Anbessa heard. Leaning from the thin-cushioned sofa, cocking a penciled eyebrow.

"Why didn't you tell us? We'd have..."

"Met some guy who wanted to try it out." From her purse, Reina pulled a small flask and up-ended this. The smoky mezcal burned on the way down, leaving a chili pepper and chocolate aftertaste. Pollock reached for the flask, but Reina turned it upside down, giving it a shake — empty.

"Pig," the beta cat voice Reina had once loved.

"Get me a refill, and I will share," handing him the leather-bound aluminum flask.

Taking this, he disappeared toward the bar on the other side of the dance floor. "Where were you?" Anbessa asked.

"Next door at the carpark, like I told you." Anbessa leaned back, rolling her eyes.

"Fine, if you don't want to tell me or you don't want him to know," motioning toward the bar and Pollock, "I will play along."

"Where is Rolando and Ava?"

"Last I saw, they were dancing."

"There they are," pointing to the side exit. As Anbessa spoke, Pollock was pushing through the throng beside the dance floor waving the flask over his head; in his other hand, he had a bottle of mezcal. Anbessa waved at Pollock, pointing to Rolando and Ava. Understanding, he collected them with a low swoop. Ava resisted until she saw the mezcal. Looping about Pollock, she snatched at the agave. Ava had the worst drinking problem in the posse. At nineteen, she was the youngest. Reina was a full five years older — Ava, though, could have passed for a hard thirty while Reina not much more than twenty in the club.

When the group first met Ava, she was by far the most beautiful. Her long black hair, thick and shiny, reached the base of her spine. Ava's eyes had been clear and healthy. Now, the hair was no longer shiny; the eyes no longer clear; the skin, once soft and unblemished, sagged. Her belly, though still beautiful, showed signs of becoming potty. Most zemmoans had not yet taken notice of what the drugs and alcohol were doing to her.

Ava, from one of the better families in the city, had not had an easy life. Her father, before he died, had been distant with her and abused her mother. Ava's brother, whom she loved, had been a stranger to her since being sent away to boarding school, after this to the military, meeting again only after his service. Her mother, to deal with the physical and sexual abuse, had become an alcoholic years before. When her father died, her mother retreated into the bottle. And when her brother returned, to take over the family business, Ava had been swallowed by the somnambulant cloud of alcohol and drugs.

Soon after Harold returned, he announced his engagement to the daughter of an impoverished patrician family. Although Harold insisted Ava remain at home, she no longer felt comfortable there with a woman she did not know well and liked less. There were arguments, threats, tears, and broken crockery. To Ava, it appeared Harold was picking up where their father left off. She did not believe he would become abusive. However, there was a strong feeling he would become the same patriarchal humanist. Ava was uncertain what she meant by patriarchal or humanist; it was one of the many terms she heard at the women's meetings she attended after papa's death and the disintegration of her mother.

When Ava developed a functioning definition of patriarchy, though phantasmagorical, she applied this to any man or non-binary leaning toward toxic masculinity. Still young, these tirades did not bother the men and non-binaries — as long as she would do whatever it took to help them reach completion.

None assumed Ava long for the world; many zemmoans believed she would burn out within a year, two if lucky. Harold had often attempted to get her help. Whenever committed to hospital, however, Ava used her charm to escape. Her stays were never long enough to dry out. Harold had attempted to strangle her trust fund, but the lawyers that set up the trust had not expected the need to control the younger Diez. When Harold's wife, though, became pregnant, his interest in Ava plummeted.

Harold loved her, wanted the best for her, and attempted to do what he could through doctors, lawyers, and mental health voodoo. None of it was good enough. On her own, for over a year, Ava had descended into drink and drugs with a ferocity frightening even the most hardcore zemmoan. Rolando, though, loved Ava all the more for the damage and perhaps because she was not long for the world. A happy man, with a good life, a good education, and a good career, Rolando enjoyed the waif's nihilism. He did not wish her harm, but he did not want Ava better. If cured, he supposed the sex would become pedestrian. As it stood, the sex was the best he had ever had.

The zemmoans embraced Rolando because he was funny, sensitive, and had connections in city government. It was rumored, by Pollock, Rolando also had federal connections. There was no evidence of this, but given they were zemmoans, it was unlikely any would experience a direct connection to the federals. It was not that their group was chaste. Depravity was writ large and scored upon the hearts, minds, and souls of each member. The zemmoans had not started out this way. At university, they were committed to a better world through justice and peaceful demonstration. This did not long survive graduation. Quickly, it had become about sensation and escapism. It turned out the world did not want to be saved. Each generation discovers this for themselves.

The zemmoan posse's response to the discovery was alcohol, sex, drugs, and nihilism. All became narrative; all became dream; all became filmic. Rolando never embraced this reality — this narrative. Their great hanger-on was little more than a tourist. By day, he was part corporate lawyer and part criminal stooge, enabling the great perversion that was the South. Flopping on the sofa next to Anbessa, Rolando kissed her cheek, glancing at Reina. "Hey my beauty, where d'you get to?" Reina sighed.

"I've been here." Anbessa scanned the room. Though late, many tables were filled and the dance floor choked.

"I'm bored." Rolando pulled out a cigarette.

"This is Zemmoa. It is the definition of boredom. Isn't it why we are all here?" Anbessa said.

"What should we do?" Rolando exhaled a thick plume of smoke.

"Cancer is not a chichi way to die," Reina sniped. In response, Rolando blew a plume of smoke in her direction. She popped him hard in the arm.

"I repeat, what should we do?"

"Chin's Review," Reina said.

"The last show finished hours ago," Pollock observed.

"I thought, since we're already blasted, we might play dress-up."

"It has the advantage of never being tried before — by us." Rolando did not appear enthusiastic.

"How do we get in?" Ava asked.

"I have a key." Reina produced this from her purse. For another half-hour, they bickered, but Reina had her way. Less because the posse wished to follow her than there was nothing else to do. And if nothing else, Chin's Review had no alcohol in it; no drugs, either. That would add a few hours to Ava's short life. None cared whether the young woman lived or died. What they cared about was being in the immediate vicinity when this occurred. All were known to Harold, and her brother had connections.

Bornler had seen great years. Years of plenty, years of wonder, years of industry, years of dominance. With the Great War, these ended. The end was not abrupt or certain. After the war, there was confusion about the future of industry and who would control it. With the nationalization of industry and the crushing malignancy of national pride, following the Great War, economists, politicians, and the electorate turned in upon themselves. From out of this populism emerged the Great Collapse. Many historians, economists, social scientists, and cultural anthropologists became obsessed with what triggered and sustained the South's Great Collapse. Bornler was the most obvious casualty of the implosion.

Ava's brother, Harold, had studied the Great Collapse, hoping to manipulate the economics of the depressed nation and its geopolitical relationship to the northern empires to help leverage it out of perpetual decline. As far as Ava knew, there was little support for Harold's plan in parliament or industry, both of which were doing well with their connections to one or more of the northern empires. The great political and economic questions were concerned with an East/West divide, but this was fiction. What facts concerning divides there were, though, had always been marshaled along the North/South axis. Racial imperialism fed the fiction of the divide among the northern states and later empires.

When imperial wars and the following frigid peace gave way to new economic prosperity, it was clear the loser had been the southern hemisphere. Bornler was a microcosm of this. There continued in the district remnants of great mansions from the time the South had reached between East and West to siphon off staggering fortunes. The Gothic mansions, the early modern monstrosities, modern functionality, the death of humanism, the collapse of religion offering meaning, purpose, and community, all had a hand in the rise and fall of the city, along with the Southern states. There remained those, such as Harold and a marginal knot of parliamentarians, that cocooned their investments, wealth, and families.

These were no one-percenters, in relationship to the northern states and the informal empires that grew from them; these individuals (business leaders and politicians) were little more than affectations. Bornler with its fragmentary cobbled streets, ruined mansions, desperate hangers-on, faded dreams, and the festering nightmare of the Komodo refusing to permit the city to rest easy in its precipitous psychological, economic, and social collapse. True, emigration was at an all-time high. True, there were more old people and criminals than young entrepreneurs. True this and more. Bornler, experiencing en masse evacuations, had been hollowed out. The Komodo traps expressed the desperate need festering in the mythic cavities expanding beneath the city.

It was unknown by the remaining Bornlerites, zemmoans, or the great in their rickety halls of power what was happening in the Komodo. Also, there was no clear designation for the Komodo. Sometimes it was *the* Komodo, sometimes Komodo or Modo. If Harold was correct, the source for this information, the questionable competence and memory of Ava Diez, not even the well-positioned and wealthy, who controlled much of the government, were clear about what was happening beneath their city streets. In effect, if not fact, the Komodo was a world apart. Disappearances in Bornler were blamed on the Komodo.

That said, the evening found the five friends tripping through the side streets between Zemmoa and Chin's Review, passing the vanishing mezcal between them. Reina had wanted to go to Chin's Review to keep Ava from another vicious, drunken episode. But now she was leaning over the remnants of a railing, all baling wire and rust, expelling what little food she had taken for dinner. The episode passed, and Ava was once again back with the posse. Reina looked about the street and breathed. "Do you smell that, Rolando?" Stopping in the middle of the street, putting his hand on the back of his hips, he inhaled. Rolando Seifert was tall, at six foot two inches, but slender and effete in manner. This effeminate quality disguised the fact he was a patriarch of toxicity. With eyes and hair a black that was a kindness to the void, Rolando had smooth skin with a light dusting of rich black hair on the backs of his hands and well up his forearms.

Though not muscular, Rolando was toned from a five day a week regimen at the gym. The goal had always been stamina rather than bulk. His skin, thanks to an Iberian past, had a gentle olive complexion. He insisted there was none of the Moor in him. Rolando was utterly European in sensibility; where this would have embarrassed others, to Rolando, it was an affirmation. He was the ultimate stooge. For all these qualities, reprehensible to most, he also possessed a sense of humor and a bent compassion making him a fit for the zemmoan posse. The zemmoans were persuaded they were all racist. Most assumed an Iberian or North Atlantic heritage. Rumors abounded of a distant mestizo connection, but in the hearts of each, this was an anxious nod to the South's troubled past. The posse, while admitting to a genetic xenophobia, were not proud of the fact. Rolando attempted to hide it, but he was certain, whatever the others were, he was European; he was Iberian.

"The Komodo," Rolando pulled a folding blade from his back hip pocket. Snapping this open, he stepped to Reina and the others clustering about Ava.

"It means nothing," Pollock said.

"That's true — most of the time." Anbessa pulled a nail file from her purse. Reina smirked at the file. If there were komodoans about, they would have laughed at Anbessa, reducing her to an appetizer. Over the last weeks, perhaps months, the Komodo had become a fret. While the labyrinth had been diverting, inspiring political lyricists and poets, now the narrative had gained mainstream support.

Online and print were carrying front-page stories of the Komodo, where it had once only published in the strange and unusual sections. The Komodo was also given substance through unnamed police and government sources. On her better days, Reina thought this absurd; now she was not so certain. "It's coming from the alley," Pollock said, stepping across the street to the rear of Chin's Review. The others followed, Anbessa and Rolando steadying Ava.

"Iktan," Ava called Reina, using her nickname.

"What?" Reina's tone sharp; when the young woman did not answer, she turned. Ava was pulling back from Anbessa and Rolando. Her sallow face approaching ashen. "Are you okay, kid?"

"It smells terrible."

Releasing Ava, Rolando followed Pollock into the alley then

staggered out. Halting beside two upended bins, he vomited. "What do we do?" Pollock wiped his mouth, suppressing a belch.

"Get..." Three police cruisers turned the corner. Rolando folded his blade, tossing this to the gutter.

"I am Rolando Seifert," raising his hands. Ignoring him, the uniforms ran down the alley. The police found Pollock at the end of this, past the stage manager's ruined car. Before the zemmoan was the night bird. The glasses, platform shoes, billfold, and identification were all gone.

"You sick fuck," a baton swung toward Pollock's head, stepping aside the baton connected with the foot of the night bird pinioned to the decaying, wrought iron fence enclosing a small, abandoned garden. With a quiver, the body collapsed.

"I didn't do this," Pollock held up his hands.

2
———

THE QUETZAL EFFECT

"Get up. Do you hear me? Get up." The woman threw the blanket back, slapping the sleeping man. Naked, he turned over; she rolled her eyes. "There's a call for you."

"Who's calling, pumpkin?" running a hand down his chest toward his belly, both chest and belly thick with black hair. The chest was barrel, the abdomen was softening, and a small amount of fat had collected above the hips.

"Captain Slank." Leaning against the windowsill, she lit a cigarette, looking across the street. Swinging his legs from the bed, he sat up, taking his head in his hands. "Whiskey?"

"What?" looking up. "French brandy." Stepping over to the window, he leaned down. She turned away, and he snatched the cigarette from her fingers.

"Fuck you," pulling her hair back into a hair tie. Drawing on the cigarette, he stared out the window. Their condo was on the west-side, near the west-end of the core. Charles and Ramira had been here for about a year and a half. The move had meant to be a fresh start. The fresh start felt more like a sepulcher. Ramira had gone from disaffected to bitter to hostile over the eighteen months on the west-side. Though poorer, they had been happier on the south-side.

Charles had been happier; Ramira had complained less. Ramira's happiness had been a mystery. In the beginning, she appeared content, but over the course of their five-year marriage, this changed.

Charles was uncertain when the change had begun. Though he first experienced the complaining on the south-side, this focused around the quality of the apartment. In response, they found a condo on the west-side near the core to be closer to the office. However, the better condos were in the suburbs. These were newer, with superior specs. The disagreement over where on the west-side to settle triggered their first major fight. Ramira had even threatened to return to her mother's. Charles thought Ramira might do this but for two reasons: first, she hated her mother, and second, the old woman lived seven hundred miles to the South.

According to Ramira, Gemma Sanchez was a harridan. Charles had not seen it that way. When he met Gemma, she was not only charming, but more attractive than Ramira. The flesh, at forty-eight years, was not as firm as Ramira's, but she had taken care of herself. Even after four children, two boys and two girls, you could crack an egg on her ass. Noticing the attraction, the following fight should have been a red flag.

Still, the first year of marriage had been good. By the end of this, there had been talk of children. This had surprised Charles, for when they first dated, Ramira had been adamant about not wanting any. In the beginning, he had not been interested in marriage. Having only been promoted to CID Inspector, Charles wanted to focus on his career. After a few months of dating, however, he was transferred to the capital. His closure rate had been higher than anyone else in the provinces. This would have been enough to bring him to the attention of the provincial government, but after cracking the case of a northern pedophile ring, his name was mentioned in parliament.

Afterward, there was no choice but to bring Charles to the capital to deal with a crime wave. Upon learning of this, Ramira launched a campaign both obvious and brazen, announcing she was reconsidering her position on children. Charles had also learned the capital police force preferred their investigators and ranking officers settled. Either Charles found someone else, or he had to go with Ramira. A beautiful woman at twenty-three, there was little to warn him off. Charles assumed, at the beginning of the relationship, Ramira was establishing boundaries.

Charles was certain he loved her. To be *certain* is to experience the emotion. Whether it lasted was beside the point. He *thought* he loved her, so he loved her. Practical, Charles assumed knowing a thing was the beginning and end of any argument. It was not that he did not understand emotional knowledge but preferred reason. This had not saved him from a fraught relationship. Ramira had taken the pair of them to highs and lows he had never known. Growing up, his parents, both science teachers, had privileged reason and proof. What had been surprising, to many, was both were classic liberals.

Samuel and Leticia had always been moderate in their political and economic views. In itself, this was unusual, having grown up during the Great War and the collapse that chased them throughout the rest of their professional careers. Samuel, however, invested a small inheritance, from a distant uncle, in a northern stock exchange. Though no great sum, the investment had flourished and provided his parents with a comfortable retirement in the nation's reduced circumstances. With the Great Collapse, the country's economy had not so much imploded as stumbled, reducing the condition of the majority without destroying the nation's political order.

Revolutions, or the threat of these, emerged and collapsed often over the course of Charles' life. Samuel and Leticia, nonetheless, had and continued to have an easy retirement. His father would turn seventy in two years, while Leticia would turn sixty in another three. The difference in their ages was not great, but his mother had been honest with Charles after his first failed romance at fifteen. Telling her son she had not married Samuel for love but friendship and security. Love came later. This was helped by a sensible attitude to money and a benign paternalism. It had not hurt the inheritance came through after their vows. Charles often wondered, though he had not asked, whether Mother had fallen in love with Samuel's practicality or inheritance.

Raised to be sensible, anything interfering with his commitment to order disturbed him. Life with Ramira, however, was everything he had grown up avoiding through the example of his parents. But they were married: the deed done, papers signed, die cast. If Ramira, sometimes, supposed they should end the marriage, Charles was not prepared to entertain the idea. They attempted counseling, but this was only an opportunity for Ramira to spend an hour screaming.

After the fact, the sex was always great. The problem was Ramira saw sex as an opportunity to exhaust the confusion, frustration, and anger preceding it. To Charles, her concept of sex and love were strategies of avoidance. Ramira was not a foolish woman. She had not attended university, but that was the norm, except for the upper classes. Gemma and Leticia were neither. Though not destitute, as many in the rural south, their situation became complicated after the death of her father. Only years later did Charles enter their lives.

If there was much to regret in the marriage, Charles was certain he owned as much blame as Ramira. He had married her to advance his career. That their life had not been all she may have wished for, it was better than the life she would have had with Gemma. Charles supposed Ramira had forgotten how fragile her situation had been. Why she was unhappy, now, had more to do with how those native to the capital treated them. Provincials were looked down upon. It did not matter that Charles possessed a Master's in Criminology; he was a provincial. Because of this, they were treated, Ramira was treated, poorly. Charles, successful in his career, however, had absorbed the insults. Ramira had not.

"Hello, captain?" Charles said, staring at Ramira. Sitting on the couch, legs crossed, and twitching a foot. With another cigarette in her mouth, making a show of not looking at her husband.

"Yeah, what's up?" Slank asked.

"Heavy night."

"Ramira at it again?"

"It's my day off, captain," Charles sighed.

"We've a bit of a bother in Bornler."

"Big district, where exactly?"

"Chin's Review — the alley behind."

"This is a CID matter?"

"There may be a Komodo angle." Turning from Ramira, he cradled the phone in his shoulder.

Picking up a notepad and felt marker, Charles took down the details. There were few. Those Slank had, he shared. The details ruined a day that had already begun badly. "That it?" Hanging the phone up, Charles turned to Ramira.

"Let me guess, no therapy today?" Jamming the cigarette butt into the saucer beside her coffee, swearing beneath her breath.

"You can yell at me next week."

"I've never needed an excuse to yell at you, hit you, spit on you, or any of the other things you like me to do."

"Aren't you getting that backwards, pumpkin?" Ramira leaned forward on the sofa, propping her elbows on her knees, cocking an eyebrow.

"Careful now..."

A quarter of an hour later, Charles was at the door, crockery still flying. Turning, coat over his right shoulder while he adjusted the holster of his Heckler & Koch. "Ramira...Ramira, get out here," placing a hand on his tactical baton. At such times, Charles had to remind himself he loved the Southerner.

"What?" the natural husk in her voice breaking high.

"No more hysterics," snapping open the tactical baton.

"Keep threatening me and I'll believe you won't use it."

"Don't believe you are safer than I am. Now, listen," taking a step forward, pointing the steel tip at her.

Folding her arms, she looked away. This was as close as Ramira came to submission. "Go to the therapist; take the time for yourself."

"I don't need..." She didn't finish, throwing her right foot out and grinding the heel into the carpet's tight weave.

"We both need something; I don't know what..." Ramira looked at him. Folding the baton, he slipped this into its case on his hip.

"Goodbye."

"Will you be home for dinner?" Ramira stepped about the remains of their second-best China.

"There's been an incident in Bornler."

"That's a no, then?"

"I don't know; there's talk of a Komodo angle, but I won't know until I get there." Ramira went white.

It took a lot to make a Southerner pale, but Ramira was proving she was as fair as any of the northern women who looked down on her. They did not look down on Charles. Ramira was certain more than one of them had tried to take him from her. Charles had attempted to dissuade her of this, but his attempts to comfort her only made Ramira suspect him the more. Or worse, perhaps he wanted to leave. If one or the other of them were to leave, Ramira needed to be the first out the door. But the Komodo put this all to the side. Taking her husband by the upper arm, she pushed up on her toes and kissed him. "Be careful," the words little more than a breath.

Bornler, especially the side streets and minor arteries, did not experience much traffic. Chin's Review was one of the few businesses on the east-side that still attracted attention. Even so, the parking lot across the street from the main entrance was usually only half-full. This evening, though, the side street near the alley behind the Review was choked with vehicles. All belonged to the city: police, emergency services, fire department, and three municipal SUVs parked near the end of the circus and closest to Chin's Review. There appeared to be three plain-clothes officers functioning as minders for the politicos.

The latter were not in evidence. Charles closed the door of the department supplied car, an aging Korean import, rusting about the left front tire. The transmission had been rebuilt three times and the rear axle replaced six weeks before. For three months, the department had promised to replace the car. Their excuse for not doing so was as valid as any: budget. Resting his arms on the roof,

Charles looked about the street. No police cordon had been set up. Perhaps it was felt no one in Bornler would be foolish enough to show up or announce they had seen what happened.

"Inspector Lane?" a voice from two cars down.

"Yes," turning, he stopped; the woman's face was ashen with a tincture of khaki green. Charles had seen her around CID a few times but had exchanged only peremptory greetings. Charles thought she was one of the deputy mayor's assistants.

"We're down here," pointing to the alley before buckling over and retching.

"Are you all right?" Charles locked his door and stepped forward.

"Yeah," wiping a handkerchief across her mouth.

"You are here with the deputy mayor?" She nodded, taking his hand.

"Sorry, I've never been to a crime scene before. Are they all like this?"

"I suspect this is worse than usual — otherwise they'd not have called me in on my day off." Charles put an arm around her shoulders, and either she was too afraid to be offended or did not care. Working for the deputy mayor, Charles supposed she had grown used to offense. Insults may have been the least of it. The mayor and deputy mayor, and many high level staffers and key supporters, had a long and ugly reputation. If it had been anyone else but politicos, Charles would have been asked to investigate.

"I've only seen the head."

"Dismemberment?" She nodded. "You're Ada Trantor?"

"I've heard of your memory."

"Where's your boss, Alistair Bun?"

"He's giving an interview around the corner; the police aren't allowing the media near the crime scene." Pointing down the street, her hand shook.

"Doesn't look like the police have set up a cordon," speaking to himself.

"Deputy Mayor Bun did not believe it necessary, as long as he kept the media in front of the Review."

"The deputy mayor is in charge of the investigation?"

"As I understand it, that's your job. However, you weren't here; there were no ranking officers here at all. None of the constables appeared to know what to do or who was in charge. There was also an argument between the police and fire departments about who was responsible for what. Then there was a disagreement about whether anyone should be sent into the Komodo." Holding Ada at arm's length, Charles stared at her.

"They didn't..." She shook her head.

"Alistair wouldn't allow anyone down until the chief investigator arrived. I don't think he wants the responsibility for what may happen."

"Cruz, Ortiz, Ramos — get over here." Charles waved at three uniformed officers standing outside the alley passing a bottle in a brown paper bag back and forth. Cruz dropped the bag behind him; there followed the sharp sound of breaking glass. It was going on 10 a.m., and these fools were already drunk. Either the scene was that bad, or morale was that low. Since coming to the capital, much had changed. The crime wave had been brought under control, but that had exhausted itself by the time he had arrived. Much of it had to do with more foot patrols, community policing, and broader powers of search, seizure, and detention. There were rumors, as well, of extra-judicial flying squads operating out of abandoned warehouses, shuttered factories, and the backs of east-side clubs.

Even if Charles was not responsible for the end of the crime wave, he was touted by both municipal and national politicians as the source of their salvation. The initial result was he rose faster in CID than he had a right to. A backlash followed his rise amongst those with seniority and in the secret flying squads that had done all the heavy lifting and broke all the skulls. Along with the skulls, there were to have been small necropoli littered about the remnants of the industrial zones in the East and South. There were also hints of the desecration of small town and village cemeteries, near the capital, to dispose of bodies when space became tight.

Lionized by politicians and alienated from the police force,

Charles understood how fragile his position within the department was. One misstep, one failure, one angered politician, and he would be finished: not only in the capital but the country. Charles had not been as fortunate as his father. There were no investments to fall back on; there were little enough savings to rely upon. Ramira did not have expensive tastes and was aware their position in the capital was tenuous. However, moving to the west-end had eaten most of their savings. Even if they were to sell up and move back South, they would lose money. Realtors could smell blood and desperation better than any shark.

Charles could grift with the best of them, but there was no better grifter than a realtor for carrying a good lie and spinning this into myth. If the Christ had been a realtor, he would have fared better. The point of this, for Charles and Ramira, was they would not recoup their losses following a misstep. How far behind the collapse of his career would be the end of his marriage? Charles should have cared about this, but he did not. His cell phone buzzed: *be careful — Mira.*

If Ramira was borderline crazy, it was not a genetic accident. If crazy, it was from frustration with her position in the world and the need to rely upon someone superiors or coworkers could destroy. What would she do then? In two years, she would be thirty. What then? Divorced, post-thirty, infamous because of her connection to Charles, and without a means of earning her way in the world. True, she might strike up friendships, but how many years could she do that? Marriage was the safest place for her. If the economy turned around, she could be a waitress, factory worker, housekeeper, or sales clerk. There were other possibilities but not in this world.

The couple's situation was not desperate, Charles was certain of that (Ramira less so), but this business at the end of the alley worried him. If it concerned him, that text from Ramira suggested she was close to panic. When that happened, he was uncertain what he would find back home.

Cruz, Ortiz and Ramos took a little time getting out the police tape and pushing back those not involved in the investigation. Since few were from Bornler, they found most of those being evicted were city employees. There was a level of pleasure in this the three had not expected. If they had known better, they would not have thrown back the politicos, but they did.

"Bad business this, you've heard of the Komodo connection?" Alistair, still holding Charles' hand.

"Captain Slank was concerned."

"No," Alistair leaned in, lowering his voice. "Slank is not worried; to him, this is the death of a no-name zemmoan." Both knew what zemmoan meant. Where the zemmoans would have thought of themselves as the cultural avant-garde, Alastair and Charles saw ruined members of a dying upper class.

Alastair was what remained of the upper-middle-class. He was contemptuous of those beneath him and terrified of those above. Even if depraved, the deputy mayor was not foolish — Charles saw Ramira in the deputy mayor. Trapped by circumstances and having to deal with the underemployed masses and the disinterested upper classes, his choices were limited. "What are we looking at?" Glancing down the alley, several sheets hung before the manhole. Three constables stood before these, armed with shotguns.

"If it were only the death of that creature," pointing past the sheets, "then I would agree with Slank. This is not all we are dealing with — he told you about the Komodo?"

"Only that there is, or may be, a Komodo angle." Alistair dropped the inspector's hand.

"*May be* and *is* are the same thing in politics."

Not for the first time had Charles heard this argument. Since being adopted by city hall and parliament, the inspector had learned there was little difference between maybe and is. Narrative was all — if a thing looked bad, it was worse. If it was worse, they were all dead. Dead, politically dead, was the sum of all evil. Evil for the political class was losing power; evil was the failure of narrative; evil was the bacillus in the body politic. The body politic would not, could not, abide a bad case of the shakes today. *Today* was an infinitely more metaphysical concept than temporal mechanics would have it. Today referred to the political mess the country was in, referred to the economic catastrophe they had lived with for generations.

"Yes sir, I agree. What do you need me to do?"

"We need you to be our man on the force." Alistair, not a large man but portly, rocked back on his heels, hands stuffed deep in his pockets. The thin paisley vest bulged over his abdomen, and the buttons appeared to be straining to hold the world together. If they failed, the politician's viscera would spill over the alley.

"I think I know what you mean."

"Good — you have been around long enough to understand what may and may not be said, what may and may not be attributed to city hall or parliament."

"Mr. Bun, it is true I suspect what is going on and what you need of me. I'm happy to offer that, but it would help if you could be clear."

This was not why Charles had studied crime; this was not why he had gone to university; this was not what Samuel and Leticia had hoped for him. It was bad enough he had disappointed them in marriage. Nonetheless, Charles was stuck with his reputation and his indebtedness to those like Bun. He did not hate the deputy mayor. The inspector, though, would have loved to go after the deputy mayor, mayor, and all their senior staff for what the likes of them were doing to Ada. It did not matter whether she had been willing or unwilling. Charles understood complicity; he was no less complicit in the perversion of justice than Ada.

"Easy peasy: we need this business with the Komodo to end." This was not what Charles had been expecting. Something over-the-top, but this was asking him to debunk a myth: Christ, Shiva, the Great Spirit, Gandhi, Martin Luther, Alexander, Sun Tzu, or Confucius. Charles enjoyed lists more than he enjoyed statistical analysis, more than he enjoyed sex — maybe not that.

"How do you propose I deal with something that does not exist?"

"Prove the Komodo does not exist; prove the deaths are accidental. Take this poor creature at the end of the alley — place the blame for his death, his murder, where it belongs. Take away the stink of the Komodo."

"His friends?"

"Not Harold's sister, Ava Diez."

"The rest?" The deputy mayor shrugged.

"If I can put them in the frame?"

"This is the east-side — you should be able to find many villains to suit your purpose."

The two men shook hands, and the deputy mayor, collecting Ada, took his leave. Charles stepped past the sheets and toward the end of the alley. There he found what he was looking for, and it was a bloody mess.

Daniel Slank was fifty-eight. He had spent thirty-four years in this building. Daniel had come South from the Northwest and never explained what he had been running from. Inquiries had been made, reports filed, interviews held, and bribes accepted. Whatever it was he had been running from had been buried. Daniel had come south when corridors of internationalism still remained. The economy and politics of the country had been damaged, but Daniel had money and connections. Whether the connections were his remained uncertain. Over the thirty-four years, those connections either died of natural causes or found encouragement to remain silent by whatever it was the captain held over their heads.

When young, the captain had been slender, but with a strict regime and diet, Daniel beefed up. The connections then gained for him a position in CID. Fifteen years before, an administration position became available; Daniel had turned it down in favor of remaining in CID. His closure rate had not been as impressive as Charles', but the rate was genuine.

There were many in the division that found Charles' inexplicable rise disconcerting. To Daniel, there was nothing disconcerting about it. Movement in the department had always been a matter of who you knew and expedience. Charles' rise was a byproduct of political need. Being overtaken by municipal and national politics was not the inspector's fault. However, most did not see it that way. Daniel believed all the young inspector need be held accountable for were the cases he solved in the South. This business with the Komodo, though, could be a death sentence for his career. There was reason to believe, given political interference, this could extend beyond career death.

Rumors surrounding the Komodo had always had a flavor of political manipulation — perhaps adventurism. If the first, the Komodo investigation would be a matter of greasing the right palms. With the deputy mayor involved, however, there was a good chance of crossover political agendas: Bun being involved in municipal, provincial, and national politics. What pies Bun did not have his fingers in were of no interest. His goal, as far as Daniel could see, was the mayor's office then an MP's chair. Whether Alastair Bun was interested in becoming the prime minister, he could not be certain. Daniel assumed this would be the goal but was also aware, the further one climbed, the slipperier the pole became.

The deputy mayor was a man of profound contradiction. On one hand, he, the mayor, senior staffers, and major supporters had a reputation as fearsome predators with malignant appetites. There was another hand, this one as contradictory as it was possible to be. Alistair Bun was obsessed with improving the lot of the poor. That said, he was not above taking advantage of a beautiful woman — or teenage girl. Daniel had seen reports, he believed, that suggested the deputy mayor may also have an interest in prepubescents. Did he believe these reports? On days like this, he did. On others, when the deputy mayor and the mayor's office increased his budget, looked the other way when his officers went further than was conscionable, and promised him a free hand, Daniel was less inclined to accept rumors and reports.

Today, Daniel was of the opinion Alistair Bun was first cousin to the antichrist. Not that he had any faith left. Daniel had little faith in people. Not being able to trust them, how does one trust a sky-god? At fifty-eight, though, the captain had taken an interest in what was next. He had been accompanying his wife to church. Catholicism, with its pagan intersections, was filled with rituals that felt nearly erotic. If he did not come away with a deeper sense of faith, the return to church had improved his sex life — not only with his wife. The confessional embraced all manner of sin, scrubbing the soul clean for a few circuits of the cross. Daniel Slank did not believe but wanted to. How could one not believe in a faith that allowed one to speak one's wickedness and be forgiven?

Leaning back in his chair, Daniel spun about looking over Sonando, the city core. The high-rises still stood, but shabbier than they had been only ten years before. Fewer repairs were being made, but the glass still shone even if the stonework was worn. A thin layer of smog cut across the taller buildings. It was a brownish yellow haze that had returned to the city twenty years before with the weakening of pollution laws to lower productivity costs. It had worked; the cost of productivity went down but so did the health of city workers and citizens. However, people still flocked to the cities for employment, entertainment, and to hide. To hide from families, the law, and failed marriages. To hide from this and more.

Everyone was hiding. Daniel was hiding, but after thirty-four years from what? The reason for him to be here was gone. And everyone who had a hand in it was dead or in prison. Still, he stayed. Stayed because his life was here, because his wife was here, because moving, returning, made no sense at his age. Everything he knew was occluded. Blindness was how each of them, Daniel, Alastair, Charles, the mayor, parliament, city hall, and the Komodo, got by. There was a rap at the door. Turning from the window, Daniel pushed from the chair. "Hi, Charles," taking the younger man's hand.

"It's a mess." Charles took the seat the captain offered, his face drawn. Daniel slipped back into his chair and leaned forward, hands crossed upon his desk.

"Have you been to see our guests?" the captain asked.

"After securing the scene and taking control of it from the deputy mayor..."

"What?"

"There was no one down there in charge of the crime scene." Charles detailed his conversation with Ada.

"But it's sorted now?"

"If by sorted, you mean we have control of the scene," the captain nodded, "yes, we do. Cruz, Ortiz, and Ramos are out there and mostly sober."

"Drunk again?"

"And just going on ten."

"I know what you want me to do, but everyone will know where it came from. Do you want any more weight on your name?" Charles shook his head.

"What of those zemmoans in lockup?" The captain tapped his finger on the desk.

"Said Quetzal Martinez, name of the victim…"

"Victim?"

"Preliminary assessment."

"Yours?"

"Originally, yes — but when the corner examined the scene and body, what remained of it, the preliminary finding is now death by suicide, misadventure, or murder."

"Why murder?"

"An actress ," looking at his notes, "by the name of Mala Garcia reported the incident."

"She was with the zemmoans?" Charles shook his head, returning to his notes.

"Mala was with her boyfriend, Petr; they are both actors in whatever extravaganza is playing at Chin's Review. The pair were arguing and heard a noise come from the roof opposite the Review. She is certain they saw two people fighting on this."

"If this Mala and her boyfriend, Petr, were not with the zemmoans, and you didn't pick them up at the Review, how did you find her?" The captain returned to the office window, hands clasped behind his back.

"Mala Garcia made the call anonymously — from her cell

phone." Daniel turned from the window, smiling. "She and Petr saw the fight and fall. An old fashioned murder, maybe accidental death."

"What of Petr?" Daniel leaned on the side of his desk, arms folded.

"We're still looking," Charles stood, flipping through the images on Mala's phone. "Here he is," handing the phone to the captain. Returning this, Daniel nodded.

"Contact Chin's Review and get his information...if you don't have it in the phone."

"It's here, but he's not responding to calls, texts, or social media posts."

"Dead?"

"Could be in the wind," returning the phone to his breast pocket. "We are looking into it. A car is also sitting at his apartment."

"Sort those actors out and deal with the zemmoans. Bun has contacted you?" Charles nodded, and the two men went over the conversation.

3
____

MENDELSSOHN'S INK

"Mites." Twisting around, he bit at his shoulder.

"Steady, or I'll drive the needle into your junk." Dante sat up.

"Amok, I tell you, amok."

"Caspar, calm down." Dante set the needle on the tray beside the ink and pulled off his latex gloves. From the top drawer of the utility cart, he pulled and sparked a blunt. Looking out the window past the neon sign, Mendelssohn's Ink, it had been raining all day. "Here," passing the blunt to Caspar.

"Go on, take it," stretching out his arm and waggling the wrist. Turning from his shoulder, Caspar eyed the blunt then Dante then the blunt. Caspar's eyes were pinpricks in the center of a lunar sphere, pockmarked cheeks peppered with blackheads, active zits and grime overflowing the divots of tissue. The black hair was thin, almost stringy, and receding. There was a large semicircle of hair missing from the front of his head: this suffering a natural secession. Caspar did not appear to be infested. The nose that grew out of the center of the face and appeared tumorous was red, veined, and bulbous.

Irregularly shaped, this gave the appendage a malignant appearance. Broken several times and cut a couple more, the asymmetry of the nose was disturbing. Taken together, the pinprick eyes, the pockmarked cheeks, blackheads, zits, receding hairline, and the Dumbo ears, Caspar made most uneasy. The discomfort Caspar created in others continued beyond the face to the head, which appeared more a celestial satellite than a structural container for navigating the world. His body, strange for a homeless man, was doughy while the legs were spindle thin.

The feet were aquatic flippers that, in the water, would have worked well. On land, these long, broad supplements were clumsy. On more than one occasion, Dante had seen Caspar wandering the streets with his feet wrapped in rags and sometimes paper. No one cared to speculate about Caspar's shoe size. His origins were unknown, but his accent suggested the Northeast. Standing at over six feet, Caspar was imposing but was an emotional child. Many considered him an imbecile, but his only deficit was problem-solving skills. Because of this, finding and keeping work was a challenge. Dante, having known him for years — going back to when his father ran the shop, attempted to find Caspar work where possible. When he could not, Dante tried to give him work around the shop: sweeping, putting orders away, and security when necessary.

Caspar was a physical coward, but his presence limited drunken disturbances. Drunks made up a big chunk of Mendelssohn's business. There were several bars and clubs close by, and Zemmoa was only ten minutes away. An even larger chunk of the business came from zemmoans. He knew most of these by name, and those that had chosen the lifestyle of radical ink, implants, piercings and scarification were close friends. The latter for no other reason than they kept a roof over his head and food on the table. Those choosing the radical lifestyle, he interviewed before beginning a major job.

If the client was looking for a transformation, top of the head to tip of the toes, Dante wanted to be sure they understood what this would mean. Usually, it would be difficult to find work, to find a partner, to maintain friendships. If the interview went well, Dante would begin. These radical transformations could take anywhere from months to years. It would require several consultations over the course of the inking. Also, there was the issue of allergies. There were non-allergic inks, but these were more expensive. The inking would run into half a year's salary for an electrician. Dante loved these jobs. More than the smaller commissions, or walk-ins, these radical inkings were his bread and butter.

Caspar had expressed an interest in getting tattooed frequently. However, two problems prevented this. First, he never had enough money. Often, Dante would turn him down because it would have been a choice between the tattoo and eating. Second, Caspar had a profound aversion to pain and needles. One of the few instances in which Caspar spoke of his childhood was when he explained to Dante the origin of the fear. When a child, he had many illnesses, not least of which was cancer.

The giant spent most of his childhood in pain. Needles were a reminder of this. Eventually, Caspar overcame his fear, and Dante got him in the chair. Perhaps this was because Caspar was distracted by the mites. The blunt, now finished, had helped. As Dante returned to inking the lower abdomen, Caspar continued to glance out the window. Leaning back, placing the needle once more on the tray then wiping the excess ink and blood away, Dante examined his work. "What's wrong?"

"Wrong?"

"First mites, now the window. What's out there?"

"They bite," running a hand over a massive chest.

"There are no bite marks." Dante examined the big man.

"Under the skin, they crawl, they twist, they dig."

"When did this begin?"

"Two days ago, I was down near Chin's Review." Dante nodded. "Something was in the alley." Caspar stopped. A large, meaty hand with sausage fingers went to his face.

"What is it?" taking away the giant's hand.

"I saw Zavala and Zhenli running from the alley...I think there were two actors as well — she was pretty, but I was drunk." When drunk, Caspar thought everything female pretty.

"What happened then?"

"Nothing, I sat across the street for maybe fifteen minutes — maybe longer, I'm not sure."

"But you went over?" Dante asked, pulling two canned beers from the mini fridge next to the utility cart. Passing one of these to Caspar, he cracked the tab and downed the beer. Crushing the can, he tossed this into the garbage across the room.

"Noises were coming from the alley. They were wrong. Never heard noises like that coming from Chin's before. I hid behind the dumpster."

"Yes," when it appeared Caspar had finished.

"There was something at the end of the alley, near the fence. I heard breaking and tearing noises."

"Someone was being hurt?" In Bornler, this was not unusual. Dante had never heard of it occurring around Chin's. The theater was one of the few places the street people left alone because it was a good place to panhandle. Chin's was also good for casual work. Because of this, no one risked pissing off the theater.

"Not hurt — torn and broken...pieces, really. I think it was eating."

"It was eating an animal?"

"Thought so, but then I saw."

"You saw what?"

"I moved closer, to get a better look, and I saw it was eating a man."

"*It?*"

"The thing was bigger and stronger than me, weird shape, and it moved funny. It made no sense, but I think it heard me because it turned." Caspar looked at the fridge, and Dante gave him two more beers. He downed these in quick succession.

"What did it look like?"

"A piece of jaw was sticking out from a hood pulled low over the face. When I saw it knew it was being watched, I ran." Dante leaned back, putting on a new pair of latex gloves.

"Let's finish this." Caspar smiled, a big loopy, baked grin that took his fat lips close to his ears. The teeth exposed were yellowed in places, blackened in others, and two were missing from the smile.

An hour later, finished with Caspar, Dante closed the shop and went upstairs.

His father, Victor, had bought the shop from old man Mendelssohn forty years before. The name was well-respected, and his father had apprenticed under the old man. Mendelssohn's sons had not wanted to go into the business even though, in Bornler, it was one of the safest professions. Competition was low and job security high. Everyone below the middle classes wanted ink, and even those in the middle and upper classes wanted a little — to be transgressive. There were only a few of the middle and upper classes any longer, but those that still existed were hungrier than ever for tattoos.

I am not my parents; I am not the problem; I am with the people.

Dante, as his father, only believed in his family. Victor was a man of few beliefs, few dreams, fewer loves. Victor loved his children and his wife, Lola. Beyond this, Victor only cared for the business. Once he had even opened a second shop near what was now Zemmoa. He remained certain Bornler could support a second shop. There were a few tattoo studios in Bornler; there was even one on the west-side and another on the north-side. Though problematic, tattoos were common enough to make owning a studio, maybe two, worth the investment. The second studio, however, had not fared well. Management and employee issues plagued Victor. Then there was the black economy.

Since Victor could not pay his artists as well as they thought their due, many took on side jobs. This would not have been bad if they had not been using the old man's ink, needles, and studio. It reached a point where he either had to close the shop or make Dante manager. At fifteen, Dante was qualified but lacked management experience. Although reluctant to close the studio and put his artists out of work, Victor had no choice. It was from this point Dante marked his decline. Victor lived another seven years but over those years put increasing responsibility for the studio in Dante's hands.

Near the end, Victor came to the studio less and less. Now,

whenever Dante took the stairs, he thought of his father — five years dead. Where Victor was not a romantic and never a sentimentalist, Dante was both. Taking care of the family, his mother and three sisters, though, beat much of this from him. Of the family, only Beatrice, the youngest, remained troubled by her lot in life. Juanita and Eyrie, both older than Dante, were close to being settled. Juanita, the eldest, was engaged and planned on marrying as soon as her fiancé finished his apprenticeship. Eyrie was in a serious relationship with a close friend of Dante's, a framer by trade. Beatrice, however, was five years younger than Dante.

Lola's late pregnancy had been a surprise. Beatrice, the baby of the family, was spoiled. Dante was left dealing with the consequences. Beatrice was certain she had a right to anything she wanted, believed she could do whatever she wished. Well enough for a child, but that was years behind her. Now she needed to consider her future. Difficult women had trouble finding a man — no matter how beautiful.

Reaching the top of the stairs, Dante locked the staircase door, kicked off his shoes and called to the women. Lola shouted from the kitchen; she and his other sisters, not Beatrice, were cooking dinner. He could smell the stew on the stove and the fresh baked bread in the oven. "Strange days," Dante said sitting in the chair. His mother placed a short glass of wine beside him and a heel of bread with a dollop of fresh butter and sliced garlic beside him.

"Why strange?" Juanita asked from the counter where she was cutting vegetables for the salad.

"Got Caspar in the chair, at last." The news silenced the women.

"What did he get?" Eyrie asked from beside the fridge. She was collecting plates from the cupboard above this.

"The charm I suggested — right, Dante?" Juanita asked. Dante nodded, beaming.

"Juanita has a secret admirer," Eyrie chided. All laughed; Juanita reddened but said nothing.

"That was what you meant, Dante?" his mother asked.

"Yes and no." Dante finished the wine, taking a bottle of water from the fridge.

"Which is it?" Lola asked, propping a hand on her hip. Not huge, the kitchen was big enough to fit the family with room to spare. The table where they took their meals was the biggest thing in the room. When not eating, this was pushed back against the wall.

"That business down at Chin's Review — remember, Mom?" She did.

"Caspar was down there; he saw?" The murder of Quetzal Martinez was everywhere online and in the resurgent print press. As the economy became tighter and hope less common, many had given up on mobile devices and computers — returning to paper.

"Says he was."

"Do you believe him?" Eyrie asked, hands knotted in a drying towel. Her knuckles had whitened where she had wrapped the fraying towel about her hands.

"Calm down, child." Lola put a hand over Eyrie's and an arm about her shoulders.

A vacantness had taken hold of a face normally filled with life. Eyrie's large black eyes were pulled tight as she trembled. "Daughter, we are safe here, and it was only that fool Quetzal."

"I wouldn't call him a fool, Mom." Standing, Dante had stepped to the other side of Eyrie, putting his arm around her.

"It could have been an accident; the paper says as much." Juanita said from the kitchen sink, dish scour in her right hand.

"Your sister was right; it could have been an accident. You know how much Quetzal liked to drink; how he loved drugs; how he loved dangerous partners."

"Everyone knows about Quetzal," Juanita said from the sink; she had turned back to washing the prep dishes.

"What did Caspar see?" Eyrie asked.

"He saw people running from the alley, that's all." Not having realized how frightened his sister was, Dante saw no reason to introduce Caspar's monster.

"Caspar is more than a little crazy," Lola said, looking to her son for support.

"That and more; I love him, but he has his troubles." Dante took Eyrie's chin in his hand and smiled down at his sister. Eyrie smiled up, but there were tears in the corners of her eyes. A fat one spilt down her cheek; Dante brushed this away.

"There are rumors about the Komodo," Eyrie answered, thicker tears following the first.

———

"I blame television," Lola said, knitting needles clutched in one hand. Sitting beside the living room window, looking down over the street, Lola held the drapes with two arthritic fingers. At sixty-three, the years had not been unkind to her. Although she was having trouble with her fingers, the arthritis had not spread to her other joints. Knitting had become a challenge, but as long as she did only an hour a day, the pain was manageable. She also took a cat's claw medicinal tea twice a day. There were other remedies, but the healthcare system had imploded with doctors and hospitals on a pay-as-you-go basis.

If you had money, this was fine; if you didn't, you learned to die with as much dignity as possible. Lola had been lucky; the cat's claw was managing the pain. With Mendelssohn's Ink doing well, she had visited a doctor on the north-side. The visit cost the better part of half a month's profits from the studio. A visit to the hospital was out of the question. Dante would have had to go into debt if he could find a bank that would lend to him — Bornlerites were high credit risks.

Dante worried what would happen if any of them became seriously ill. Lola did not want to risk the studio for a few more years, though her children opposed this. Unlike his sisters, however, Dante understood this might be necessary. He hoped it would not, but as he watched his mother work the needles attempting to hide the pain, it was obvious the choice was not far off.

Lola, still, wore the years well. Though she had crow's feet in the corners of her eyes, her skin was still tight. The hair, at one time thick and black, was streaked with gray. What black remained was closer to iron than pitch. Her eyes were still black and energetic; the nose was straight and narrow. Although thin, her lips were pink and healthy. His mother's chin was pointed and the jaw squarish. Not tall, at five-foot-six, Lola was well put together with a little padding offered by the years and four children. When alive, Victor continued to take a lively interest in his wife. His death had been hard on Lola, one the children feared she would not survive. It took six months, but she returned to them.

"Why do you blame television?" Dante asked. His mother was sitting in her favorite chair: Victor's reading chair. Lola preferred this one to be closer to Victor. Beneath the table next to the overstuffed reading chair, she kept a photo album with all her favorite pictures. When she thought the children were not watching, Lola would leaf through the early years when she and Victor were courting.

"There's nothing on, nothing the young would enjoy," tapping the flat-panel monitor with her needles.

"Juanita and Eyrie do not seem to have that problem."

"Beatrice demands more. The other girls are fine. They are more like me, but Beatrice has always wanted more."

"What you mean, Mother, is we spoiled her." Lola frowned, twisting the needles and looking toward the drapes. Pushing from the chair with effort, she attempted to hide this from her son. Dante saw the pain. The other girls, least of all Beatrice, who was too involved in her own life to notice anything, spent no time worrying about their mother. Both Juanita and Eyrie loved her, but they were not prepared to admit Lola was becoming frail.

Lola had been spending more time with the album for the last months. All she had left were her memories, and these were not enough. As far as Dante could tell, all Lola wanted now was to see the girls married. They had talked of Dante marrying, but he was not prepared to take that step until his sisters were settled. Juanita was well on the way, and Eyrie was making a good stab at it. Beatrice, however, seemed more interested in men, clubs, drink, and escaping her life.

Dante, however, enjoyed reading history and biography. Though born to the lower orders, he and Victor did their best to squeeze as much profit, meaning, and joy out of life as they could. Books were a way to achieve this. Victor passed on to his son a belief that only in understanding people and the world could you ever hope to rise. Because of this, Dante had developed an interest in biography and history; he also maintained an interest in business and economics. Beatrice never wanted to work her way out of Bornler. Rather, she would prefer to marry her way out. Dante loved his sister, but it was difficult to like Beatrice.

He never found liking Beatrice more challenging than when he and his mother had these conversations. This one would be about her actions. It did not matter these actions flowed from her beliefs: specifically, the world owed her whatever she wanted. Settling in the cushion next to Dante, Lola took his hand in both of hers. Like his father, Dante's fingers were fine, thin, long, and strong. The backs of the hands were dusted with light, soft black hair.

"You want me to find her?"

"Beatrice is your sister; with your father…"

"With Dad gone, I am responsible for the home." Dante wanted to say family, but he was uncertain Beatrice was. His sister, yes, but family — she had long since ceased behaving as though related. The family were an embarrassment to Beatrice — and a tattoo artist for a brother was more than should be asked of her. Pride in workmanship meant nothing to Beatrice. For her, there was nothing to be proud of in tattoos and tattoo artists. Most of those with tattoos were losers or criminals; most who inked them no better. Beatrice, not shy of her opinions, never bored with telling Dante just what she thought of him and Mendelssohn's Ink.

"Yes." His mother tightened her grip on his hand, as embarrassed by Beatrice's behavior as her sisters. Dante was no longer embarrassed by her behavior — anger was his point of departure.

"Where do you think she is?"

"Dinner with friends, I suppose. Maybe one of those clubs she likes so much in northern Bornler."

"She'll be home soon — she always comes home, even if it takes a few days." Lola looked away, releasing her son's hand. This part of Beatrice's life her mother would not discuss. Though open-minded, Lola was still a product of her time and faith. She never missed a Sunday service, often attending during the week. Dante assumed, closer to the end than the beginning, his mother needed faith's security.

"Please, find her." Dante pushed from the sofa and got his coat.

"Don't wait up. I'll be late."

<hr>

Dante took the motorcycle. He had considered the SUV, but given the side streets he would look for Beatrice in, it seemed a poor choice. Before leaving the house he collected the automatic from the studio. Since policing had gone by the board in Bornler, many business owners, not only in the district but the country, had returned to do-it-yourself self-defense popular before the state intervened, promising all equity under the law. Most companies had private security. Because of this, business and industry combined forces to change the gun laws. Before, it was difficult to own a handgun and impossible to possess an assault rifle. After the lobbyists finished with the politicians, anyone who wished to own a handgun or rifle could.

This had not gone down well with the Left, who had been hoping to resurrect Socialism. The Left made three abortive attempts to keep violence within the hands of the state. Liberals and Conservatives crushed each vote in parliament; even the Green Party voted for legalizing weapons. Fear, and a need to placate the electorate, had gone a long way to informing these choices. There had been a series of articles written on this topic five years before, shortly after the death of Victor. Dante, aware of how dangerous Bornler and the rest of the country had become, remained unconvinced by either side of the argument. The Left, however, forced a referendum before the final vote.

The referendum had coincided with the populist revolutions

sweeping the world. Whether on the Left or Right the populist governments had consumed the Center. Talking heads from all networks and many podcasters had their theories on what had happened to the Center: jobs/economy, immigration, fear, and the collapse of the international consensus. The last was too metaphysical for most viewers and readers, but there was a sense the elites were behind it all. For some, these were bankers; for others, there were more exotic theories. The illuminati a go-to standard, the Jews were trotted out if only for the sake of shorthand, then there were the fringes: voodoo history, gnostic dementia, hollow earth, aliens (especially the reptilian sub-genus).

No matter the definition of populism or on what end of the political spectrum it located itself, the world was coming apart in dribs and drabs. Dante bought a 9 mm; over the next six months, he practiced daily. On the weekends, he took instruction from former military officers. When finished, Dante was comfortable with the handgun; whether he could put it to use was another matter. When he left the house, however, he took the automatic.

Dante had served two years in the Army but was trying to put this behind him. He enjoyed the close quarters combat training and shooting the weapons then there was his tour on the frontline. After being wounded, he spent the rest of his enlistment in filing and bookkeeping. This worked out well when it came time to take over Mendelssohn's Ink. As a teenager, he loved a good fight and even carried a knife. Now, though, he was twenty-seven years old and responsible for his mother and sisters.

For the next three hours, Dante went from clubs, to bars, to restaurants, to parties. Twice he used the automatic to bluff his way through the door. In all but one case, the bluff had worked. When the Nine's presence did not work, he pistol-whipped the ad hoc security guard at a private party. Eventually, he found someone who had seen Beatrice. She had met a young man from the west-side; he had taken her to another party. It took more digging, but after blowing out a speaker with the Nine, Dante got the address. This party was six blocks into the north-side, but road blocks, or checkpoints, had not yet appeared: this was only a matter of time.

Bornler did not make up even half of the east-side. There were several other smaller districts, but for years, Bornler and the east-side had been conflated. This worried Dante. There was a chasm emerging between those that had and those that wanted. Crime was bleeding out from the east-side to other districts. Dante supposed it to be only a matter of time before municipal and national governments moved against them. Bottling up the problem would not solve it, but that was not Dante's immediate problem. Pulling up to the last address, Dante moved the automatic from the breast pocket of his jacket to the back of his pants.

Though on the north-side, it was another weathered apartment building. The first floor apartments were lit, but the second and third floors appeared vacant. There was no security on the entrance to the building. Several cars on the street were too good for the east-side, which suggested slumming north and west siders.

There were two parties, one on the left side of the hall and another to the right. Dante took the door to his left first. Beatrice was not there, and some men, all from the north and west sides, attempted to throw him out. The automatic cowed the impulse, and he was directed across the hall. Next door, most were baked. Many of the women were nearly unconscious. In the corner of the room, a woman was spread-eagled on the floor beneath several men. They were not holding her down, and she was moaning as if enjoying herself. Dante kicked the first off, and the others scuttled away.

It was not Beatrice.

He next checked the kitchen, where more of the same was occurring, but no Beatrice. What Dante found in the bathroom, he preferred not to think about. Still, no Beatrice. The apartment had three bedrooms. In the first bedroom were three sleeping couples in a post-coital and drug induced haze. Dante had been there often enough. When a teenager, he had enjoyed partying with slumming northerners and westerners. There was a core of women that slummed, but most had been men. This was during a time in Dante's life when he was rebelling against his father and his lot in life. He came out of this rebellion wiser and with a deeper understanding of human anxiety, hunger, and depravity.

He had slept with what was to be expected: women, men, trans, and fluid. For the first months, this was fun. Slowly, however, a weight settled upon Dante's chest. This ennui should not have weighed him down, but it did. In response, Dante rediscovered his mother's faith. Though reactionary, what it offered in exchange was community, meaning, purpose, and acceptance. Acceptance for what could not be changed in his and the family's life — without a lifetime of hard work and some good fortune.

The door to the master bedroom was unlocked; several voices were coming from behind this. Throwing this open, he found Beatrice in the center of a lit bed with two men and a woman. At the end of this and to the side were two men with expensive camcorders. Also, around the bed, men and women were using their phones to take stills. Wading into the group, Dante slashed left and right, beating a path to Beatrice.

4

THE ATMOSPHERE IS LETHAL

"Sancho, you are no longer on patrol." Calling to the first sergeant, Charles leaned against the car. Two weeks previous, Sancho Korn, twenty-six, arrived from community policing. He had finished his training the day after the Quetzal murder. The press was still referring to the murder behind Chin's Review as a regrettable incident that was all too typical of Bornler. Sancho requested partnering with Inspector Lane even though Charles was hard on partners. Investigators, interested in advancement, did not want partners — these basked in the reflected light of superiors.

Charles was ambitious, and Sancho was less a partner than a competitor. It was clear Sancho had requested the pairing to advance his position. This meant any work Charles did would reflect on the young first sergeant. Unlikely as it seemed, if Korn had a well-positioned mentor, it could occur. The first sergeant may have been partnered with Charles to spy on him. If improbable, it could have been Korn was placed with the inspector to evaluate him, with a view to replacement. If the government no longer felt they were getting value from the manufactured hero, they may look elsewhere.

For the past two years, Charles had known of Sancho Korn, having run across him as a patrol officer at multiple crime scenes.

The young patrolman had secured the sites well enough, was useful canvassing the neighborhoods, had an effective interview technique, was not intimidating, had a decent education for a patrolman (he had completed high school), was intelligent, and self-effacing — the last, perhaps, a mask. To be elevated to first sergeant after five years on the force was unheard of. To Charles, this meant he had a mentor. Sancho would need watching and, when the opportunity presented itself, gotten rid of.

There were methods for disposing of partners. These ranged from the innocuous, to the tragic, to the villainous. Charles favored one or two: the tragic being distinguished from the villainous by the journey. Tragedy, however, dogged the department. Only a few patrol officers reached retirement. Often because of a life on the front lines: community policing placed officers up against fallen civil society. Since the consequences for transgressive citizens were severe, there was no reason for those accused not to take direct action.

Frequently, patrol and community officers were bought off. If this was not possible, or out of the price range of the accused, then more direct action resulted. This rarely happened but often enough for both to be on edge during an arrest. Attracting new recruits was difficult because of the violence dogging a law enforcement career. The department overcame this by offering higher pay, better benefits, excellent insurance, and access to the best doctors and hospitals in the city. All good, but attracting recruits remained problematic. The educated classes wanted nothing to do with policing — as patrol officers, investigators, or administrators.

Administrators were seldom on the streets. Uniforms, though, were neon targets. Gang members had been known to be initiated through officer assassinations. Often, patrol/community officers were targeted for ease of access. If an administrator had been causing trouble, or available, they were targeted. Afterward, the department would crack down on gang activity. Soon enough, the overtime would cripple the budget, and the government would not increase this. Gangs knew of the timeframe; the better ones exploited the financial pinch and the natural tension between politicians and bureaucracy.

Charles would have to be cautious in how and when he disposed of the young Korn. Moving before command believed all was right with the partnership could trigger an internal investigation. These went nowhere if the department and fellow officers had your back. Slank was the only one that would stand up for him. Charles could not trust the politicians because they only moved out of self-interest. There was also the worry the same politicians may attempt to replace him with a newer model with a lower profile. Concerns may have been raised that Charles was not as malleable as he had once been. In CID, Charles had to worry about not only working for those that had placed him in the department, but command and fellow officers.

From this emerged the need to protect and advance his position. The politicians that had placed him in CID could be nervous about a conceptual independence. Charles did what he could for those he owed favors to, but with politicians, there was always another favor, always another corruption, always another humiliation. He was their man and understood this. But did they?

So, Charles and Sancho were partnered. The partnership could have been following a necessary departmental policy: all investigators were to have partners. The policy applied to Charles. He had preferred to work alone for years and only seldom took on a partner. The Komodo angle on Quetzal's murder could be the reason. Being uncertain exposed Charles.

Ramira saw it this way on learning of the partnership. That had been a difficult conversation. Ramira was already on edge because of the Quetzal and Komodo connection. Komodo, more than anything else, ratcheted up Ramira's anxiety. There was also the worry about their marriage, the worry about Charles' career, and now the worry about this young man placed with her husband to destroy his career and take his position. Charles was catching it from three sides at once: department, government, and wife. Any of them could destroy him.

Sancho trotted across the street, a hand on his holster. The first sergeant had put his holster on incorrectly and was paying the price. Armpit holsters challenged most officers new to plain-clothes:

Sancho was wearing his for the first time. The suit was straight off the rack and cheap. Because of this, the automatic was obvious. People always knew when they were speaking with the police, but Sancho's suit was a flare. Charles would have to speak to him about getting a better suit then check him out on the holster. It was too soon to have him shot. Charles would have preferred a simpler way to rid himself of Sancho. Even if shot, though, the wound need not be fatal.

Shooting and not killing Sancho would be the trick. Pushing the first sergeant through the door first would not be difficult. At twenty-six, he would have much to prove, as much to the world as himself. Charles could work with that. Still, getting Sancho shot would be dangerous. Controlling the outcome of the shooting would not be possible. It could be nothing more serious than a flesh wound; it could cripple him; it might kill him. The first would be preferable while the second and the third would expose Charles to an internal investigation and heighten prejudice. Who he was and how he got to the capital remained an issue.

The puppy dog grin on Sancho's face was disturbing. A handsome man and at five foot eleven inches, he was not short. Like everyone else, he had black hair, black eyes, and a gentle olive complexion. His nose was finer than most, the lips not too thick, the jaw squarish. Sancho's musculature was sedate, making the suit fit well. Not yet married, with the CID promotion, he was planning on this. Sancho, therefore, would fight hard any attempted reassignment, placing Charles in a precarious position. Liking what he knew of the first sergeant, he did not wish to harm him. However, did Charles like him enough to risk his career, freedom, and life? This would not be a good day.

"What?" Sancho asked, stepping up from the deep gutter. Bornler streets had gutters that reached a third as deep as a man's shin. The purpose was to collect runoff and offal during the rainy season. Many Bornler neighborhoods also had bricked or cobbled roads. Here cobbled, many of the stones chipped or split, and the mortar had long since decayed. Trotting across the street, Sancho tripped over a missing stone. Almost doing a header into the middle of the street, solving Charles' problem, a delivery truck swerved. Sancho righted himself but almost overbalanced, going head first into the edged gutter. Another missed opportunity. Charles slipped his hands into his hip pockets, revealing the automatic's grip. Passersby, noticing the weapon, quickened their pace. Adjusting his tie and jacket, Sancho pulled the holster back under his armpit.

"The streets are wet." Reddening, Sancho looked away.

"What were you doing over there?"

"Best fruit stand in Bornler. I was hoping to get a bag before the interview."

"You want to go to an interview with fresh fruit?"

"No, the fruit was for later."

"You were stealing?"

"Stealing?" eyes hardening.

"Paying then?" Glancing up at the apartment windows, Sancho buttoned his jacket.

"We are on the third floor?" not answering the inspector's question.

"A minute there, first sergeant," reaching out and placing a hand on Sancho's arm. "We do not thieve. If you are going to last as my partner, *we do not thieve.*"

"It's not — oh, what's the use."

Charles stepped back, looking about the street. Most were ignoring them, but across the street, the peddler, with a brown paper bag, eyed the detectives. He was not holding the bag up but was not looking away either. Charles had seen this many times when other detectives and patrol officers extorted local businesses. The owners could not resist, if they did not want to end banged up — the economy, however, was in near chaos, and few legal standards remained. Peddlers, business owners, corporations were all in the same position. Still, the police and inspectors were not above reapplying the laws, still on the books but no longer enforced.

Sancho had been attempting to apply the laws to leverage a bag of fruit. So typical was this amongst patrol/community police, no one thought anything of it. Charles knew business owners did but no one else. "What does that mean?" watching the young detective.

"It's not thieving."

"If still in uniform, I'd agree, but you're in CID now. We're above extortion. Look at me, first sergeant." Sancho turned from the apartment. "Do you wish back into community policing?"

"You can't..."

"Sancho, I don't want you, or anyone, here. I work alone. As long as you're here, though, we do things my way. Got it?" The younger's mouth tightened.

"You are correct in thinking I cannot bounce you from CID, but if you keep that up," motioning across the street, "I will have you charged with extortion."

"If you can get anyone to testify I was extorting the peddler."

"I've been in this gig a long time. Fought my way out of the provinces. I know people on the street; I know people in the department and municipal and federal governments. Do you really believe," leaning in, "I cannot fuck you?" Charles expected Sancho to trot out his mentor.

Stiffening, Sancho raised his chin. Bornler's din evaporated. The first sergeant's hand did not move toward the automatic or tactical baton, but he struggled with the impulse. There was a controlled violence in him. Charles saw an opportunity. Violence found a way of expressing itself, and he wondered what Sancho's expression would be: those he was to protect or women? Could have been both. The inspector was determined to find out with whom Sancho shared. "Well?" When the first sergeant did not answer, Charles placed a hand on his hip and smiled.

"I know about you — everyone knows. You have no pull in the department. If you did, I would not be here." Not attempting to hide the smirk, Sancho's hands drifted to his hips, slipping his thumbs between shirt and pants.

"Good, you're not stupid. I can build on that — but we will do it my way. I would not use my political connections to deal with you, but I'd see you slip down a stairwell, fall into oncoming traffic, meet an unfortunate end because you had to be first through the door, or something else — something creative, something embarrassing." Sancho's reaction was muted. It was plain the first sergeant came from nothing or close to this. In comparison, Charles had been a member of the proto-middle-class. Most would have seen his upbringing, because of the money and his parents' jobs, as solid middle-class. The inspector did not see it that way, but it was difficult to argue against.

Sancho's background would have been harsher — he only had high school, which was more than many, and this would have led to radically different experiences. Coming to the police, as a career, Sancho could not have had much by way of choice. This was his way out. The chances of him making it to retirement were slight. That said, almost no chance was better than none. The capital gutters were a hard place to live. With the struggle continuing, Charles looked up at the third floor, keeping Sancho in his periphery. "You would be investigated."

"That took you long enough."

"You would not get away with it, sir." Charles smiled, not turning back.

"CID, command, and officers have attempted to get rid of me many times — I'm still here." Sancho stepped about Charles and toward the door.

Thunder, great rolling, beating drums ripping across a black sky. No rain, no moisture, only the smell — a sour, funky urinal on a hot summer night. To the left and right was nothing but rocky landscape, flat and punctuated by potholes. In each of these holes, someone stood in ragged clothing. A few wore trench coats and ties pulled down to the second or third button over gray-white shirts. Even from a distance, the smell of the others was thick and rank. Their hair was greasy, neither brown nor black. None appeared to be one thing or the other. They were manifestations of the void, fragments of nothingness.

The scream fell flat, having bounced off an atmosphere thick with absence. How nothingness offered resistance was unclear, but the sound, the energy of this, crawled about stunned and bleeding on the barren, rocky ground. Thoughts and actions were manifest across the landscape. So the scream took on form, possessing sinew and tissue. Within this was an eccentric skeletal structure holding organs in place, allowing for the possibility of locomotion. All figures were pinioned to their potholes: some deeper than others, some reaching their waists, others reaching their chest, and some reaching toward the neck. There was a ululation that had become white noise over the time spent in the wasteland.

When focusing, it was possible to separate the individual moaning. That done, the grievances became plain: the pleas, cries for redress, demands for justice, and justifications for wrongs. These never ended, and when it became clear, as they attempted to communicate with the others, that none wished, or could, speak with them, the white noise returned as a vague whisper on the hot, dry wind drifting, then ripping, across vacancies of rock and troubled inmates. This was a prison. New internees blipped into holes, but none escaped.

Flailing followed with consciousness but did no good. In time, the struggling ended, and the voices subsided, leaving the dry, hot wind. They were all alone yet not so. This meant something; there was a trope here, a metaphor, an interpretive mechanism that did not want to step forward. Another roll of thunder: harsh, sharp, repetitive. Not the normal thunder rolling through a luring sky — this was something else. There was a pause, and they could hear in the pissed stained air the harsher, closer rumble repeat itself. As the noise rose, they had to cover their ears and cower. The sky shook and the clouds split, releasing a torrent of filthy rain on those in the rocky desert. The stench was hideous.

Consciousness collapsed then split wide, reached down and tore the quake of self-identification out of the oubliette.

. . .

Cleaved from the crown of her head to the back of her throat, the pain broke with the light; behind this was a thundering rap. Reina pushed up on an elbow and slid back with a low moan. Her throat and mouth sealed, fumbling over the nightstand, her hand fell on a bottle of water with three fingers remaining. As the knocking continued, Reina finished the bottle, dropping this on the linoleum with an empty rattle. Sliding off the bed, she used this to prop herself up. All she had on was a faded T-shirt stained about the armpits. The boxers, ill-fitting, she had worn for the last seven nights. Reina tended, now alone, not to care about how she slept. At Zemmoa, she had done the best possible with a diminishing wardrobe.

A beautiful woman, however, when between boyfriends and the occasional girlfriend — or whatever the fluid genders were defining themselves as, Reina had a tendency to let go. Clothing littered the apartment, a one-bedroom with kitchenette, belonging in the laundry or hamper, wrappers, boxes, and the detritus of a couple weeks' worth of living. In nearly a month, she had not swept or run a vacuum over the floor. Whenever she struck up a friendship with someone at Zemmoa or a local bar, Reina went back to their place. If that was not possible, she took them to a hotel. Reina's looks were such that she could still get them to pay if coming from Zemmoa. She always looked better under black light.

Reina's hair, a dark brown and coarse from an overabundance of product, hung to the middle of her back. Normally, she swept this back and sometimes parted it in the middle. Each morning she woke, often with a hangover, this was sticking up, makeup smeared across her face and pillow. Grabbing her phone, she flipped to selfie mode. The makeup smudged, the lipstick halfway up her cheek, and her eyes appeared a raccoon mask. In the center of the mask were two milk chocolate eyes, light as those of northern ancestry.

There were few in the capital and fewer in the provinces. Even her closest friends suggested Reina may have the North in her. As much as everyone railed against the northern empires, they all wished it were part of them and, failing this, to have some DNA attributed to the North. Reina's skin was lighter than many others.

Not the khaki olive many supported in the northern districts of the country. In the South, most ranged from a light to dark brown. There was a genetic subset of those descended from West Africa, but they lived in the Southwestern districts along the coast. This was the most deprived area, and for generations, they had either been subsistence farmers or worked the fisheries.

There was no excuse for the exclusion the darkest felt from the rest of society, but it did not alter the racial hierarchy. This was not the only hierarchy: economic, professional, social, cultural, and geographic were also in play. All could be transcended within a few generations if families decided their lot in life was inadequate — before the Great Collapse. Since the collapse, social movement had become difficult. This only increased the marginalization of those of African descent. Before the Great Collapse, a few of those had made it out of the Southwest and into larger provincial towns. Some even found themselves in the capital. They were never quite integrated but sometimes married into the lower strata of the lighter skinned. Skin color was the unofficial social marker of the country and most of the southern states. With the collapse, the unofficial social marker became more important. In consequence, many of African descent were no longer welcome in the capital or provincial towns.

The bulk returned to the Southwest. Of these, many became small business owners, while others went into politics. Those clinging to the economic frontiers of provincial towns often ended their lives as bandits or pirates. Piracy along the West Coast had been increasing as the depression deepened. When it appeared this was what they should expect for the rest of their lives, marginal behavior increased. Southwestern piracy the most romantic expression of this despair. The pirates, in the beginning, did not last long: at most five years. About that time, the depression began to be referred to as the Great Collapse, and the alt-economies emerged as significant challengers to democratic capitalism. Socialism never took off, except among the beta-academics, because it left everyone poor.

Poverty was fine for those that could slip into a genteel variety and were from old families in which a Faulknerian decay was admired. Where one came not from the upper classes, poverty was brutally woven into the body. When their caloric intake dropped below 1,500, and closer to 500, it was impossible to deny what was happening. Starvation, often, had been restricted to the poor rural areas. Within the capital and major provincial towns, starvation occurred, but national and regional governments were canny enough to understand having too many skeletons tottering through the streets was destabilizing. In these areas, the government fed the people. In rural areas, the problem could be ignored — this was dangerous and despicable, but the population was small enough that any destabilizing influence would be minimal.

Reina's skin color and the shade of her eyes had earned a lot of attention from wealthy men. However, she had never been willing to translate this into marriage. She was youngish, and for now, that was enough. If she had not been a zemmoan, if she had not been a member of the posse, Reina may have been more thoughtful about her future. Those attracted to the zemmoan lifestyle had little concept of the future. True, as well, the country was having trouble imagining this. Where most struggled with possibilities, zemmoans remained indifferent. Partly because they considered themselves artists. Some were, such as Quetzal, but most only talked about painting, sculpture, their novel, play, screenplay, and whatever ephemeral piece they were contemplating.

Dropping the phone on the nightstand, it bounced and toppled to the floor, striking the linoleum with a sharp crack. Reina looked down, but the screen was still intact. Using the bed, she pushed to a kneeling position, the rapping urgent, then stood. Still bent over, Reina, based on brutal previous experience, slowly unfolded. Whenever a bout of vertigo began, she halted, waiting for this to pass. When it did, she would experiment with the next couple of degrees. If successful, two more while shouting came from the door. Not answering, for fear of throwing up, Reina went vertical. Turning to the door, she combed her hair back. Stopping at the full-length mirror hanging from the bedroom door, she examined the fallout.

With a wet wipe, Reina cleaned what she could from her eyes and wiped the smear of lipstick from her cheek. Though the material beneath was haggard and aged beyond her years, she looked better without the ruined makeup. Her breasts were not large nor small. She had considered augmentation but could convince none of the rich men she dated to pop for this. They seemed to think her breasts were fine. Reina broke up with one over the issue, but when the others would not foot the bill, she gave it up. Lip augmentation they were happy to pay for. Wiping the lips clean, both a full, gentle pinkish-brown. Stepping back and taking in her full figure, an argument having broken out on the other side of the door, the muscle tone in her legs was good and her belly flat. Perhaps there was a little fatty tissue below the belly button and above her hips, but only a little. She needed to go on a diet again. Reina was good at these — but better at vomiting.

Her skin was still smooth with a light chocolate tincture when spending time in the sun. Reina avoided this, and since she had not been to an East Coast resort in two years, there was not much opportunity to get any sun. Most resorts had closed down or were operating on limited seasons. There was not much wealth, and northerners were no longer coming down for fear of kidnapping, torture, and murder/assassination. Still, a few remained open, but the territory between the capital and the East Coast was dangerous. Those that still frequented the resorts flew, but even then they risked armed incursions and assassination. Of the resorts still in operation, they appeared more like fortresses than holiday venues. Even if businessmen and politicians went, they took along a security contingent, composed of former Marines and Special Forces. The cost of security was ruinous, and even the rich were now careful with their money.

Reina, hesitating to open the door, examined her nails. She needed another manicure. Attempting to smooth her hair, again, she looked about the room. There were half-read magazines on the coffee table; on top of these were used, dirty cups. A pair of jeans hung over the side of the sofa. Balled up socks were before the window with more under the kitchen table. Empty bottles of wine and mezcal were on the table, and another was under the coffee table. Shrugging, she took hold of the front door, where the knocking had begun again. Throwing on a smile, she opened this. The smile collapsed. "Fuck me."

"Not on the job," Sancho said.

"Ms. Noche?" Charles asked.

"You have forgotten me so soon, inspector?" Reina stood back, holding the door. The two detectives stepped past her. Sancho looked about the room then toward the kitchen, frowning.

"I'm not much for housework."

"We're not here about your apartment." Charles pulled a chair out from the kitchen table, sitting in the middle of the living room, and sat down on a small stack of magazines and newspapers. Pulling these from beneath him, he tossed them on the table and took out a notebook. Sancho moved toward the bedroom door and eased this open with a heel.

"I'm alone."

"Not surprised," Sancho said.

"We have a few questions for you, Ms. Noche." Charles frowned at Sancho.

"Please, sit down." Sancho motioned toward the chair beside Charles.

"You are a member of a group?" Charles looked up from his notebook.

"I don't belong to any groups."

"I believe your group is — the zemmoan posse?" tapping his pen on the tabletop.

"Not a group, they are friends."

"The ones we picked up behind Chin's Review?" Sancho moved toward the table as Charles asked the question. Tucking a hand into a pocket, this exposed the butt of his automatic. Reina noted the weapon and stiffened. She had not much experience with police but had seen enough to be cautious. When they exposed their weapons, a message was being sent.

The detective, with the notebook, frowned up at his partner and he backed away. Were they playing her? What was next? Something was coming but what? Accusation? Arrest? "Yes — may I have a bottle of water?"

"Of course," Charles said.

"Thank you, Detective...?"

"I'm sorry. I thought you remembered me from the interrogation," Charles answered.

"I'm trying to block out everything from that night — from the moment we entered that alley until we were released."

"Why, are you hiding something?" Sancho pulled out a chair, legs scraping against the linoleum. Reina flinched from the younger detective.

"I am Detective Charles Lane, and this is Detective Sancho Korn." Charles again flipped through the pages of the spiral bound notepad. He had several note apps on his phone, but preferred to use paper and pen. There was something about the physical notebook he liked. Also, the notebook put suspects off their game. Tapping on the phone was not the same as rippling through paper and scratching on this.

Reina looked at the paper, the pen, the thumb of the detective moving against the tabletop covered in magazines and newspapers. "So you are all friends?" Charles looked up from the notepad, twirling the pen in his right hand.

"You know the victim?" Sancho leaned on the table, and the legs groaned.

"Everyone knew Quetzal."

"Everyone?" Sancho eased off.

"At Zemmoa — and hangers on," Reina said, having gotten a bottle of water from the refrigerator.

"Hangers on?" Charles closed the notebook and slipped the pen through the spiral top.

"Everyone not making art."

"How many at Zemmoa are *making art*?" Sancho, again.

"Fewer than are fucking." Charles leaned back, a long, low chuckle slipping from a half-closed mouth.

"Which are you?" Only Sancho would have asked the question. Charles was wondering how effective his interview technique was. Not answering the question, Reina turned to Charles and waited for the next.

"Are there many at Zemmoa making art?"

"Most talk about their work, but Quetzal was one of the few making any. He's even had a show at the National Museum."

"Yes, it was a success I hear." Charles had seen the show with Ramira. He had not liked it; the paintings were reminiscent of mid-twentieth century European cultural deconstruction. There was in the art a lack of hope and no sense of purpose. Perhaps it was where they were, culturally, but it was unpleasant. Reina nodded in agreement but offered no assessment.

"So..." Charles' phone buzzed, interrupting the interview. He opened this and for about half a minute scrolled through a series of images. "You are familiar with the ink Quetzal had done?"

"At Mendelssohn's Ink?"

"Yes." Charles continued to flip through the images.

"A full back tattoo?" She nodded, leaning toward the phone. "You do not want to see what is left of him," sitting the phone face down next to the notebook.

"I already have," a sigh coming from deep within the woman's chest.

"Zemmoans are believed to have connections to political dissidents and, it is rumored, revolutionaries in the South and Southeast." Sancho stepped back into the conversation.

"I was wondering when you would get around to that." Reina hit back.

"It is a matter of concern; can you help us understand what Quetzal might have been doing on that roof?" Charles asked.

"I've no idea why he was up there or what happened after he fell."

"Ms. Noche, you remember we spoke of the fall and the dismemberment?" Charles was aware there had been more than simple dismemberment but kept the information about predation out of the news. He was hoping for predation but feared cannibalism.

Until the coroner's office completed the report, he could not be certain, but from what he had seen, it appeared to suggest what had got at the body was too large to have been vermin or dogs. Reina nodded, without looking at the detectives. Instead, she stared at one of Quetzal's paintings, hanging askew, on the wall above the sofa.

"It's the political connection we are interested in." Sancho was not letting the bone go.

"The *posse* isn't political."

"I see, and what are your politics?" Charles asked.

"Mezcal."

"We were hoping for more," Sancho said.

"None of us are political. The closest we get to political is Harold — and he's reactionary."

"Harold Diez?" Reina nodded. "Will other members of the posse back this up?" Charles continued. Another nod. "Right, thank you for your time, Ms. Noche." Charles pushed from the table, pocketing his phone and notebook. The younger detective followed him to the door, where Charles gave a card to Reina and asked her to call him if she heard any rumors about what happened to Quetzal on the roof or afterward. That was it. They were gone. Alone, she slid down the back of the door — staring at the card.

"We are so fucked."

5

I AM A STONE

"Call off the hounds — Charlie, where the hell have you been?" The inspector smiled down.

"Tahira, you missed me."

"Missed you, I've been ringing every precinct in the district. Where did you get to?" Tahira was in her early thirties with a Japanese father, a bureaucrat who had retired five years before and had moved with his wife to Bali. One of the few retirement options in the country that still worked was for national bureaucrats. Given the option of a monthly stipend or a tax-free payout, Haruto, considering the state of the country, took the payout. He and Tahira's mother now owned a Bed & Breakfast, catering to upscale backpackers and retirees. They had attempted to bring Tahira out, but she had something on. Charles was one of the few who knew what this was.

Because of her ancestry, Tahira had a look that most found hard to resist. She had her father's eyes and cheekbones — while her mother's hair, breasts, and hips. Unlike her mother, Tahira exercised, did not smoke, and was only a social drinker. The hair was normally done up in a bun but, when down, reached the small of her back. Black, soft, and shiny, it always turned heads. However, Tahira was not married and had no boyfriend. In the six years she worked for

Captain Slank, the woman had no boyfriend. Standing, she pouted. This pushed an already full lower lip out, and behind the burgundy red lipstick was the moist pink of her inner lip. Beyond the lip was a row of perfect, bleached-white teeth.

"Needed a little time away from the new wife," Charles said.

"Oh, Sancho?" smoothing her dress and stepping from behind the desk.

"Yes, I need to talk to the captain about what is going on."

"He's been looking for you; the sixteenth floor has been..."

"I've done nothing...or have I?" Charles rocked back on his heels, staring up at the ceiling.

"You are often up to something. That's how you got here, but that's not what he wants to see you about. Charlie, you went missing on Sancho, and everyone's been looking for you...I've been looking for you for the last couple of hours."

"It took you two hours to ring up the precincts in Sonando?"

"I was talking to Ramira."

"Comparing notes."

"If it were only that way between us — I might even leave Daniel for you."

"Then we'd have to leave the country." Raising a hand to her mouth, she tittered. This had been an inside joke between the two of them for four years. After coming to the capital, Charles and Tahira had a brief fling. It was on one of the many occasions he and Ramira were on the outs. He never considered it an affair, two weeks and it was over. Tahira had been attempting to get Daniel to leave his wife. But they had been married for over ten years and had three children. Perhaps if it had not been for the children, he would have left her.

Charles was happy with this choice more often than not. When not, Ramira could make his life a misery that might only be imagined in Hell. At such times, the frost on her ass was enough to wilt Satan, and Charles was but a man. To deal with these mini ice ages, he would spend more time at the gym. He could pick up with another Tahira, and Tahira had hinted at picking up the relationship, but with Ramira's temper, this seemed suicidal. In fact, if Ramira found out about them, she might kill him — then tell Daniel and, after Tahira lost her position, take up with him. It was not as if Daniel was incapable of hiding murder — Charles knew of several occasions when he had done so for municipal and federal politicians. Charles had been pulled in on two of these to fiddle the forensics and offer an alibi.

Only part of Charles had bridled at the corruption, but it offered him leverage. The alderman had since lost an election and was back in the private sector. However, the parliamentarians were still in office and looked as if they would be career politicians: these debts Charles protected. "So, the captain is upset his new stooge can't find me?"

"Daniel," Tahira looked about, "had nothing to do with the assignment." Tahira thumbed upwards.

"Command?"

"I'm uncertain. The call did not come through my desk."

"Landline or cell?"

"Cell."

"We are all in deep doo-doo."

"Understand why we are nervous?" Charles nodded, looking over his shoulder toward the captain's corner office.

"I better get in there," Charles said.

"Whoever he has been talking to, they put the wind up him." Tahira touched his upper arm and stepped back behind her desk, putting on the dictation headphones. Charles took a breath; it would not be the first time he was chewed out over ditching a partner. This time, though, if Sancho had been placed with him by command, it appeared serious. Charles wondered if it might be worth leveraging one of his parliamentarians on who was moving against him.

"Captain Slank?"

"Skorna, get in here." The captain slammed the phone down, bolting up. Pointing at the chair in front of the desk, he pushed his chair out of the way. "Do you have any idea about what's been going on this morning?" Charles sat, crossed his legs, placing a hand on top of his knee and looking about the office. Do not let them see you sweat — Dad's first and best advice. His second best advice was always have a fall guy. One out of two was not bad, but the second bit of advice was perhaps more important than the first. Not sweating, though, was a good way to buy time until you worked out what the second bit of advice should look like.

"You and Tahira have discovered the Kama Sutra?"

"That's your volley?" Charles examined the nails of his right hand. Pulling out the pen he used for notes, he flicked this open and dug a wad of grime from beneath the nail of his forefinger. "She has, but that's not the problem."

"If it is — I've got a few *poppa's little helpers*."

"What...oh, no...we're getting along fine."

"Marriage, again?" Charles asked.

"No, the wife's not shown much interest in anything after the last child. She's happy enough spending my money."

"So, all's right with the world, and the angels are dancing on the head of that pin once more."

"The angels are dancing on my head." Charles put his pen away.

"Tahira tells me she's been burning up the phone lines."

"She even talked to Ramira...not happy, is she?"

"Ramira is worried about this Sancho fellow."

"First, Sergeant Korn is not some fellow — he's your partner."

"That's why I'm here."

"You've been missing for two hours and change. Charlie, you left a note on your car — *back soon, don't forget to feed the fish*."

"Don't want them to die, do we?"

"He's your partner, not your roommate."

"I needed some me time."

"For two-plus hours?" Charles pushed from the chair, stepping to the wall of commendations. Before he had transferred off the street, the captain had been the most decorated officer in the department. Slank, although an excellent administrator, had always been a better detective.

"I wanted to catch lunch then come to see you." Charles turned from the wall.

"What you wanted to do was to see what would happen if you

ditched Sancho." The captain sat back down, tapping the intercom. "Tahira," waiting for a response. "Please let the chief know we've located Charlie. Once I sort this mess, I will be in touch."

"The chief, that's how far this went...chief of detectives?"

"Chief of police." The captain propped a foot on his desk, loosening his tie and popping the first button of his starched white shirt. "You knew, didn't you?"

"Who is Sancho?" ignoring the question.

"Who you think he is."

"That doesn't tell me who he is...or what."

"Korn is an ambitious first sergeant."

"Is he someone's bastard child?"

"That I cannot say, but he has an excellent arrest and conviction rate. If he has been chosen for more, it was not because of his parentage."

Charles stepped to the window and hummed to himself. "I do not care who fucked whom. What I care about is where he came from, who he is, and what he's doing riding shotgun."

"I've told you who he is, and you know where he came from. Why he's sitting next to you, I can only speculate."

"What do you believe?"

"The chief requested the partnering. What's that tell you?"

"Up to my chin, aren't I?"

"Unless you can dispose of him...not involving violence or a problematic death...any death."

"This still doesn't answer the question, what he's doing with me... Sancho's been placed beside me by the chief, but that does not explain why they want to stick it to me or who behind the chief wants me to fail, so I can be replaced."

"It has to be about more than replacing you," the captain said.

"Thanks, I'd not have expected that much truth."

"Charles, I don't want a rat in CID. When he's finished with you, his next step would be me."

"Then what do we do?"

"Sancho's from community policing — he's bent, right?" Charles nodded. "Give him the chance to step into a frame…don't push it, don't set him up, do nothing that might blowback on you…or me…if it comes back on me, I'll throw you to command."

"You know his interview technique is shit."

"Feel your pain; nothing I can do — find me something actionable, something he cannot wiggle out of."

"That's it?" The captain nodded. "Better text him."

"Now, get out of my office. I've a call to make."

"You've got the car. What are you complaining about?" Charles said.

"I could have picked you up," Sancho answered.

"Let's be clear. This is a professional relationship. When I need time alone, I'll be taking it. You send the captain after me again, and we've a problem."

"We don't have one now?" Sancho adjusted the armpit holster.

"Here." Charles took off his jacket, demonstrating the correct rigging of the holster system. "Got it?" That done, Sancho tested the holster and nodded. The look in the first sergeant's eyes told Charles what he needed to know: not only did he distrust him, but there was a malevolence behind the suspicion. How the detective got this far was a wonder.

Whoever was behind the first sergeant had to be working hard to keep him out of harm's way: Sancho alone appeared incapable of this. "You left me a message under the wiper to *feed the fish*. What was I supposed to think?"

"That I'd be off-book a while — don't get literal."

"Literal?"

"A gag."

"We're partners. During the shift, I need to know where you are."

"You don't, and you're Junior."

Charles stepped to the first sergeant, pushing his face close. "Slank chewed me out because of you and whoever you're working for — they put the chief on him." Taking the young detective beneath the tie knot, using his forearm, Charles pinned him to the car door. Attempting to pull free, Charles slammed his forehead into the bridge of Sancho's nose. A gout of blood burst over the young man's lower face, tie, and white shirt. Twisting around, still holding the tie, Charles threw Sancho to the ground. Flipping onto his back, Sancho reached for the weapon and stopped, palm tightening over the grip. Putting his free hand to the bloodied nose, he stared at the inspector. "Feel free to report this — I'd love to know who's behind you."

"If you weren't," Sancho began.

"But I am, Sancho." The detective scrambled from the sidewalk. Several people were watching from across the street. When nothing happened, they turned away. Such damage, once done, is difficult to repair. To recover his reputation, he would have to do something extreme. Charles assumed as much — part of the plan. If Slank was correct, and he could not push Sancho through a door, the next best thing would be to trigger violence. "Now, go get yourself a clean shirt. Can't have you interviewing like that. After this, I'm taking the afternoon for myself — family business."

"But ..."

"I've cleared it with the captain." Charles adjusted his jacket and tie.

"You'll be in tomorrow?"

"See you in CID." Charles stepped onto the cobbles. Halfway across the street, the engine kicked and coughed.

Not looking back, Charles stepped up to Mendelssohn's Ink. An electronic bell sounded as the detective entered. The studio's display room was filled with samples, and several flip racks lined the far wall. On the wall to Charles' left was a large whiteboard with a price list. To the right of this was a laminated list of custom prices based on design, color, and size. There was a small counter in front of him standing chest high, behind this a small desk, to the right a till. On the wall in back of the counter and right of a door with a beaded curtain were photos of family, friends, and customers. Some photos were old; these had yellowed about the edges and faded. Some cars and bikes in the photos looked forty or fifty years old. Other photos appeared to have been taken within months.

With a clack of beads, a woman stepped out. Young, early to mid-twenties, she was five-foot-five; the eyes were narrowish, the pupils black and empty. Beneath her baggy clothes, she had a good body, but her face was coarse — it would not age well. Though not dark, her skin was on the brownish side hinting at a transitional, hirsute mestizo. Not two yards apart, Charles could see the beginnings of a light mustache. This had been dyed, but the translucent hairs stood out against the brown skin. There may also have been stray hairs on her chin.

None of this caught his attention. What stood out were the bruises on the left side of her face, running down her neck. The left eye was swollen; what could be seen of this was laced with broken blood vessels. In a heartbeat, she recognized he was a detective. Stiffening, her left hand covered the damaged eye. "Yes," pushing back against the door jamb.

"What is it?" a man called.

"Inspector Lane for Dante Skorna," Charles replied. A scrambling clatter of cupboards and drawers was followed by a shuffle of leatherette slippers.

A hand reached out, pulling the young woman into the backroom. Flinching away, she was pulled off-balance and through the door. Stepping out and jamming his hands into sagging pockets, he waited. His features were like those of the young woman — the face was common, the eyes narrow and pupils a deep black; the mouth was perhaps a little fuller and the jaw wider with the chin coming to a deeper point than the woman's. Though taller, he was a hair under six-foot. Well-built and in his late twenties, he appeared strong and trained in close-quarters combat — ex-military. Going against type, he had long sideburns and a close-cropped goatee.

"Detective," inclining his chin.

"You are Dante Skorna?" Charles pulled out his ID.

"Yes," stepping around the counter into the storefront.

"What happened there?" motioning with his chin toward the

back room. Looking at Dante's scuffed knuckles, the jaw, on closer inspection, was bruised at the hinge.

"My sister, Beatrice, got into trouble a couple nights back; had to fetch her home."

"Where?"

"A few blocks north of the east-side." Not following up the incident, Charles opened the images of Quetzal's back.

"This is your work?" Charles said.

"Shit, Quetzal."

"So, your work?" Dante nodded. "Looks new."

"Parts of it, other parts date back two years."

"That's how long a fullback takes?"

"Six or seven months, if you've the money. Quetzal was often short. I finished it maybe three months ago."

"You knew the victim well?" handing the phone to Dante, allowing him to flick through the images.

"Yes, I suppose," voice distracted. "Quetzal was hard to know. He kept himself to himself — friendly with everyone but close to no one. Perhaps I knew him a little better than most because of the time we spent on his back."

"Do you know if he was involved with anyone?" Charles asked.

"He had nothing long-term — and wasn't particular about sexual or gender identity. It was enough if you were beautiful and willing — bent helped."

"Did he spend time with anyone in particular?"

"The zemmoan posse, have you heard of them?" Charles had. "Quetzal would not have been close, but he played with them a fair amount."

"Yes, the posse had good things to say about him, but I spoke with them after his death. Most people want to speak well of the dead to the police."

"He was murdered then?"

"What makes you ask?" Dante returned the phone.

"That doesn't happen from a fall. I've seen falls; that's not a fall."

"Military?"

"A while back."

"Damage appears postmortem."

"Looks as if something was gnawing on him."

"There's been some speculation, but the Coroner's Office has yet to submit their findings."

"With Bornlerites, I'd not be holding my breath."

"Too much press for a broom, and the victim had an exhibition at the national museum — that means more attention than the police or government want."

"Political?"

"If we don't close this case soon. I need to know as much about his life as you can tell me." Over the next hour, Dante recounted how he met Quetzal and what little he knew of him.

"You're late," Ramira said.

"Why are you out here then?"

"The doctor will be with you in another ten minutes," the PA (personal assistant) said. Ramira looked from her husband, recrossed her legs, and stared at a "Water Lilies" reproduction beside the office door. The decor of Dr. Cote's office was a confusion of styles: utilitarian pastiche, 70s faux-wood paneling, and a visitation of classic Iberian architecture. Dr. Neda Cote had often complained to Charles, during their private sessions, the office was an embarrassment. Dr. Cote was from what remained of the upper-classes. With the Great Collapse, her family had fallen on hard times.

The family, though, had rescued enough capital to pay for her education. Unfortunately, the fall had made her unappealing to those remaining in the upper-classes and many in the upper middle-class. Neda ended up marrying a teacher that had risen from the skilled working class into the lower-middle. How he had managed this in the wake of the Great Collapse remained a mystery. This had not prevented Ramira from speculating after each couple's session. Charles suspected this was an attempt to push back on her fears for their marriage: leaving Charles feeling like a stone — he went where kicked.

Dr. Cote, during private sessions with Charles, hinted at political connections — which he took to mean extortion. Charles knew nothing of her ex: after the divorce, he moved to the Northwest. This had happened ten years before when the Northwest was reckoned safe. At the time, there had been another revolutionary scare. A cabal of officers from the Air Force believed they possessed enough support in the military and government to replace the Prime Minister. For a week, it appeared they had been right. Then the Army surrounded the capital, and the Navy refused to join.

In principle, the Navy had agreed, but failed, when the need was great, to support the Air Force. The Army had always been behind the government. The coup d'état failed. After a series of show trials, the nation stuttered forward. Afterward, anyone who could, got out of the capital. Dr. Cote's husband was part of the exodus. By that time, their divorce papers had been signed, and the doctor stayed. Not because she trusted the future, but because he thought leaving a good idea.

Nor could she bring herself to head northeast or southeast. There was no possibility of heading south or southwest. These areas, after the Great Collapse, were infested with bandits, pirates, and criminals of every persuasion. Neda, though, did not think of herself as a racist or a xenophobe; most liberals and socialists (Neda was an intellectual leftist) had a hard time admitting to their in-group preferences. This spoke to her social angst and liberal guilt. Both of which were a compensation mechanism for dealing with the fact she had more than others and was ashamed of this. Still, Neda and others of her class were unprepared to part with the bulk of their wealth — or what remained. Nor did many marry into the disenfranchised classes.

Neda's marriage was an anomaly — perhaps failing because of this. Even the manner in which Dr. Cote spoke of her husband made the detective suspicious. Their marriage appeared to abrade the doctor's sense of class and tribalism. Charles inclined to a tribalist answer but did not push for details. Now in her late forties and childless, Neda was lonely, frightened, and bitter. Charles assumed this was because she was alone.

During their private sessions, Neda would often flirt with Charles. The inspector, though, did no more. If this helped him during couple's therapy, Charles worried, by doing more, Cote would have expected more. Not only did his fear of Ramira make Charles reticent: the doctor worked for the Police Department — if she went off on him, that would be his career. He was already facing threats to both marriage and career. The first he needed; the second was necessary to keep the first.

Charles sat in a worn wooden chair with a cracked leather seat, three chairs down from Ramira. For a long time now, he only saw his wife as his wife. Ramira, however, was a beautiful woman. Where Charles was a northerner, Ramira was of the South. When comparing his mother to Ramira, Charles found Ramira swarthy — never using the word aloud. She was not the darkest of the southerners, with no obvious African DNA, but she was dark. Being raised in the South, Charles found southern women attractive. Differing from his mother was part of the attraction. Leticia, though handsome, was not a small woman — not fat, but not a small woman. Broad of hip and large of chest was how Charles thought of her. Ramira, though, had narrow hips and a small chest; she was athletic; her face held telltale indigenous markers about the cheekbones, jaw, forehead, and eyes. Charles loved these.

What he had trouble with was the woman inside. This woman had brought them to their present state: marriage counseling. Turning from Ramira, he looked back to the PA who was a youngish woman, plain of appearance and very much of the capital. About to push out of his chair, the doctor's door opened. Dr. Cote was also of the capital. Here they were not as fair as northerners nor as dark as southerners. Those of the capital tended toward a blend of ethnic and racial identities. It would not be fair to call the capital multicultural or multiracial and definitely not post-racial. What could be said: the capital represented the ruling elites and the brutalized underclasses. The PA was not quite the latter but neither the former.

Since the Great Collapse, the confusion of ethnicity and race was sparking tension within the capital. Many of the older families, reduced in circumstance, now moved into the upper-middle-class and middle-class neighborhoods no longer able to afford estate upkeep. The upper-middle-class and the middle-class also moved downward to skilled worker districts. Skilled workers moved to unskilled districts. Where the unskilled moved was a matter of debate. Many appeared to be creating enclaves within skilled labor neighborhoods. These ghettos were typified by a lack of utilities and services. Most times, there was no garbage collection, no electricity, minimal water, and everything else that made life possible.

Alcoholism and drug addiction were rampant throughout the country. In the capital, however, these had reached crisis proportions. Substance abuse had always been a problem for the upper-classes. In the past, this had been hushed up with afflicted family members sequestered in quiet hospitals, recovery clinics, and sanitariums. This was no longer possible — with the collapse of the economy, the business models failed. At first, the closures were sporadic and often accompanied by scaled-down re-openings. As the economy continued to unravel and the upper-classes were unable to support face-saving retreats, the failure rates increased.

Family members, once packed off, appeared in public hospitals or wandered the streets where they mingled with other indigents. As their ranks swelled, so did the troubles. Accompanying these were destitute young men. Amongst these groups of the addicted, destitute, and bitter emerged demagogues. With these, the government could no longer feign ignorance. Their initial response targeted the marginalized. The effort only inflamed tensions between classes, ethnicities, and races.

From these tensions emerged a radicalized collection of lower and middle classes — Cote's PA belonging to the latter. While the doctor, once upper-class, was also embittered. Of the last, most did nothing — but not all. These found voice and comfort in demagoguery: although the causes were complex, most emerged on the frontiers of political identity. For the middle-class and elements of the upper-classes, the demagogues on the right were most attractive. Of these classes, many were of northern extraction and their sensibilities reactionary. The former middle-classes, who considered themselves centrists, found comfort in the demagogues left of center. With the center long since abandoned, these were few.

Many who had been progressive middle-class centrists now found more comfort in socialism, communism, and even anarchism. Of these, most grew up angry and the demonstrations that had grown from this were quick to embrace violence: on the right fascists, on the left communists (and a wild variety of improv-anarchists). It was left to the municipal government to deal with them. The city failed, forcing the state to step in with broadening police powers, increasing loathing of the police and National Guard.

Charles and Ramira stepped into this cultural and political morass.

Ramira, anxious of her place and the new threat to her husband, had spent the hour screaming and ranting as she attempted to make sense of the Quetzal affair. There was much Charles could not speak of. If he did, Dr. Cote would have to report him. Soon after, he would have found himself out of CID. It already appeared as though more than his fellow officers wanted him out of this and the capital: perhaps the force.

As the session winded down and Ramira's litany of complaints faded, there had been little forward movement. Dr. Cote noted the new condition: Quetzal. However, the doctor sided with Charles' silence. In response, Ramira accused Dr. Cote of being a political shill. Though remaining calm, the doctor's response was short. Angry not only for the insult, but because Ramira was close to the truth. Cote's job was to maintain a functioning Police Department. The health of the Lanes' marriage was of secondary importance.

Charles did not envy Dr. Cote's next session with Ramira.

After the session, the couple made new appointments with the PA. This done, Charles took Ramira for coffee two blocks over, spending the next two hours calming her. That done, Charles took her home. After dinner, there would be sex — Ramira's preferred manner of righting all wrongs. Truth was, the marriage was dying. Charles tried not to admit this to himself for fear of what this would mean to his career. He doubted Ramira would leave, but her rage would chip away at him until he did. She wanted to be the first out the door, but would not be — Ramira would hold on to the bitter end. Once that came, Charles would be the villain.

6

KOMODO'S VOICE

"Zhenli, hold up there."

"Move your ass, Zavala." Neither knew how many days, or weeks, had passed since Chin's Review. They had moved at night when word got around the police were looking for anyone in the vicinity of Chin's Review when the night bird tested the air. Evening held its own dangers since the Review, but there was a lot more on the move in daylight to worry about. The police were not the only problem. The pair were warned a reward had been offered for information leading to the arrest of the individual or individuals involved in the death of Quetzal.

Zavala let slip the pair had been behind Chin's Review when they saw a night bird. Jumpers were called night birds, and the news spread. Soon the police were looking for them. Rumor had it a reward was on offer for the two. Not by name, but the police had descriptions. From this, it was only a matter of time before they were picked up. To avoid this, the pair moved at night, gave up hostels and squats. Everywhere it was the same problem — people wanting to make a little on the side. The two had to get creative: abandoned warehouses or those with no security. Failing this, they found shelter in alleys, rooftops, storage rooms, condemned buildings too dangerous for other squatters. Even going so far as two nights in a burned-out factory.

Charles and the department did not understand why locating the pair was taking so long. The swollen ranks of the homeless should have made finding Zavala and Zhenli a simple matter. Desperation had made the two cunning, and life on the street had given them a brutal courage Charles did not appreciate. While throwing the net wide, these two were slipping through the mesh. Composite sketches were circulating. Still, these sketches were being shown to the mentally impaired, addicted, alcoholic, derelict, broken, or those terrified of the police. Here was Zavala and Zhenli's edge, though other troubles dogged them.

The duo had brought an unusual amount of heat onto the community and were unwelcome. Zhenli reckoned this as well since they would have soon been turned over. What did they have to fear from this? Zavala asked several times. "What if they think we're connected to the night bird?" Zhenli answered.

"We've done nothing wrong," Zavala said.

"We have done nothing wrong — ever?"

"What do you mean?"

"They might find something else we could be done up for...or what we did to it." Zhenli was referring to his strangulation of the dying Quetzal.

Zavala ran a hand over his face, the stubble almost a beard: reddish-brown with streaks of gray. His face, narrow and long, was a haggard dark brown with thick lines running down the cheeks. With long, delicate fingers scored with fresh and healed injuries from years on the street, Zavala pulled his coat close and shivered though the night was hot. His hair was not the typical black. Almost the same reddish-brown as the beard. Like Zhenli's, the hair was long, matted, and greasy. The homeless had a problem with staying clean. The only place they could safely shower were the hostels; there the pair faced other dangers.

Theft, assault, and rape were common, but there was also trouble with staff and police. Many of the staff had been homeless and brought with them the same values and vices. Assaults by staff were not unusual, only, in turn, to be accused of assault. When the police arrived, this ended in arrest and conviction. Anyone catching a beating, robbed, raped in the hostels by the staff knew to remain silent. Even to Zhenli and Zavala, this was obscene, but nothing could be done. There were periodic explosions of moral outrage from what remained of the middle and upper classes. Afterward, the abuse would disappear for half-a-year, but it would always creep back in.

Zhenli's hair, though matted as Zavala's, was a deep, thin black with flecks of gray in this. He too had a beard, but it was sparse and black with streaks of gray sprouting on the chin. Asian, Zhenli's face was round, flat, broad of nose, high cheek-boned, and with a square jaw. If more aggressive than Zavala, Zhenli was the shorter of the two by some inches. His fingers were short and stubby but not thick. There were not as many scars on Zhenli's hands as Zavala's. "The police can't lock us up for something we haven't done." Zhenli turned and stared at Zavala. "Well, they can't."

"The law can do whatever it wants — we've no home, no job, no bank account, no identity papers."

If the law was annoyed, the space between arrest and the local police station was a great, brutal distance. In this space, they could be assaulted, raped, robbed, murdered. "We need to find a place to sleep." Zavala ignored the question.

"The streets aren't safe."

"It..."

"Two nights ago, remember only two nights ago."

"The Komodo?"

"That cover was open for a reason," Zhenli said, sticking a dirty, stubby finger into Zavala's chest. There was a clatter of overturned bottles; turning, there was no further sound. Both, taking a step back, were preparing to bolt. A cat hissed, and another responded, darting across the alley onto a dumpster, leaping from this to a fire escape. Another, following the first, scrabbled over the fallen bottles slipping and flipping. The pair waited for whatever was coming, but nothing did.

"In heat," Zhenli said, squinting down the alley.

"We should be safe."

"Something was moving in the Komodo — remember?" Zhenli continued.

"And that manhole was open," Zavala remembering the night behind Chin's Review. The voice carried with it a mnemonic of dread closer to a childhood nightmare than a memory. Zhenli knew the voice, understood Zavala was working up to an outburst. A dash through the backstreets of the district would follow with a better-than-average chance of being picked up. Stepping next to Zavala, the latter's eyes large as saucers, Zhenli struck him hard. Zavala's body twisted and collapsed onto a pile of garbage. Turning back, Zhenli waited — nothing.

"Damn fool, you damn fool," looking back at the unconscious Zavala.

"Zhenli," the hollow voice echoing up from beneath them and ringing off the glass, shaking the fire escape. It had a rich baritone creep to it that niggled at the base of the skull. Zhenli struggled against the panic squatting where spine and brain connected. A throaty laugh followed. For a beat, Zhenli considered leaving Zavala to whatever the voice belonged to. Instead, he threw Zavala over his shoulder and staggered down the alley.

"Come back. You know I will find you — come back, join me; join us." The baritone echo rose from beneath the Komodo covers. Louder, fuller, and richer, the edge of the voice cut the air as Zhenli tottered away. The voice had been trailing them for days. For days, they had been hiding from it — maybe it had been weeks. Days certainly, weeks maybe, but the pair never found over two days' respite at a time. That much memory the drink and opioids had not withered.

Zhenli wondered whether it was a better idea to turn themselves over to the first cruiser. What then? What would happen in custody? Would they be safe from whatever moved in the Komodo that night behind Chin's Review? Would they be safe from the police when frustration set in over not being able to find out what happened to the night bird? Typically, the police would not care — someone from the city would show up and scrape the remains from the car; that would be it. Not now, whatever had happened or whoever the night bird had been, they had pissed off or frightened their betters. Whichever way they played this, it was a gamble.

The voice had only chased them from place to place in the back corners of the city among their own kind — mostly on the east-side, but Zhenli was not sure if they had not crossed over onto the north-side. The alleys were less nasty, buildings less destitute, and cars better. They could still be on the east-side; crossing over from east-side to north-side was not always a clear transition. Still, Zhenli had to wonder where they were. Where would determine how he acted and, if Zavala woke, how he would feel. For what might have been twenty or thirty minutes, Zhenli had been carrying the unconscious man on his back. Unable to go further, Zhenli dropped Zavala on the jutting platform of a loading dock. The voice stopped, maybe three or four blocks behind them.

Slipping down against the base of the loading dock, Zhenli pulled out a mickey of whatever distilled liquor it was he had stolen the other night. Swallowing half the bottle, which had been two-thirds full, he winced at the aniseed — a sharp, cold, licorice burn. The warmth spread out from his chest and throat. He had not remembered drink like this since dipping into his mother's stash. Beatings followed, but the rush had been worth it.

Zhenli had not thought of his mother in a long time; he would have liked to think it years but no longer knew what years felt like. Trouble was, Zhenli and Zavala together no longer knew what time was. Most experienced time as a requirement: work, family, friends, bills, mortgages, appointments, meetings, children, partners — life. These trivialities had long since disappeared for the two. Their lives revolved around food, shelter, drink, and survival. Take away the drink and they were once again hunter gatherers: same as the city vermin. Unlike the other vermin, Zavala and Zhenli could not retreat between the walls of buildings. More importantly, they could not escape into the Komodo. There had been a time, Zhenli had heard from those surviving on the streets of the capital for the past thirty years, that this had been possible. But for fifteen years, the Komodo had been dangerous. Word was, not even city workers would go into the sewers without an armed escort.

Caspar rubbed the side of his head; the lank hair, swept back from the receding hairline, hung loose over his ears and onto his shoulders. A goose egg was rising on the left side of his head where he had hammered this against a metal door, screaming. The door opened, but before he could cry for help, a sharp pain exploded between his eyes; he dropped to his knees. "What..." Another blow hit him square in the face. It may have been the sole of a work-boot. Caspar dropped onto his back, and the world faded for the beat of a heart or the drum of eternity.

If eternity, the skin was pulled loose over the rim. The flop and flutter of epochs rose and fell with the beat of the snare. Time, again, wove its way through eternity. With time came being, with being evolution, with evolution consciousness. From this last byproduct of the nervous system came sensation: rain. Beady eyes fluttered, and these opened. All the energies, physics, chemistry, metaphysics, logic, and millennia of culture collapsed into one form. Doughy features coalesced, forming Caspar's disturbing girth and malformed particulars. A hand, with sausage fingers, rose to his face then promontory forehead. The fingers traced a gash from the middle of his forehead and swept back over the pulsating goose egg.

This had not been Caspar's first beating. He had lost count of the assaults and how often he had brought these upon himself. What Caspar could not control was never certain, but it was there. An impulse, always an impulse — but what this was never revealed itself to him or the electrochemical metaphysics humming behind his eyes and down his spine. Caspar knew there was something wrong with him. Had not everyone said as much, again and again? Dante had not, but Caspar was certain he thought this. What was the difference between saying and thinking a thing? The answer was throbbing in back of his eyes but could not make it to Caspar's tongue.

What does this mean? Not the throbbing in back of his eyes but that in his head. A beating — another beating. Sitting up, Caspar felt his head for further injuries. Finding none, he tested his arms then legs and, at last, the torso. Someone had kicked him in the side when he was unconscious. The pain along the left side of his body was a familiar one. Pushing to his knees, in the driving rain, he looked out over the empty parking lot in back of the factory. What was he doing? Caspar had been after something; he knew he had been after something. What had it been? It had not been a thing. Oh, Zhenli and Zavala. They were in the factory? No, they no more worked than he — had he? Had Caspar worked? Dante gave him work at Mendelssohn's Ink — he remembered the broom; he remembered the boxes; he remembered Beatrice. Beatrice, she was not his job. He remembered Beatrice.

Beatrice.

"Stop," he repeated several times. A mantra, whenever he saw Beatrice, he repeated this. "Stop." A long, low keening escaped from the back of the big man's throat, and he leaned forward touching the bulbous forehead to the tarmac. The pain from the gash and the goose egg lit up, but he pressed harder against the surface, feeling the irregular stones. Caspar, again, wheezed out the mantra. He loved her, but there was only contempt in her eyes. That would never disappear — but he loved her. "Stop." Pulling up from the tarmac, he arched his back, threw back his head, and screamed. Pulling a flip-blade, snapping this open, Caspar drew the blade over his inner forearm. The counter-pain helped ease the longing. The longing would return; when it did, Caspar would revisit the blade.

For now, it worked — Beatrice disappeared. Caspar was himself again. He had to be okay. Dante was his only friend. Dante was the only one who saw the man. He could not think of Beatrice. Caspar attempted to stay away from Mendelssohn's Ink as much as he could, for Dante. He succeeded in this more often than not. Sometimes he would go for weeks. He was certain there were weeks between visits to the studio with no need to see her. Sometimes this would not work. When Caspar could not stay away, and there was no work, he had come up with the idea of the tattoo. It had taken little effort to convince Dante he wanted the ink but could not afford it. If Caspar had wanted the tattoo, he could have gotten the money in a matter of days. Though he preferred not to, Caspar would do what was necessary. From his early teens, Caspar had been on the streets and knew his way around the dirty, dark, gritty corners of the city — but especially those of Bornler on the eastside.

Pushing up, Caspar stood, arching his back, his heavy belly protruding over the tight belt, and leaned his head back allowing the rain to hammer against his face. "Caspar, you ferret, what are you doing here?" Lowering his face, Caspar drew the cuff of his shirt over his eyes.

"Zhenli, what's wrong with Zavala?" Caspar's shoulders hunching as he stooped. Zhenli was helping Zavala, one arm under him. Zavala's head was hanging loose from his neck; hearing Caspar's voice, he raised this. The eyes were unfocused and distant. Not distant in the sense of unaware, but as if he were looking at something a long way off. The expression on the slack face was beatific. Holding Zavala's eyes, Caspar stepped forward, further hunching, whistling long and low. Finishing, the rain stopped.

"What happened to you?" Zavala asked, attempting to stand.

"What?" Caspar's hand reached up to the gash and goose egg. "I was trying to get away...that's right, I remember...I was trying to get away."

"From what?" Zhenli asked.

"There was this voice."

"Voice?" Zhenli allowed Zavala to pull free, staggering two steps off. Zavala had to use all his focus and strength to remain upright. Zhenli did not believe he had hit him that hard; in fact, he knew he had not. Something else was going on. The dreams were back. Where Zhenli had heard the voice while waking, Zavala sometimes heard it then too. However, Zavala was more upset by dreams of a figure in a long, embroidered cloak. He could not see his face but heard the voice.

The cloaked figure, tall and bulky, would lean over Zavala, paralyzed in sleep, and with large gnarled hands would fawn over chest and abdomen. These hands had long knobby fingers, and the nails were blue-black, hooking down over the ends. As the fawning proceeded toward Zavala's abdomen, he could feel the fingers were calloused and scored. The shadow's breath was heavy, strong, and cold. There was the smell of death in the icy breath. Reaching his belt, a hand looped about this and raised him from the ground, the other hand cradling his neck and lower head. Pulling Zavala into the darkness, he could hear a whisper: a soft, gentle complaint. Before the embrace was complete, before Zavala knew the words, he would wake screaming.

"Yeah." Standing, Caspar put a hand to his wounded forehead. "The Alchymist wanted me."

"Alchymist?" Zhenli jumped in.

"This guy he works for." Zhenli scratched his chin, thinking.

"The Alchymist is not the voice?" Zavala asked.

"Says not."

"Who is the voice?"

"Didn't say...didn't ask."

"Who's the Alchymist?" Zavala pushed.

"Who he works for, maybe follows. Kinda sounds like a follower."

"A religion?" Zhenli wondered.

"I don't know, maybe — maybe not."

"Are you looking for the voice or running from it?" Zavala appeared stronger on his feet and stepped close to the big man, taking him by the upper arm. Though doughy, there was muscle beneath the fat.

"Looking for you — both of you," Caspar said.

"Why?" Zavala asked.

"The Komodo, something's going on down there."

"Like what?" Zhenli's voice slipping along the question.

"I don't know, but something wrong."

"What you want us to do about it?" fear growing in Zavala's tone.

"That voice after you two, isn't it?"

"Maybe," Zhenli's answered.

"It's been chasing us all over the east-side," Zavala said. Caspar looked about then back at Zhenli.

"We're in Harcourt — on the north-side."

"Harcourt, that's the industrial basin," Zavala said, looking over the parking lot.

"It's chased you out of the east-side."

"Suppose it has — why are you looking for us?" Zavala asked.

"The voice has been speaking about you," Caspar said. Zhenli jammed his hands into his hip pockets.

"It's been talking about us?" Zavala took a couple quick steps back from Caspar. "And you've been looking for us?" Zhenli produced a knife from an ankle sheath. Motioning Zavala back with a hand, Zhenli stepped between Caspar and the tottering Zavala.

"You working for that thing?" Zhenli asked. Caspar held up his hands, stepping back from the pair.

"No, the voice wants all of us."

"Wants us to join it?" Zavala asked. Caspar nodded.

"You joined it, Caspar?" Zhenli waggled the long thin blade between two fingers, while pointing this at Caspar. There was a nonchalance in the gesture, but Caspar sensed a bloody mindedness.

"No, I want to destroy it."

"Destroy it?" Zavala asked.

"*Him* — sounds like a him," Caspar said.

"You know what that means, don't you?" Zhenli asked.

"Means finding *it or him*."

"Finding the voice will not be a problem."

"I've been looking since Chin's Review." Caspar squatted on his haunches, resting his wrists on his knees, hands dangling over the edges of these.

"Chin's..." Zavala never finished the thought. Stepping next to Caspar, he squatted.

"You were there?" Zhenli's said.

"When?" Zavala asked.

"Before you and those actors took off."

"You stayed?" Zhenli stood in front of Caspar, looking down at him, hands on his hips. Caspar nodded.

"Why?" Zhenli kneeled on the parking lot, hunching down to look into Caspar's eyes.

"Why what?"

"Why did you stay?"

"You may have left stuff." Zavala chuckled, placing a hand on Caspar's shoulder.

"You are one of us."

"There have been questions about you for a long time," Zhenli said, no longer attempting to catch Caspar's eye.

"What do you mean? I've lived on the streets since I was, I don't know — maybe thirteen or fourteen."

"Everybody knows about you, Caspar — since you've been on the street," Zhenli said.

"What do you mean?" Caspar's hand did not reach for the flip blade, but he noticed Zhenli's eyes change focus and narrow. The street had taught each of them the micro cues necessary to survive.

A simple shift of focus in one's eyes, the narrowing of these, easing a hip in one direction or another, cocking a head one way or the other, or taking a breath the wrong way all showed trouble was on the way. "Easy there, big guy," Zavala cooed, attempting to ease Caspar's anxiety. A breath, the beat of a heart, and one more glance between the men as the heat returned. Caspar looked up as the clouds parted and the sun came out. The early summer sun beat down on them; Caspar pulled out a handkerchief and ran this over his face.

"What kind of questions?" Caspar asked.

"Oh, all kinds — but mostly questions about where you stand," Zhenli answered.

"I stand where I have always stood, on my legs." Zhenli and Zavala exchanged glances. When Zhenli picked up, the voice was slow and careful.

"No, Caspar, that's not what I meant. Your relationship with Dante Skorna and his family is odd." Zhenli watched as Caspar stood, unbuttoning his trousers.

"Whoa, there," Zavala jumped up, putting a hand over Caspar's. He brushed Zavala's hand away and continued; unbuckled, he dropped his pants to his ankles. Pulling the threadbare paisley boxers down below his bellybutton, Caspar exposed the tattoo.

"This is what I'm doing there."

"Not finished, is it? But you've been going there a lot longer than it would take to finish that," Zhenli said.

"I sometimes get odd jobs — unloading a shipment, sweeping up, putting boxes away, and sometimes security."

"Security?" Zavala asked.

"Mostly drunks, but sometimes." Not continuing, Caspar picked up his pants and re-buckled the belt, sucking in his gut as he did.

"People talk about your relationship with the Skorna family. Some believe you want off the street, some that you never belonged," Zavala said.

"Belong? On the street?" Zhenli nodded, taking a step back. "Who *belongs* on the street?"

"Not everyone does, that is true. Was a time, not too many years ago, when this wasn't the case. People who came to the street belonged here, had belonged here all their lives but could not come to admit it."

"Don't, Zhenli." He looked over to Zavala and shrugged.

"Don't what?" Caspar asked.

"He's got a whole philosophy on what belongs and don't belong on the street."

"*Who*, not what."

"Zhenli, we're all *what* — the who got left behind when we stepped off the world."

"You're soft in the head, Zavala; always said it."

"Since when am I soft in the head?" Zavala's voice rising with an uncharacteristic break at the upper end of the register.

"Didn't I carry you halfway across the district?"

"Since when am I soft?" Zavala asked.

"Since that damn voice."

"That's different; the thing has crawled into my head."

"Get it out."

"Would if I could."

"Better find a way because I'm not carrying you for another night."

"Then we had better kill it, that voice of yours," Caspar said. The two men looked at Caspar then one another.

"That thing ain't natural," Zavala shook his head, looking away from the other two and over the parking lot to the street beyond. "Won't be too many more hours 'til dark." Zhenli eyed Zavala but said nothing.

"More unnatural than either of you know, unless you hung around."

"You mean Chin's?" Zhenli asked. Caspar nodded. "We didn't."

"Shoulda, you'd have seen what came next."

"Someone was on the roof with the night bird; they saw us, so we ran."

"Would've run faster and all the way south if you had seen what came out of the Komodo. I had not reached the bird — maybe halfway between the mouth of the alley and the manhole." Caspar stopped, appearing unwilling to continue.

"What did you see?" Zavala asked, and Caspar shook his head.

"It came out of the sewer: black like I ain't never seen. At first, I thought it was something weird with the light, but the floods at the back of the Review were on full, and still the darkness moved over the road then up against the wall. Strangest thing I ever saw. Thing was not right; no way that thing is right anywhere."

"Right, *not right*, got that, but *what* was it; *who* was it?" Zhenli's voice edged.

"Zavala's got that right. It ain't no *who*. Whatever that thing is, it moves like nothing I've seen before."

"What is it, a troll, fairy, mutant?" Zhenli would not let it go.

"Moved like it had no weight, nothing to hold it down, nothing to stop it from dancing through the damn air," hands going to his eyes, attempting to wipe the image from these. "Not until it took hold of the bird. When that thing got its hands on the bird, there was a tearing sound: part bone and part meat. Next thing I knew, a leg was flying over its shoulder. Then it shifted to its side, and I could see the cloak better. Along this, where it should meet in the front, was gold embroidery. There were weird symbols or images mixed in with the gold that I couldn't make out."

"How far away were you?" Zhenli asked.

"When that thing came out of the manhole, I ran behind the dumpster where you two were earlier."

"And you *stayed*?" Zavala hugged himself, walking a circle around the men.

"I wanted to run but was afraid it would hear. What was stranger was whoever was on the roof had not moved away. It looked like they had squatted down on the ledge and were watching." Zhenli had pulled his handkerchief, mopping the sweat from his face.

"Who pushed him?" Zavala stopped, staring at the two.

"Didn't see what was going on until the night bird hit the roof."

"What were you doing across the street?" Zavala asked.

"Watching the two of you; what were you doing behind that dumpster?" Caspar seemed happy for the distraction.

"Looking for scraps until those two came out the back. We dove for the dumpster. I was thinking maybe they would have a little extra silver," Zhenli answered.

"Then the night bird," Zavala said. Chuckling, Zhenli jammed his hands into his front pockets.

"That bird sent those two scurrying faster than I've seen any two people move that weren't running from a rape gang." The other two nodded. Young indigent men had long since formed gangs in which they preyed on anyone too young or slow. Rape was just one thing that happened and not the worst. Sometimes they would beat their victims, other times set them on fire, other times torture them to see how long it would take before they died. The worse the economic and political situation became, the worse the behavior.

Great lights of the city and nation bemoaned what had become of upper and middle-class values, especially middle-class, but had hardly a word to say for the poor and none for the homeless. These were the canary in the coal mine. The disenfranchised were becoming vicious and terrified at the same time. In the past, these had relied upon the state and charitable organizations to carry them over the course of a lean season where little or no work was available. As the government tightened its belt, the first programs to go, the first resources to disappear, were those supporting the poor and homeless. In response, their behavior drifted toward criminality.

As long as this remained limited to the homeless, there was little outcry, but as it crossed over into street crime and violence that affected the voting public, the government had no choice but to act. They could have restored the affected programs; instead, they chose to invest money in aggressive policing. Turning the streets of the city and many major provincial towns into armed camps. There were little or no avenues of redress for the poor. In effect, if not in fact, the poor were guilty, and it was up to the police to decide what they were guilty of. When brought to court, if ever brought to court, they were convicted, and sentences had become stiff — borderline hysterical.

This draconian approach had the effect of getting more criminals off the street and swelling the populations of already bloated prisons, but it only made the problem worse as more people joined the streets. These new street people were not only from the lower orders, but also came from the lower end of the middle-class. Amongst these were elements, small in number, of the professional and upper classes. These people did not know how to suffer as they were expected to. One of the many ways the demagogues were created was through introducing the upper classes (middle, professional, and upper) into the street.

Zhenli, Zavala, and Caspar all had heard, and sometimes followed, one or more of these demagogues. There was a feeling, for Zhenli, what they were chasing was something not far removed from these demagogues, if on a new order of magnitude. Not prepared to say anything, Zhenli kept the idea to himself but never far from his thoughts. "Street preacher?" Zhenli said.

"What do you mean?" Caspar asked.

"This Komodo voice. Doesn't he sound something like the street preachers?"

"It wants to kill us," Zavala said.

"I didn't hear it say so. Did you?"

"You want to follow it?" Caspar asked.

"Didn't say that," Zhenli warming to the notion.

"What are you saying?" Zavala stepped away from Zhenli, not far, but the movement was noted.

"What I'm saying is this Komodo thing sounds an awful lot like those street preachers we've been hearing for years."

"Same ones that bring down the police and National Guard on us?"

"Yeah, a lot like them, maybe just like them."

"What are you saying, Zhenli?" Caspar asked.

"I'm saying, maybe we should ask around about it."

"It's been chasing us up and down the east-side..."

"Out of the east-side," Caspar interrupted Zavala.

"Unless you're willing to crawl down into the Komodo to say *hey*, then we need to get smart about this. Running ain't doing no good — and crawling down into the Komodo is plain stupid. Have either of you heard of anyone, *anyone*, coming back out?" Zavala and Caspar exchange looks but did not answer.

"We can't wait around until he gets bored and comes after us," Caspar pushed, his enthusiasm evaporating.

"Has it? Has the Komodo Voice come after us? Caspar, have you seen it outside of that time behind Chin's Review?" Caspar had not, even though he had been visited by the voice occasionally: this always appearing to emerge from the Komodo covers. "It could be recruiting, not unlike street preachers we've seen all over the east-side — even on the north and west sides. How about the three of us stick together, get ourselves some weapons, and the next time it shows up, we have ourselves a little conversation?" With his hands jammed into his front hip pockets, Caspar looked about, not answering.

"This will not end well." Zavala, animated again, walked up and down behind the factory, fingers knotted in the front loops of his pants.

"This is the street," Caspar said. Zavala stopped and turned back to him.

"What's that mean, *this is the street*?"

"Means, ain't nothing here going to end well. Best we can do is to deal with the situation," Zhenli answered.

"So, how do we *best* deal with the situation — I've got this fucker in my head, and he ain't showing no signs of wanting to move on."

"All the more reason to talk to the thing. We can't run away from it; we can't climb down into the Komodo and hope to survive...no one else has that I've heard of. Can't hide. Can't fight. The only thing left to do is talk."

7

ZEMMOA AGAINST THE WALL

Bornler was an industrial wasteland. With the Great Collapse, industry emigrated to the West Coast. Factories, though, held on in the north-side of the capital as family and employee enterprises serving local demand. Even so, the roads were becoming difficult for transportation. Not only had highway infrastructure collapsed, but bandits and revolutionaries infested these between major cities and towns. Not two months went by that a new bandit did not throw in with one revolutionary casus belli or another. These political postures ranged from far Right to far Left.

If vacant of heavy industry and populated by low-end service culture, fast food, clothing shops, and food stores, Bornler also boasted bars, clubs, escort agencies, theaters, reviews, and street performers. Zemmoa ranked the greatest of these and Chin's Review a distant second. Since the death and mutilation of Quetzal, the Review lost many patrons, and performers no longer answered casting calls. In the weeks since the incident, euphemism won all when facts on the ground screamed helplessness and the whereabouts of Petr Novotny remained unknown. The official line, Inspector Lane supported this, insisted he went south or left the country. No one bothered to inquire how he got out of town, let alone the country, with a bank account barely able to cover next month's rent.

Such questions were no longer asked. Such inquiries would have raised too many difficult issues. Not only were the police and government unable to answer them, but the people did not want to hear this. All suspected what happened to Petr, but with one dead artist, and this one with some fame for a showing at the National Museum, there was no need to add an obscure actor. Neither belonged to groups the government and the wealthy would miss. Actors were a dime a dozen and artists little dearer. The National Museum planned another show with a new zemmoan artist, with a handful of Northside exhibitions to their credit, but nothing in either the west-side or Sonando.

The capital's public relations department moved at warp speed to put Quetzal's murder behind it. The lack of movement on the case and the fact it remained high profile made the move essential. Parliament, holding its breath, avoided questions about the murder. Quetzal's was not the only murder in the capital: these ranged from daily to weekly events depending on the season. Still, the federal government worried, and this fear translated into pressure on City Hall, which shifted this to the CID and Captain Slank then Lane and Korn.

Reina, curled up in a small alcove across from Zemmoa, had been the direct recipient of Inspector Lane's focus. Along with the professional pressure brought by the inspector was First Sergeant Korn's approach. Sancho's attempt to wring a confession from Reina drove the woman from her apartment on a couch surfing expedition across Bornler and the north-side. Soon enough expelled from these sanctuaries by Sancho's relentless hounding of friends and what family still spoke to her. Zemmoans did not have good relations with their families, but Reina's relationship with her mother was so bad the old woman gave a scathing interview to an online scandal rag. This gave the police more ammunition, leading, again, to her detention and interrogation.

After this, Reina found sanctuary in an old apartment in Chin's

Review, at one time used by the original owner some hundred and fifty years ago as a place to entertain actresses, mistresses, and rent boys. Back in the day, he brought the boys to the apartment. Women he could acknowledge, but men, or boys, were dangerous. Even today, living an openly homosexual life remained problematic and an appetite for fresh meat suicidal.

Reina had brought in a new mattress and washed and dusted everything else. She had heat, but the summer made this unnecessary; along with this was running water and a toilet. When she had moved in, the old cleaning lady had shown her a secret entrance and exit to the apartment. As long as Reina kept her supplied with mezcal, she would keep her secret. That was until a reporter found her and made a better deal. Reina supposed she had a few weeks, maybe the summer, before this became a worry. By that time, she hoped to have another solution. Her immediate problem was slipping unnoticed into Zemmoa.

Reporters and the police no longer staked out the club, but paranoia gripped the zemmoans, which left her with few friends and many that would not mind turning her into a night bird. Zemmoans, an ineffectual lot, would be unlikely to follow through with the attempt. If they tried, Reina liked her chances. There were, though, hangers-on of questionable origin that would not only have been capable but professional. The Dark Web continued to reach all corners of the globe as the international system imploded. If the Internet could survive a nuclear war, it would not be brought low by the collapse of trade.

"Reina?" Jumping, she pulled deeper into the alcove.

"Anbessa, don't do that." Reina took hold of her chest and stuck her head forward, the orange sodium light of the streetlamp catching this.

"We've got the side door open and a room in the back. Here." Anbessa passed a large, felt, floppy hat to Reina. "Keep this on until you get into the back room."

"What's going on?"

"You're not popular."

"I've never been…"

"Not like this." Anbessa waggled the shapeless hat in front of Reina. She took this and jammed it on her head.

Since going underground, Reina only went out at night and then only to places she trusted. Even at night, she wore huge sunglasses that disguised much of her face and only shopped in places they did not know her. In the short time she had gone dark, Reina was already missing the restaurants, nightlife, and Zemmoa.

Anbessa took Reina a block up, and they circled behind Zemmoa coming up along the side and into a door wedged open. A thrum of bass leaked from the crack; as Anbessa opened this, the music blasted them. Reina smiled from behind sunglasses and hat. "Stay close, and whatever you do, keep the hat and glasses on." Taking Reina by the hand, Anbessa led her through the door and along the back wall toward the private rooms at the other end of the building. There was a long table in the room, scratched, worn, old; sofas with thick cushions surrounded this. Pollack was the only other posse member. Harold and Ava would not be joining them because of Harold's position. Since the CID began digging into the group's past, Rolando made himself scarce.

This, which interested Inspector Lane and his partner Detective Korn, was the left-leaning social justice clique of pseudo-intellectuals that attached themselves to the posse. The relationship had faltered within months when the leftists called for demonstrations and action against the state. These always rubbed Rolando and Harold the wrong way, but when they called for action, the rest of the posse revolted. All the zemmoan posse ever wanted was to play, dance, drink, and fuck. Having the right political sensibilities was one thing, having to act upon them another. However, the connection between the zemmoan posse and leftism had been made. A few of the leftists had later been arrested during violent protests in Sonando. That was all Lane and Korn needed to bring the full weight of the CID down upon them.

Anbessa snapped the door closed behind the pair, and Pollack stared up from the table. Of the posse, all that remained was Pollack and Anbessa. Ava would have been there, but her brother had placed her in another sanitarium. It was only a matter of time before she broke out, but for now, she remained locked away. The present rumor had Ava tucked up in a high-security home for wealthy, troublesome, and violent patients. Pollack affected to believe this would be the last they saw of her, but Anbessa was not so sure.

"What do you want?" Pollack asked.

"You could say hello, first."

"Hello; now, what do you want?" Anbessa continued. Reina slipped behind the opposite side of the table from Pollack and Anbessa.

"No Rolando or Harold?"

"No, and I would not be expecting either for a good long while — at least not Harold. Rolando, who knows? That guy's so bent he might just come back," Anbessa said.

"I'd be leery of him if he did." Anbessa turned to Pollack, cocking an eyebrow. "He's a climber. Will do anything to make it up that next rung." Anbessa and Reina nodded. "What do you want, Reina?"

"Pollack, we've known each other for years."

"You brought the state down on us."

"I didn't do that. Whatever happened with Quetzal was the cause. Those detectives only need someone to blame so they can get off the hook."

"It doesn't matter." Anbessa shook her head and drummed her nails on the table. "They've torn our lives apart, and only two days ago did the police take the cruiser from outside of my place."

"But they are still investigating us and our connections to those leftists, along with you," Pollack said.

"I warned you about those people." Anbessa and Pollack exchanged glances. It had been true. Reina cautioned everyone about getting involved with the politicos. Quetzal had been engaged with his show on the west-side and escaped the taint. Too bad he had been murdered. No one else, except Harold, who was only a nominal member of the posse, and Rolando found the wherewithal to be elsewhere. Ava, though, could not get enough of them. There was something about wannabe revolutionaries who never got beyond the coffee shops and clubs that checked all her boxes. After Ava, only Pollack and Anbessa had been drawn to the socialists.

Reina hung around, but she was only in it for the fun, and there was not much of that. All they wanted to talk about was politics and social justice; sex was an afterthought. They never checked out the fun in the bathrooms or the car park behind Zemmoa. Reina was certain they were offended by the casual sex and drugs, making excuses to avoid either. She heard somewhere revolutionary types tended towards puritanism. It could have been, and this idea came from Harold; they were more interested in building a New Jerusalem, while the posse in deconstructing flesh and re-imagining mind. The two groups drifted apart because of an incompatibility of politics and identity.

The posse was decadence. Not a manifestation of an unruly psyche, not a cry for help, not an unchained libido. Zemmoa's posse was about the erotic destruction of the flesh, aided by the pharmacological unhinging of identity. There was no final explosion where the two came to blows, for the zemmoans would not have known what to do with violence when not attached to sexuality. Instead, the politicos stopped coming around when they discovered there was no one in Zemmoa to convert. Harold and Rolando warned, when the socialists left, if they succeeded in any of their revolutions, the zemmoans would be locked away in a variety of nunneries.

Their relationship petered out as oddly as it had begun, with no more fanfare than a casual ghosting. The zemmoans had soon forgotten their erstwhile revolutionaries. The drink, drugs, sex, and mindless debaucheries of the soul recommenced. Quetzal, with his exhibition over, drifted back into the group. Ava, always in love with him, had recounted the conversations and revolutionary goals. Quetzal listened, nodded at all the right moments, and fucked Ava in the car park outback with half a dozen other anonymous zemmoans.

Reina supposed no one would remember Ava from the exchange, either. Part of the woman believed Quetzal remembered no more than the experience required. He had floated over the posse and Zemmoa as if they were a dream and he the sleeping god. Perhaps he never woke from the dream; perhaps his flight as a night bird did this. Pollack got over himself and pushed back. "And you have been right so often in the past we should listen to you? Isn't that right, Anbessa?" The woman threw back the green colored liqueur. Anbessa's purple streak shook as she snapped her head back, running a hand through a knotty mass of coppery hair. There was a rooster quality to this Reina had not noticed before.

"Bitching is getting us nowhere. The CID and those two detectives want to jam us up." Pollack jumped on this.

"Us? I see none of us in their investigation. They are focusing on you and only because you can't come up with an alibi."

"I was in an orgy."

"Someone should remember you," Anbessa said.

"They should. After what I did with them, they should. I've been thinking about that. These zemmoans," indicating the door, "don't like the CID and will do anything to avoid having to answer questions." Pollack stared at her but said nothing.

"You mean those people are hiding their involvement and knowledge of you to avoid further CID questioning?" Anbessa inquired.

Reina nodded. Anbessa pulled out a flask and poured a light golden liquid into the liqueur shot glass, knocking this back. She placed a hand to her mouth, suppressing a cough. "Sounds reasonable," a hack following this. Anbessa was about to pour herself another, when Pollack put a hand over the flask, shaking his head. With a shrug, she put this back in her jacket and thrummed her nails on the pressboard table. Reina glanced from Pollack to Anbessa.

"Thought you may want to help find out who remembers me."

"The CID just finished with us," Pollack's voice ticking up against the bass vibrating the door.

"They aren't done with you, any more than me," Reina said.

"What do you mean?" Anbessa asked.

"I'm part of the posse. If they banged me up for this murder, they will look at you. You'll be called to testify, if not charged. How long do you think it will be before our idiosyncrasies become public knowledge? Not only us, the media and police will deepen their examination of Zemmoa and Bornler. All will become public knowledge. The washrooms, outback, the car park, and everything happening in these private rooms — not to mention what we've seen happen on the dance floor and tables will be exposed."

"You mean," Anbessa shifted uncomfortably, "you'll make certain they learn of it."

"Throw me under the bus and I'll drag you along." Reina pulled off her sunglasses and felt hat. The hat she tossed at Anbessa; the glasses she dropped on the table. Reina reached across the narrow table into Anbessa's jacket and pulled out the flask. Slamming back half the contents, tasting of cold fire and licorice, Reina closed her eyes and waited for the pain to subside. As it did, a warmth spread out from her chest and washed up the back of her head, reaching forward and clouding her eyes. The room shifted, settling in a haze of primary colors.

Anbessa and Pollack exchanged a quick glance. Tapping the flat of his hand upon the table three times, Pollack stared at the woman, eyes hooded. "All of us?"

"What do you... Oh, I see. Yes, all the posse, so you best get in touch with the others — especially Harold and Rolando."

"Why them?" Anbessa asked.

"They'll be able to exert pressure, right Reina?" Pollack pushed. She nodded.

"Why don't you call them yourself?" Anbessa said.

"They're not taking my calls — Harold's even blocked me." Pollack chuckled before replying.

"He's done the same with us. Why, I think he's locked Ava away for good. Appears the posse has taken him beyond his comfort zone."

There was a sharp rap on the door before Reina could respond. The door opened, and Juan was standing there. Behind him were two of Zemmoa's largest bouncers. "We need to talk." Stepping in, he closed the door on the bouncers. Juan looked at Reina for a beat, slipping in beside Pollack. "You've been barred."

"We can fix this," Reina began, "with a little help from Harold and Rolando." Juan rubbed both hands over his face, placing these on the table. He was well into a shoddy middle-age, potbellied, doughy, a bulbous, pocked nose with dark, red veins, eyes protruding saucers. Swollen veins laced the backs of his hands; on the right hand was a white scar. Dirty nails tipped the callused fingers.

"Harold and Rolando have had enough of Zemmoa. My backers are finished with the zemmoan posse. You," pointing at Reina, "are barred. Do you remember?" Reina nodded. The rumors about Juan's backers were the stuff of legends — Reina had no wish to test this. "Why are you here? Those men outside," motioning toward the door, "do not work for me. I think you know who they work for."

"We do," Pollack answered for Reina, "but we may have bigger problems."

"Bigger problems than the CID crawling over my books and interrogating my patrons?"

"It's too late," Pollack continued, "to put a wall between ourselves and Reina. It is well-known she was a regular here, also that she was part of the zemmoan posse. We have to deal with the fact of her presence and the lack of an alibi. Everything she got up to here will be exposed if we don't get her an alibi. Not simply Reina, but what zemmoans consider fun."

"There is no reason why..." The words died in Juan's throat. "What do you need?"

"I need people to come forward and tell the truth: that I was at the orgy."

"No one will want to do that because of what may happen to them professionally, then there's the matter of family and friends. People come to Zemmoa to be anonymous, to let loose. I'm not sure it will be possible to get anyone to admit to seeing you — even if they had."

"If no one comes forward, it is likely I will be charged, at least implicated in Quetzal's death." Reina said.

"I cannot force anyone to vouch for you."

"Juan, if you find no one that will confirm my alibi, the CID will turn my life upside down. They have already found socialist connections with our group and Zemmoa. How much further will they have to investigate to expose your connections? The CID will want to make certain there is no conspiracy."

"They may," Pollack stepped in, "wish to suggest a conspiracy if only to dislodge your backers from Zemmoa. It's never bad politics to go after organized crime."

"Criminal connections have never been proven with any of my investors."

"Definitive connections will not be necessary, though I believe the CID will be able to either find these or invent them, if they so choose. What will be necessary is to make a show of speculation. The detectives will throw their research to the news media, and that's chum in the water."

"That's a dangerous threat; none of you have met my investors or would wish to. If you push, Reina, this may trigger a reaction." Juan leaned over the table, nudging the bulbous tip of his nose forward; Reina smelt garlic and liquor. Behind this, cigars and weed, the heart note of the weed softening the cheap cigars. Though Zemmoa made money hand over fist, Juan appeared to be scraping by. He never dressed well, was often unbathed, possessed little by way of manners. It was as though his investors had picked him up off the street and put him in charge of Zemmoa on a whim. Juan was more than this, however. In the years running the club, he had made Bornler a going concern.

Juan indulged the wealthy, made certain plenty of beautiful, young bodies from the poor and arts communities were available. Though not always working out, it did often enough for the rich, arty, and poor that few complained. Only when the CID inserted themselves into the lives of the well-to-do did this become a problem. Quetzal's death, so near Zemmoa, and Reina's inability to produce an alibi had exposed the club and patrons to an examination neither could afford. How to move forward after their exposure was an issue Juan could not solve. His first strategy had been to bar Reina, but that did not slow the CID. With Reina between their teeth, it appeared detectives Lane and Korn planned on using her to hammer Zemmoa from existence.

"Without your help," Pollack responded, "it will not matter what any of us do because the CID will tear this club apart and the lives of everyone in it." Juan sighed, folding his arms over the top of his belly.

"Anything happening to me will appear suspicious," Reina pitched back.

"Possibly." Juan turned away with the word.

"Possibly this will intensify the CID's interest in Zemmoa." Anbessa sparked a short, half-burned, cigar.

"This is why Reina is still breathing. Oush this too far and the cost-benefit equation may alter." Pollack, examining Juan, scratched his chin, staring at the space above the manager's head.

"Why not give her an alibi?" Pollack turned from Juan to Reina and back. "If she gets an alibi, the CID will no longer have a reason to turn the club upside down, and your backers will no longer be looking at an investigation: that is if there's no other reason for the police to be interested in Zemmoa."

"I have experienced resistance to the argument."

"What kind of resistance?" Reina asked.

"Many worry pushing against our patrons may create a backlash."

"Backlash?" Pollack sat up, and Anbessa paused making smoke rings.

"Choose the wrong people to come forward and the police may not believe them; choosing those who are believable may anger their families — that could be more dangerous."

"Say you don't: all the dirty bits about Zemmoa and zemmoans will spill into the press," Pollack warned.

"No matter what is done, exposure is unavoidable. This is preventing the investors from deciding. The danger may be too great — some believe eliminating the problem," looking at Reina, "may be more efficient."

"We've all had our say. Now, what are you going to do?" Pollack asked.

"I'll propose we give Reina here the alibi."

"What weight will your recommendation carry?" Anbessa blew a large smoke ring toward the ceiling.

"A lot of trouble continues to rain down on Zemmoa for lack of a decision. The longer the investors take, the more trouble the club will be in; the more trouble the club is in, the more our patrons risk exposure. They've needed a push since this thing began — Reina's exposure may be that."

"Sounds like a big maybe." Ava dragged on the cigar and winced.

"Best I can do." Juan stood. "Reina, you need to keep away — and close to the Chin apartment." The woman bolted upright. "We never lost you — with friends, the motels, squats, and now the Chin apartment. Don't worry, but you can't hide from us. Even if you leave the city and head south, we would find you."

"How long have you been in the cubby?" Reina shrugged, not answering Anbessa's question.

"We've another of your zemmoans outside. Shall I let them in?" Pollack nodded. Juan opened the door. From behind the bouncers peeked Ava. As Juan stepped out of the door, Ava slipped between the two men and into the room. "I'll see what I can do; can't say for sure, but something has to give." Juan closed the door behind Ava.

"What the fuck are you doing here?" Pollack slapped the table.

"I win. Pay up." Anbessa held out a hand; Pollack slipped three bills into this.

"How did you escape?" Reina had pushed from behind the table and embraced Ava.

"We all know how she escaped." Pollack stood in for the answer. "What I'm wondering is what this will cost?"

"What do you mean?" Ava smiled at Anbessa, who returned this as she slipped behind the table next to Reina.

"Does your brother," Pollack began, "know of your escape?"

"Broke out two days ago, so I suppose he's known at least that long."

"You took that long to get back?" Reina ran a hand over the girl's arm.

"The sanitarium is about four hundred miles north of here, up in the mountains. I had to steal a bicycle in the village below the sanitarium. At the highway, I hitched a ride to the next town but had to wait around for a day to find a ride here. Things are terrible outside the capital. You would not believe the things I've seen."

"How bad will your brother want you back?" Pollack continued.

"Harold? Poor Harold, he worries so about what people think."

"But how bad will he want you back?" Pollack's voice ticking up.

"Depends how worried about his reputation he is — how worried his wife is. Pollack, get me something to drink." Reina placed a hand on the young woman's shoulder.

"Not here; not now — things are slipping."

"What do you mean?" Ava threw her arm about Reina's shoulder.

Reina filled Ava in on what had happened since Harold deposited her in the sanitarium. On learning Reina had been barred from Zemmoa, she had a difficult time believing it. Then came the news Reina was the primary suspect in Quetzal's murder. With a long, low whistle, Ava perked up. "I can give you an alibi."

"You weren't there. You were seen by us on the dance floor and at the bar," Pollack said.

"The police don't know that."

"Thanks, Ava, but the police will investigate your story, and if they find out others saw you in Zemmoa, it would come back on us both." Reina, stroking her hair, realized Ava, though wasted from years of clubbing, was thinner than before and her eyes vacant. The stare was not the byproduct of the drugs used to keep her manageable; there was another disconnect in the look.

Reina wanted to say more. Ava, of all the zemmoan posse, was the one least likely to be believed by the CID. Her behavior in Zemmoa was legendary, and her appearance spoke to the excesses. There were bags under her eyes; the eyes were bloodshot; thick lines ran from her nose to the corners of her mouth. The hair, in Reina's hand, was brittle to the touch. This was more than a lack of conditioning and whatever industrial shampoo they were using on her. There was something unhealthy in the touch. Reina hugged her, thanking the young woman once more. "What is to be done?" Ava glanced from Pollack to Reina then Anbessa.

"Juan will speak with his backers to see if he can get them to okay a plan to have select zemmoans give Reina an alibi." Pollack did not go into the details or the argument.

"For now, you had better come stay with me," Reina said.

"Unless you believe it is safe to go home?" Anbessa asked.

"No, if I go home, Harold will end up sending me back to that place — perhaps somewhere worse. He's gone around the bend on this whole Quetzal matter, now our behavior in Zemmoa has come under a microscope. Last time I saw him, I thought he would have a stroke."

"Going to him for help is a bad idea?" Anbessa wondered.

"Yes, any zemmoans coming near him he'll turn over to CID," Ava said.

"What do you think of Rolando?" Reina inquired.

"He would be subtler," the corner of Pollack's mouth turning up.

"Rolando's always been so nice to me." Ava picked at the table with the broken nail as she spoke. "Hard to believe he would turn on us."

"As a social climber, Rolando needs the goodwill of his betters. If he's political ambitions, and I believe he does, he'll not know a bottom," Pollack said.

"Where are you staying?" The perk in Ava's voice disconnected from the conversation.

"While hiding from the police, I found a small apartment in the back of Chin's Review," Reina answered.

"You mean that place is real?" Twisting round, Ava took Reina by the hands.

"You know of it?" Pollack asked.

"Heard my father used it to meet his actresses and girlfriends. It's a family story, but I thought it was only my aunts gossiping."

"The place is real," Reina replied, "but I had to do a lot of cleaning. The place looked as if it had not been used in a long time."

"This is wonderful; Harold will never think of looking for us there — even if he believed it were real, he would never think to look."

"Sorry to break in," Pollack apologized.

"What is it?" Reina asked.

"Should we attempt to find out who killed Quetzal?"

8

FLESH & BONE

"Wʜᴀᴛ ᴀʀᴇ ʏᴏᴜ ᴅᴏɪɴɢ, Dᴀɴᴛᴇ?" Lola squatted on an overturned crate. He looked up from between his fingers, running these through his hair, massaging the scalp. Lola's knees cracked as she drew her feet in.

"Should sit in the chair, Mom."

"I'm not so old I can't squat on a box. What's wrong?"

"How's Beatrice?"

"She's healing."

"From what I, or you, did?" Dante sat in the tattoo chair, extending this.

"The new chair is nice." Lola ran a hand over the faux leather.

"Don't change the subject."

"I can't figure out what to do with Bea. We gave her the best, more than most in Bornler get, but she's never been satisfied. Bea could get herself a rich husband and be happy half a dozen years together, but it wouldn't last. That girl knows no such thing as enough. So I beat her." Lola stared at her knobbed, arthritic fingers, flexing her hands. "Not the smartest thing I did. My hands still hurt, but your sister needs to learn her place."

"Are you ashamed of her?" Dante shifted in the chair, leaning on an elbow.

"Yes, but not for the reasons you think."

"This world offers few opportunities for people like us. When they present themselves, we must hold tight. The more dangerous her behavior, the fewer opportunities she, and the rest of us, will have. The future of your sisters would be ruined if it was ever learned what she got up to on the North side. Juanita needs a husband, and she is close. For six months, Eyrie's been dating the same man. What do you think would happen to them if the men learned what Beatrice did?"

"Mom, you are overreacting."

"Perhaps, but with your sisters so close to being settled, I am not prepared to take any chances. I understand why you refuse to marry or date. We need Juanita and Eyrie settled; I fear Beatrice never will be."

"I'll find someone," the conversation moving in an uncomfortable direction.

"Not until the girls are settled. Beatrice, I fear, will never be — not in the way either of us would choose. I've known women like her." Lola wrapped her hands about her knees. "I had a sister like her; after she left, no one spoke of her."

"First I've heard of it," Dante's voice tippling up.

"Just your father knew, and he only found out when it became impossible to hide her disgrace."

"Were you married?"

"No, and that bothers me." Dante waited for his mother to continue, but she did not.

"Why, what do you mean?"

"Victor didn't have to marry me, not after what Helen did. Everyone, in both families, would have understood if he left me. Your grandmother even said he should break the engagement. Your father, though, wasn't having any of it. When your grandmother insisted, he said that either she accepted me or she would lose a son."

Dante pulled the chair upright, resting his elbows on his knees. "Grandma, wanted him to dump you?"

"Don't blame her, Dante. There was pressure from all sides in the family, and she was class conscious — most of us in Bornler are attempting to get out of this mess, and the collapse only made matters worse. Victor attempted, in opening the new shop, to do this, but it didn't work. He was ashamed of that. I think it aged him before his time and then..." Lola stopped, putting a hand to her mouth and choking back a sob. Dante jumped from the chair, kneeling before his mother, and put his arms around her.

"It'll be okay, Mom." Lola wrapped her arms about him, and he rocked her.

After five minutes, Lola stopped crying. Dante sat her in the chair, giving her a box of tissues. Lola continued, "What's wrong, Dante?"

"Caspar has missed two sittings."

"His tattoo?"

"What's that mean?"

"You realize why he keeps coming around, don't you?" Dante shrugged. "You can be so simple," resting a hand on her son's hip.

"What are you hiding?" placing a hand over Lola's graying crown. She looked up with an expression that was half-grin and half-condescension.

"Bea is why he comes around." The pieces fell together, not that he believed them. His mother assumed a certain prescience neither Dante nor his father would admit to.

"Mom." Lola jumped on the thought.

"You've got your father's look about you, same one he pulled whenever I spoke of things he couldn't understand."

"Caspar can't even meet Beatrice's gaze...and you know what she thinks of him?"

"Yes, and if it weren't for the fact he cannot look at her, I might think I'm wrong. But whenever she passes, while he looks at the floor or the ceiling or anywhere else she isn't, he reddens and his breathing quickens."

"Beatrice abuses him. Remember the time she took grandfather's razor strop to him for breaking that box of complimentary coffee cups? It took me and Juanita to pull her off."

"I believe that made the fool love her more. He's a good heart, no matter his other faults. Beatrice, though, will have nothing to do with him; if she was the poxiest whore in the city, she'd still turn him down."

Lola gave it up and pushed forward. "You are worried."

"No matter why Caspar is coming around, he has never missed two appointments together. There was also work for him unloading a shipment today. He's never passed up work before." This gave Lola pause, and balling up the tissues in her hand, she pushed from the chair, dropping this in the garbage.

"What are you planning to do?"

"Check out his cubbies."

"Those places aren't safe." Lola stiffened.

"I'll take the automatic."

"Am I supposed to feel better?" Dante rested against the wall and stared at the floor.

"Perhaps not, but I need to find out what's happened to him."

"You may fool yourself, son, but not me." Lola laid a hand upon Dante's chest. "You're chewing on what happened on the North side."

"He's a friend."

"Caspar is an excuse; as excuses go, not a bad one."

"I'm not lying, Mom."

"That's true. You, though, are not being honest with yourself. Nor are you the first Skorna unwilling to face facts," thumbing up to the family apartment and Beatrice. "You, however, are doing it for the best of reasons."

Dante, hands curled within the pockets of his jacket, tapped the floor with the toe of his boot. He preferred wine colored work-boots with steel toes and soles and wore these year-round, unless there was a special occasion. It was over a year since his last date; still Dante had worn his favorite boots. It had not gone well, but she had been a friend of Beatrice's and about as difficult. For weeks afterward,

Beatrice had bothered Dante about when he would ask her out again. Eventually she gave up: the distance the two now shared he dated from this time. If there had been another way to end the relationship, Dante would have, but Theori was every bit as tenacious and entitled as Beatrice. Dante, finally, had to be cruel.

Afterward, he buried himself in the studio. About the same time, he stopped going out with friends: no more bars, clubs, or women. Caspar, at this time, began to come around more often. When Dante thought about what Lola said, it made sense. Caspar had followed Beatrice about the studio with his eyes when he believed no one was watching or when he could no longer control himself. He never did more and never struck back when hit by Beatrice. If his mother was right, Caspar was not dangerous. He was also one of the few friends Dante had left. That was why he was going after him.

"Dante," his mother called again, and he turned. "Where d'you disappear to?"

"Caspar and Beatrice: still not convinced, but it's possible."

"How long will you be gone?"

"I'm going out now, taking the bike."

"What about the shop?"

"The weekend starts tomorrow, so I thought I'd see if I could find him."

"You are closing the studio for the weekend? Sunday I could see, but Saturday is busy."

"Yes, but we've done enough business over the last couple of months to carry us for a few more. So, a day here or there won't hurt." Dante stroked the top of his mother's head, and she leaned into his hip. Lola felt frail and tissue thin. How much longer she would be with them he could not say but assumed she was staying only to see the older girls married.

"You're sure taking the automatic a good idea?" Lola asked. Dante pulled the weapon out of the holster fastened to the inside of the cabinet beneath the cash register. Checking the clip, he slipped this back in; from a drawer next to his inks, he pulled an armpit holster.

"I'm uncertain where Caspar is or what trouble he might be in," slipping the armpit holster on.

"You believe he's in trouble?"

"He's missed two appointments and a job — something's wrong." Not arguing, Lola pushed from the chair and embraced her son.

"You'll be gone all weekend?" Lola tapped him on the chest, looking up.

"Shouldn't take longer than a day, maybe two. I know where Caspar lives and where his friends are. There are only half a dozen places he may be, most of these in Bornler."

"Those people are dangerous. I know they don't mean to be, but most of them, these days, are mad." Dante patted the automatic under his left armpit.

"I'm prepared," reaching into a drawer and pulling from this a box of ammunition and extra clips.

Lola watched Dante disappear around the corner on the bike and turned back to the studio pulling out a thick ring of keys. The largest of these a brass skeleton key, pocked and dirty. On the key's shank was an inlaid filigree Lola took to be a semiprecious stone. Before leaving the studio, she locked this. Moving around the side of the building, she came in through the family entrance. Lola sat at the kitchen table with a cup of tea, placing the keys on the table, and wrapped her fingers around the hot cup. She felt more a reptile as the years passed, but the last one took all the energy she had. Lola suspected she was running on dying batteries.

The day's heat was gone, but the evening held much of it. Though sweating, Lola was glad of the hot cup. With a sigh, Lola pulled her hair free and ran her fingers through this. She then stroked the skeleton key with its inlaid white filigree. From the kitchen, she looked down the long hall to the bedrooms at the other end. At the end of this was another door; the skeleton key fit this. It was the oldest door in the apartment; when she moved in with Victor and his parents, this was their room. Five years after the marriage, his father passed, and within a year, his wife followed.

Though Lola never spoke of this to Victor, she was happy when her mother-in-law followed her husband. Five years with a woman who hated her for what her sister, Helen, did was five years longer than Lola thought it possible to endure. To her, it appeared the old woman never missed a chance to bring up her family's disgrace. Victor either did not notice the slights or allowed them to pass in silence for fear of alienating his mother. Upon occasion, it became impossible to ignore the slights and criticisms. When this occurred, Victor always took her side against his mother. Victor's father was much as Victor when it came to women. As long as a direct confrontation might be avoided, he would choose the path of least resistance. Lola considered this cowardice.

She feared saying anything until the situation with her mother-in-law reached a point where it became impossible to ignore. This created an awkward situation all around. Her father-in-law always sided with his wife against his daughter-in-law and her family. When the issue of her family, specifically her sister, was raised, there was no holding Victor back. As the eldest son, it was his right to inherit the business. All the other sons, by this time, were married with trades of their own. It was too late to disinherit Victor, and his parents realized their son was in charge of both business and family.

The old woman, in time, gave up her hostility, but no matter how Lola tried, she would not give up her hate. Her daughter-in-law attempted to win her over with cooking, children, love, and comfort as the old woman's health declined, but nothing worked. Then came the day of her father-in-law's massive heart attack in the studio. He lingered another two days but never regained consciousness. Even then, it was difficult to afford a hospital. They got him into a local clinic for an assessment but only received a discouraging prognosis. The doctor recommended they make him comfortable at home but did not believe he would regain consciousness. This was one of the few occasions, in Lola's long life, in which a doctor got it right.

When her husband passed, the old woman withdrew into a shell. This withdrawal did not lessen her vitriol. Now and then, the hatred would explode out of her in fits of frail rage. Victor attempted to get his brothers to take her in because she would attack Lola with frying pans, knives, crockery, and anything else at hand. None would, and so they ended up doing what they could while avoiding physical injury. As her condition worsened, the old woman's violence increased, though inconstant and febrile compared to their early years together. However, the violence could come from nowhere and with no cause. Lola might be bathing her, cooking dinner, or knitting on the sofa when it would erupt.

Always grateful to Victor for taking her in when he could have walked away, she came to hate her husband during the last stages of the old woman's dementia. It took them years of work to find one another again. They did this when the children approached their teenage years. Lola never stopped liking or loving her husband, but she hated him at the same time. The anger was not always there but lurked in the background. In these years, she and Victor spoiled Beatrice. The children followed their lead, especially the girls. Lola realized, while spoiling Beatrice, this was a bad idea. Neither she nor Victor, however, could stop themselves.

When they spoke of this, on the rare occasions they spoke of anything, she could never get him to admit to the problem. In later years, when Beatrice displayed behavioral issues, after she and Victor rediscovered one another, it remained difficult for him to admit to a problem. Pointing to the spoiling of Beatrice would only cause a fight, and it would take days or weeks to bridge the pain. Lola tried everything she could as the teenage years progressed and the behavior of Beatrice became troubling. Victor would do nothing but smile and comment how much like him Beatrice was. Lola believed neither father nor daughter shared anything in common: Dante and Juanita agreed but dared say nothing.

By the time Victor passed, it was too late to change her; all Lola and Dante could do was place obstacles in her path. When the behavior became uncontrollable, they did what they were again attempting: locking Beatrice up. The room at the end of the hall had been a study for Victor. But when the wildness in Beatrice took hold, they used it to confine her through the rages. Sometimes she would rage through the night when drunk or stoned. As the situation in the city grew worse, drugs became more available and more of a problem. Beatrice, along with her friends, discovered these early on. While most grew bored with the experience or realized the dangers, Beatrice found relief and nullification in these.

Since the death of Victor, Beatrice experienced good and bad days, good months and bad. Of late, the bad got worse. When Dante returned with Beatrice, Lola locked her up in Victor's study. There she ate and slept, only being allowed out to work, use the washroom, or do her chores. Over the last two days, she calmed, appearing to have turned a corner in this latest incident. Juanita and Eyrie had been careful not to bring anyone around the house while Beatrice depressurized. New faces, or non-family members, only aggravated her condition. Lola and Dante thought of these rages as a condition. No one cared to use the term mental illness. There was no cure for this even before the Great Collapse, but now there was nothing to do but lock them up or turn them loose on the streets.

This was what Dante had gone amongst in looking for Caspar. Lola feared, when gone, there would be no one to look after Beatrice. Although Dante promised to do this, she knew he wanted a wife and family. With Beatrice tied about his neck, this probably would not happen. Eventually, she would have to find a husband or her own way in the world. It was unlikely Beatrice would find a husband, but she might find a pimp: her sister all over again. Lola ran a thumb over the shank of the skeleton key then pushed from the chair and, with a grunt, she hobbled down the long hallway toward the locked door. Although she thought squatting on a crate no big thing, it was. Her knees, legs, and back all throbbed. "Can't even sit on a crate, old woman," resting a hand on her hip and twisting against the pulled muscle.

With a rap on the door, Lola waited for a stir of footfalls, and this came with a light wheeze of floorboards beneath throw rugs. "I'm going to open the door," no reply. Sliding the key into the lock, Lola wrapped both hands around the bow and twisted. The mechanism gave with a stiff grind of metal. Into her hip purse, she dropped the keys and swung the door in and stepped back. Beatrice stood in the middle of the room in a pair of jeans and a tank top, her hair down and narrow eyes squinting against the hall light. The room had the light switches disconnected and the only functioning light switch Dante had installed on the outside of the door. The dark worked best for calming Beatrice, but if they left her in control of the light switch, this would be on all night.

"Mom, are you sure about this?" Eyrie's voice came from behind. Lola turned, and Juanita stood behind her sister Eyrie. The two women were in their sleeping clothes because of the heat; they wore only panties and thin tank tops. Their hair was down and pushed up from sleep, and both looked as though they had only woken.

"Go back to your room." Lola flicked a hand at the two. "Are you ready to behave, girl?" Beatrice's face, now that Lola had turned the light on, was bruised down the right side, and her arms and legs showed signs of the quirt Lola had used on her. Most of the bruises were now a sickening yellow with only deeper purplish stains remaining in the center of these. Beatrice nodded but did not move.

"Come out," stepping aside. Beatrice edged by her mother and into the hall, still squinting against the light. "Do you want something to eat?" The young woman nodded. In the kitchen, Lola made her fried rice with garlic, onions, and chunks of chicken breast. Lola placed the plate before her, giving Beatrice a fork but not a knife. There had been an incident the night before when she had attempted to stab Eyrie in a fit of pique rivaled only by the old woman's mother-in-law. Not even her sister, Helen, had attempted such a thing. Although not new, Beatrice and her sisters fought constantly growing up, this was unexpected. The old woman sat next to her, watching her daughter eat. "I want to put you back..." the thought interrupted when the side door, leading to the family apartment, was shattered.

"One man did this?" Sancho pulled a sliver from the wall the size of his hand.

"Looks like." Charles stood back a few paces with his phone, tapping on burst-mode.

"This fellow...what's his name?"

"Caspar is all I got."

"I realize he's supposed to be big, but isn't most of it fat?" Sancho held up the sliver, blood tipping this, and Charles took a picture.

"Should be easy enough to track."

"I understand he's well known to the Skorna family."

"You spoke with the sisters?" Sancho dropped the splinter in an evidence bag, sealed this, and dropped it in his backpack.

"Where's the son?" Sancho leaned forward, squinting up the stairs.

"Wasn't at the hospital or here. Did the uniforms find his body?" Sancho shook his head.

"But they are still canvassing. Tell me," slipping the fingers of both hands between shirt and pants, "why are we wasting resources on a Bornler home invasion?"

"Dante Skorna has a direct connection to Quetzal Martinez, and now his apartment's been broken into, his sister abducted, the mother in intensive care, and Dante missing."

"I get that, but you're certain of a link to the Quetzal case?" Charles paused taking photos and turned to Sancho.

"The longer we are partners, the more stink from this case will rub off on you. If you want to take over from me, you better solve it fast, or it could swallow both our careers."

Sancho shook his head, adjusting the small backpack, and walked across the road running beside the Skorna apartment building. In the middle of this, he turned. "I've already told you I'm not involved in that. What the higher-ups are doing, I can't say."

"A corrupt uniform with no mentor and no real convictions, beyond those forced through intimidation and abuse, gets plucked from obscurity by command and placed on a high profile murder, with political fire, for no particular reason."

"When you put it like that..." Sancho did not finish the sentence.

"There's another way?"

"I don't know what's going on. All I can say is I was to inform command of anything you did that was out of the ordinary or questionable."

"Sancho, you're a good doggy." The first sergeant stiffened.

"I'm doing my job; I wouldn't have to if you hadn't pissed off all the wrong people."

"Thing is, no one was until you showed up."

"Are you certain of that?"

"No, let's interview the sisters." Sancho shrugged, following Charles up the stairs. There was a heavy smell of garlic and onions coming from the kitchen before which another door hung broken. Split down the middle, part of the kitchen door hung on its hinges. The other half rested against the wall next to the kitchen table.

Two uniformed officers were in the living room with two of the sisters; the third was taken. "Hello, ladies, I'm Inspector Lane, and this is Detective Korn."

"Have you found our brother?"

"You are?" Charles asked.

"Eyrie Skorna, this is my sister Juanita."

"Your brother has turned off his phone. When he turns it back on, he will get the messages we left."

"Why would Dante turn his phone off?" Juanita made to stand but thought better of it and slipped back onto the sofa.

"I'm uncertain," Sancho began, "but an officer took a short statement from your mother in the hospital. She said he is looking for Caspar. Is he the same one that did this?" The sisters exchanged looks, and Eyrie lowered her head before speaking.

"Yes."

"Can you tell me of your brother's relationship with Caspar?" Sancho asked.

"He's a friend of Dante's," Eyrie began.

"A friend wouldn't do this," Juanita interrupted. "Beatrice was right about him: he's broken and dangerous."

"One at a time," Sancho cautioned.

"Your brother has an ongoing relationship with Caspar?" Charles asked Eyrie.

"He does odd jobs around the studio and is getting work done."

"Before this, would you say Dante and Caspar were friends?"

"I suppose they were," Eyrie answered, "which makes all of this so strange. Caspar broke through the outside door, I don't know how, then through the kitchen door. When I came out of the bedroom, Mom was hitting him with a rolling pin. Beatrice had run from the kitchen, down the hall toward our bedroom. Caspar struck Mom with the back of his hand, and she collapsed; he then squatted over her, striking her several more times. Juanita threw a paperweight at Caspar. It caught him in the middle of the back, and he stopped hitting Mother. Caspar then came after both of us; I thought we were dead, but he only knocked us back and went for Beatrice. When she reached the room at the end of the hall, Beatrice couldn't lock it. Kicking this open, he threw her over his shoulder and left."

"Why did Caspar take Beatrice?" Sancho asked.

"Beatrice suspected he was in love with her, though she didn't put it that way. She said he wanted her." Juanita brushed her hair back and, on the left side of her face, revealed a bruised cheek.

"Did Dante know this?" Charles sat in Victor's chair across from the sofa.

"Beatrice never told him," Eyrie leaned forward, elbows on her knees, "and I didn't believe her. Did you, Juanita?" Shaking her head, the loose hair fell over the bruised cheek.

"I don't think Dante would have believed her. Beatrice," Juanita paused, took a breath, then continued, "had problems — a lot of problems."

"What kinds? Drink? Drugs?" Charles asked.

"Mostly anger: the drink and drugs were to deal with this. Because of the anger and the fact she often verbally and physically attacked Caspar, Dante, and the rest of us, tended not to believe anything she said," Juanita continued.

"She was right about this, however?" Charles looked down the hall.

"Yes, but that after a year of abusing Caspar," Juanita pushed the hair over her cheek and looked away.

"Revenge?" Sancho inquired.

"Why else beat Mom so bad?" Eyrie catching the inspector's eye.

"Yes," Charles' answer noncommittal. "That door," standing as he spoke, "at the end of the hall has a lock on the outside and a light switch there too — what's that about?"

"It's where mother keeps Beatrice when she loses control."

"What do you mean?" Sancho asked. Juanita sighed and looked away. Sancho repeated the question.

"Beatrice has always been unhappy. Our place is too low, we don't have enough money, and the family business embarrasses her."

"What does this have to do..." Juanita interrupted Sancho.

"She's trying to find a rich husband and doing it in all the wrong ways. A little while ago, Dante caught up with her on the north-side and brought her home. Mother beat her then locked Bea in that room."

"Does this happen often — Beatrice losing control?" Charles tapped his notepad before flipping it open.

"You can see how it is for us, inspector," Juanita said.

"Help me."

"Her clubbing, drinking, drugs, and violence have been creating problems for the family, and there's no government help available. Like everyone else in the country, we are on our own," Juanita's voice cracking. Not answering, Charles continued to scribble in the notebook, stepping down the hall. After a few minutes, he returned.

"Did Caspar know how your mother dealt with Beatrice's disobedience?"

"I don't think so," Eyrie said, "but he may have heard Mother and Dante discussing her behavior."

Charles leaned against the doorway leading toward the hall and kitchen at the other end of this. "Is it possible Caspar saw this as a rescue?"

"He beat our mother so hard she's in the hospital." Juanita bolted from the sofa; one of the uniformed officers cautioned her back.

"I'm attempting to understand why Caspar took her. If I can do that, we may have a better chance of returning Beatrice."

"Who can say what that fool thinks?" Eyrie stood, putting an arm about her sister.

"He acted with purpose, and how Caspar took after your mother suggests rage. You two he knocked out of the way, but it appeared he wanted to kill your mother." Charles returned the notebook and pen to his breast pocket.

"What have you heard of our mother?" Eyrie asked.

"All we know," Sancho answered, "is your mother is in intensive care; before being taken there, she gave a short interview."

"We have to get to the hospital." Eyrie pulled closer to her sister.

"A few more questions and we'll have an officer take you," Sancho said.

"We've told you everything we know." Juanita pulled free of her sister, stepping around the coffee table and approaching the inspector. "Please, Mother's in hospital, and we need to be with her."

"Your mother," Sancho continued, "is in the ICU, and you cannot remain with her for more than a few minutes."

"But we could be with her." Eyrie's voice spiked as she pointed a long forefinger at Sancho. "If this was Sonando, you would not be keeping us here."

"This is not Sonando," Charles admitted, "and there's a connection between Quetzal Martinez and your brother."

"Is Caspar connected to Quetzal's murder?" Eyrie stepped up behind her sister, wrapping and arm about her waist.

"We aren't certain, but it appears the abduction has nothing to do with the Quetzal incident. This, however, will require investigation," Sancho said.

"That's the only reason you're here?" Juanita stepped over to the first sergeant, about to jab him in the chest with a finger when the other uniform batted her hand away.

"Enough." Charles stepped forward, holding a warding hand up to the uniforms. "Wait outside." When they had gone, Charles turned to Eyrie. "We have what we need for now; all I can say is we'll do what we can for your sister. If your brother comes home, tell him to contact us." The inspector gave Eyrie his card and scratched his personal number on the back.

"What of the apartment — it's wide open?" Juanita asked.

"Don't worry. We're leaving a uniform outside until your brother shows up," Sancho answered.

$$9$$

ALCHYMIST

THE CLOSEST DANTE COULD RECKON, he was three blocks south of Zemmoa. Most buildings were derelict factories and warehouses; there were a few carparks still working, but the abandoned carparks, factories, and warehouses now housed the homeless in a series of squats ranging from a small clan to a large village. Here, as elsewhere, the homeless banded together: there was no other way to survive. After the sun went down, they would return. During the day, the police, upon occasion, would raid these, locking up those found for a few weeks or months. Time varied based on whatever the police cared to charge.

The police avoided dealing with the homeless since there was little profit in it. However, with the death of Quetzal and rumors swirling about the Komodo, anxiety over the underclasses was rising. Fear of the lower orders had been increasing over the last generation because of the revolutionary explosions that occurred both in the provinces and capital. There was the failed coup d'état, but the government feared others. Still, most revolutionary explosions and implosions took place in the provinces, but these fires were emerging more often. This had not escaped Dante's attention, but seeing he could do nothing about them, he, his sisters, and mother ignored them.

For the past year, Dante rarely stepped foot beyond the studio or apartment, and much had changed. He had not been a complete recluse, having gone out for food and errands. There were also those times he needed to track down Beatrice, but these were few. Dante needed but call around to her friends to pick up rumors of where she disappeared to. That done, he would chase down the leads. There was not much opportunity to look at Bornler to see what had been changing. Dante had uncovered a little on his trip north to fetch Beatrice, but this time, rooting through Caspar's rat holes, Dante was discovering how bad things could be.

Making his way from one squat to the next, from warehouse to factory to carpark, Dante discovered the numbers of homeless had swollen far beyond Caspar's reckoning. Had Caspar lied to Dante? That would not be like Caspar, but it was not like Caspar to disappear for so long. In the last warehouse, he moved from one group to the next in their makeshift shelters of cardboard and wood crating insulated with newspaper. With the collapse of access to the Web, newspapers were again popular. Finished, readers would discard these. A significant portion of the refuse made it to recycling centers, those still in operation now government funding had dried up. Still, enough fell into the hands of the homeless and volunteers, from the remnants of the middle and upper classes, that anyone seeking insulating material would not go without. Stepping through the office door of the warehouse, Dante put a hand to his nose.

The smell of unwashed bodies was thick and this mixed with the odor of barbecues and barrel fires to cook what meat was gained over a day of panhandling — often this netted little or nothing. In that case, children would form hunting parties. Wherever the homeless moved, rats and other scavengers, feral dogs, and cats would follow. Dog was preferred, but cat meat was not far behind — though much harder to catch. Dogs, though, were more dangerous since they traveled in packs and some of those had been used for fighting and as guard dogs. The children often left these larger dogs to the men.

They would hunt the animals in groups with spears made from metal pipes stolen from whatever buildings they could gain access to. The points filed at an angle and the tip sharpened.

A halloo rose as he stepped from the office, and children darted across the space to the makeshift shelters running along the far wall. Dotted across the savanna of concrete were barbecues and open barrel fires. Even in the heat, people gathered about these, hands outstretched over the fire holding skewers; on the skewers were various cuts of meat. Many of these held rat or a close cousin. Some skewers held tarantulas, though the favorite method for cooking was deep frying. Where cooking oil was not available, roasting over an open fire was a common practice. Several were not dead, and as their legs scrabbled in the empty air, women and children would stick them deeper into the fire, burning off the hair.

Moving further into the savanna, Dante noticed men appearing at the far end of the warehouse, carrying spears. With his right hand, he unsnapped the holster of his automatic and loosened this. Dante raised his hands to show he was not a threat. The men stopped, but they did not go away. "I'm looking for a man," pulling a photo of Caspar from his back pocket. He did not use the digital images on his phone since this would mark him as a target. Because of this, and the fear of the phone ringing at the wrong moment, he had turned it off. "Have you seen this man?" taking a step forward.

"We haven't seen him." An old man hobbled from a small shelter on a thick knotty cane carved from a tree branch. "Now get gone." The old man turned his back and farted; the explosion reverberated from the corrugated roofing and girders. Several children laughed in their hovels.

"Can't do that. Tell me if you've seen him then I'm gone." The old man waved towards Dante and whispered something to the men, who stepped forward. Another called in a phlegmy voice for Dante to leave. Taking several steps forward, continuing to hold the photo, he slipped his free hand over the grip of the automatic.

None appeared to have recognized the gesture. One young man trotted forward, breaking into a lope. Slipping the photo into his back hip pocket, Dante braced for the impact. The youngster had little experience using the weapon for hunting and none against men. Releasing the automatic, Dante slipped aside of the thrust, grabbing the spear as it passed and knocking the young man's knee out from under him. As the youngster tumbled forward, Dante took possession of the spear and slammed it against the back of his head. There was a meaty clunk, and the young man grunted, gripping his head and rolling away. The others approached with caution.

"I only have a few questions then I'll leave you in peace."

"We have peace," called the phlegmy man moving wide of Dante, attempting to circle around him.

"This won't end any better for you — and stop right there." Dante pulled the automatic. Chances were he could handle two, three, even four. There were more, however, waiting by their shelters and further down. Several of the women and children had left their open fires, still holding their skewers, moving toward the far wall. When Dante stepped onto the warehouse savanna, there had been a hum of activity. Now there was only the crackle of the barrel fires.

Dante did not discharge a round but held the weapon out for all to see. The man, circling around him, stopped, lowering the makeshift spear. Not expecting this, he was re-calculating his odds. Looking back at the old man, who waved him off and tottered forward, leaning on the cane, the spearman backtracked. The others moved off until the old man passed them then trailed behind at a safe distance but still within striking range. "What do you want?" the old man coming to a halt and leaning upon the makeshift pommel of the cane. Dante pulled out the photo and passed it to the old man, keeping an eye on the others. Any of these could kill him if he were not careful, and he was uncertain what would happen to his remains.

Dante had heard stories.

"We knew this man." The old man returned the photo.

"Knew?"

"Word is he's gone to the Komodo." Dante cocked an eyebrow and looked about.

"Dead?"

"No." The old man shook his head adjusting his hands on the cane's pommel. "He has gone to the Komodo with another."

"He has gone down into the sewers?" The old man nodded. "No one," Dante's voice cracking, "goes into the Komodo out of choice." This was true as far as Dante knew. Only those so desperate there was no hope above ground slipped through the covers or walked into the storm drains. Shrugging, the old man looked about.

"I've told you what we know. Are you leaving?"

"How do you know this — who told you?"

"Know? We here know nothing, are nothing — even to the likes of you, Skorna."

"You know me?" Dante took a half-step forward, and the anxious spearmen matched this. "I don't want trouble, but if your people start it, I will end it." The graybeard waved off the spearmen, and they took two steps back; marking this, Dante eased off with the automatic but did not lower it.

"Caspar has mentioned you and your family," tapping the cane upon the concrete.

"He's a friend."

"Now he's gone to the Komodo."

"You make that sound different. Why is that?"

"Not different, not in the way you mean, but he has...moved on."

"Let me ask you again," Dante crossed his hands before his waist, still holding the automatic. "What is going on?"

"Going on — what is going on has been going on for years, but you people don't want to see. Maybe you can't."

With a swiftness that took the old man by surprise, Dante had pulled a flip knife and had this beneath his chin against the soft wattle. "What's going on?"

"You would kill an old man?"

"I have before."

"You fought in the South." Dante nodded, pressing the knife home so it pierced the flabby tissue, and a thin trickle of blood ran down the steel of the weapon. The others had raised their spears, once more, and hesitated. If they moved, the stranger would've killed the old man before they could get to him. Throwing a spear would be no better.

"Yes, I did." Dante shifted, still holding the old man to keep an eye on the spearmen. "Ease off," speaking to the men. Leaning over the old man's right ear, with heavy tufts of hair growing from the tragus, Dante warned him. "Ease them back, or I will use the automatic."

"Back off, Harv, and you, Limmer." The old man shifted his head, looking at Dante. "We're good, right?"

"Four more steps, all of you." The spearmen did as they were told. At this, the women hustled the children, still on the savanna, back into their shelters.

"I know who you're looking for."

"I've already told you who I'm looking for."

"Caspar has gone to the Komodo. Who you want is the one that didn't."

Dante held the old man at arm's length, placing the tip of the blade below his sternum and pointing upward. "Who — who didn't go?"

"Zavala, he and Zhenli were always together; they often were seen with Caspar." The old man shifted as the blade slipped through the thin fabric of the shirt, pressing against his flesh.

"Zhenli and Zavala? Zhenli is Asian, right?" The old man nodded. "Zavala is a bit slow?"

"Some say, but I've not found that. Still, he's the one that didn't go."

"Zhenli did — go with Caspar, I mean."

"Zavala says so. For those two to bust up, it had to be over something like the Komodo. That what you want to hear?"

"Where," Dante slowly arced with the old man held beneath the chin, "is he?"

"Not here."

"Okay, but where?"

"In a squat across from Chin's Review alley where Quetzal got himself killed." The old man tapped Dante's arm. "I can't breathe." Dante eased off, and the old man gasped. As two of the spearmen stepped forward, the old man waved them back. "You have what you came for. It is enough?"

"Yes." Dante backed the pair of them to the office. At the door, Dante released the graybeard. "If you are wrong, I'll be back."

"He was there, last I heard...maybe a day ago." The old man rubbed his throat.

"When's the best time to catch him?"

"He should be there; comes late when the patrols around Chin's Review are not heavy."

"They are still patrolling the area?" Dante closed the knife, slipping this into his front hip pocket.

"All of Bornler is seeing more activity. Haven't you noticed?" Watching the old man adjust his jacket and examine the puncture in his shirt, Dante fastened the automatic's hammerlock.

"I've been stopped a few times."

"The closer you get to Chin's Review, the heavier the patrols; there's something about the place that's got the CID nervous. There's been more Komodo activity down there than elsewhere, but since the Quetzal thing, there's been almost no activity behind Chin's Review. Can't say it will stay that way. Sooner or later, whatever, whoever, is lurking in the Komodo will come out."

"What then?" Dante adjusted his jacket.

"Then, I don't know...but it won't be good. Those that can get out of Bornler, are. Some are off to the south-side, a few to the north-side — I've even heard of a few on the west-side, in its southern reaches, but that's only rumor. Can't see the police going for that. It would set off the rich to see panhandlers on the street corners."

"Another revolution?"

"No," the old man shook his head scratching his lank, greasy hair, "but it could mean the end of everything."

"What's that mean?"

"Means what it says." Dante shook his head and stepped deeper into the office still facing the old man. At the exterior door, leading into the street and his bike, Dante turned away.

Dante stashed the bike a block away behind a dumpster and covered it with cardboard boxes and plastic garbage bags. It had taken him longer than he thought reasonable to make his way past the patrols that were heavier than the old man had led him to believe. It might have been better to wait for the next day, but if Zavala was like most of the homeless, he would not spend the day in his squat for fear of being picked up. Finished hiding the bike, there was the sound of a car, and Dante pulled more garbage bags about himself, sinking back against the chipped brick wall. A roller slipped down the street, stopping next to the alley, shining a flood into this.

The light washed over the alley and up the walls. Pausing on the bags covering Dante, the two patrol officers were debating whether to get out and check the alley but gave it up. Dante waited for this to roll down the street and turn the corner before pulling himself from the bags. For the next fifteen-minutes, he ran from alley to alcove, ducking for cover at the sound of cars. Across from the alley behind Chin's Review was another. Two doors down, there was a wire mesh basement window, unlocked. Pushing this open, he slipped in.

"Zavala?" Dante moved along the cool brick wall of the basement heavy with the smell of earth from the unfinished floor. There was no sound, no movement as Dante squatted down snapping open the knife. Before slipping through the window, Dante failed to release the velcro hammerlock on the automatic. For now, he was left with the knife if he did not want to give his position away. It occurred he had done this in calling out. Crabbing from the window, he waited for his eyes to adjust. Dull shapes presented with darker outlines against the thin light coming from the street lamps. There was a chest of drawers, a wardrobe, and what looked like a long chest.

When this creaked, Dante realized it was not a chest but a spring bed. A low moan rose from the creaking springs accompanied by the sound of a body slipping back onto the mattress. "Zavala?"

"Who," voice breaking into a hard cough. Pulling out a small flashlight, he moved the beam along the earthen floor. At the other end of the room, against the wall was the bed Dante had mistaken for a chest. A hand rose from this then floated down.

"Dante Skorna," moving between broken crockery, old pots, and cast-off clothing. Holding the flashlight overhead, Dante reached the end of the brass bed. Placing a hand on this, the frame quivered.

Pulling his hand back, Dante moved the light from the feet of the man toward his waist then abdomen. The pants, old to begin with, were dirty with tears about shins and knees. The belt was missing from the waistband. In its place was a rope tied in a sailor's knot. With the shirt open, the lower part of the stomach, covered in thick black hair, was defaced by a red welt that ran from the neck to the left hip of the pants, disappearing beneath this.

"Zavala?" Dante moved to the side of the bed and kneeled. Placing the fingertips of his hand against the carotid artery, Dante waited for a beat. It came then another and another. Though not steady, the pulse was there. Dante called the man's name again; he was far from certain this was Zavala. Dante had not seen him before and had only heard vague comments from Caspar about Zhenli and Zavala. The man's eyes fluttered open, and his head turned toward Dante, who moved the light out of his eyes but kept it on to illuminate the face.

"Who are you?" a dry hack following the question. From his backpack, Dante pulled a bottle of water and helped him take a sip.

When he stopped coughing, Dante allowed him to hold the water. "You're Zavala, right?" He nodded. "What happened to you?"

"The Komodo…it's coming…" the voice disappearing into another series of coughs.

"The Komodo did this?"

"Yes, those working for the Voice," taking a sip of water and twisting the cap back on.

"The Voice? What are you talking about?"

"The Komodo Voice, it and Alchymist."

"Right, about Caspar?"

"He's gone down to the Komodo — you're Dante Skorna?" Zavala's hand rose, and Dante took this in his own.

"You need to get home," the grip tightening.

"What — why?"

"Caspar, I'm not sure what the Komodo Voice said to him, but he wants your sister. What's her name — Beatrice?"

"Beatrice? He can't even..."

"Caspar can," Zavala interrupted, "and the Voice has given him permission to do whatever he wants."

"What are you..." and the penny dropped. "He will take her?" Zavala nodded, taking another sip of water. "Here." Dante attempted to raise the prone man, but he moaned in pain and pulled away. "I'll get the EMTs." Zavala did not answer but turned his head to the wall, taking in a rattling breath. Without waiting, Dante was out of the basement and running down the street.

The alley behind the house was taped off, along with the side door — where the side door should have been. Before the door was one of the biggest patrolmen Dante had ever seen; his shoulders blocked out the entire door and his head was higher than this. He was in full uniform wearing a riot helmet and a truncheon half as long as Dante's arm with a steel tip. "I live here." The patrolman looked him up and down.

"You are?" resting the top of the truncheon in his free, gloved hand.

"Dante Skorna." Before answering, he reached for his identity papers. The truncheon tapped him on the chest so hard he took a step back.

"Slow." Dante continued to reach for his ID papers, feeling the automatic beneath his hand. Giving the papers to the officer, he waited for these to be examined and his face checked against the photo.

"Where have you been, Mr. Skorna?" handing back the identity papers. Dante, self-conscious about the automatic, decided fear and anger were not the way to go.

"I've been looking for a friend that went missing a while ago. What happened here? Is my family safe?"

"Your sisters, two of your sisters, are upstairs."

"My mother?"

"In the hospital." The giant stepped aside. Taking the stairs two and three at a time, he found the inside door had also been broken. Part of this hung loose from the hinges, and the other was resting against the kitchen wall next to the table.

"Juanita," Dante called then called again before his older sister shouted from the hall. Eyrie called from the living room then both women were running for their brother. Eyrie, closest, reached him first and threw herself screaming into his arms. He could not understand what she was saying, and Juanita was in the same state as she reached him. "Mother?" Eyrie pressed her face into her brother's chest and sobbed. Juanita, when he looked at her, could only shake her head, face screwed tight in pain, tears running down this. "I was told she was in the hospital — is she okay?" Juanita pulled a handkerchief from the sleeve of her dress.

Wiping her eyes, Juanita stifled her sobs and choked out the words. "She died last night."

"What happened?"

"Caspar, he beat mother and took Beatrice."

"But why? Why would he do this?"

"Beatrice was always right about that idiot." Eyrie had pushed out from Dante's arms and was holding the lapels of his jacket, knotted in her fingers.

"Yes." Though it was all Dante could think to say, the answer did not explain what had happened.

"What are you going to do about this?" Juanita demanded.

"Do? Do about this — the same thing I had intended to do when I went looking for him."

"What does that mean?" Eyrie shook him by the lapels and dropped her face back into his chest.

"I have to find him and bring her back." Dante pushed Eyrie away and took off his jacket. Removing the automatic from its holster then the holster, he slipped these beneath the end table beside his mother's chair. The weapon was not illegal, but he had not registered it — that could be a problem. Next, Dante dropped the knife on top of the table. There was still no law against carrying a blade, but it was not a good idea to be caught holding one. "What did the police have to say?" Juanita ignored the question.

"How are you going to find her? The police have no idea where he is — they're hoping you may know."

"I do."

"Where is she and why aren't you going after her right now?"

"The Komodo," the single word answering both questions.

"The Komodo." Eyrie stepped away, the back of a hand covering her mouth, the other rising in a warding gesture.

"Talk sense, brother. No one, not even that fool, goes into the Komodo...hasn't for years." Juanita took her brother by the upper arm as she spoke. She wiped her tears away, shifting from grief to anger.

"The Komodo is not the empty place you think it is."

"Didn't say empty, Dante. There's every manner of freak and criminal in the deep parts of the Komodo, but only fools and madmen venture into it." Juanita shook a finger in his face.

"I met someone last night," looking back down the hall to the kitchen, Dante wondered if he should tell the patrolman.

"Who? Who did you meet last night, and what does that have to do with this?" Juanita asked. Dante ignored the question.

"What police came by?"

"Those detectives, Lane and Korn," Eyrie said. "They even had us taken to the hospital so we could sit with Mother."

"After questioning us." Juanita stepped over to the living room window and pulled the drapes back to look over the street. "The police have been down there since the break-in."

"Why would they care about us?" Dante looked from Juanita to Eyrie. Eyrie shrugged, while Juanita turned, folding her arms over her chest, working the handkerchief beneath whitened knuckles.

"They don't, said as much." Juanita ground the handkerchief in her palm.

"What do they care about then?"

"This Quetzal business, that's what they care about. If it hadn't been for the fact you did that guy's back tattoo, I don't think we would get any attention. We're uncertain," motioning to Eyrie, "whether this is a good or bad thing."

"You saw the patrolman coming in, right?" Eyrie asked.

"Yes, but he didn't tell me much."

"They'll be here soon." Eyrie patted her brother on the shoulder before sitting on the sofa.

"The police?"

"They want," Juanita said, "to know whether this has a Quetzal connection."

"I know this whole business about Quetzal is getting dangerous for them, but isn't this over the top — I mean, putting a cop at our door?"

"Have you turned your phone on?" Juanita asked.

"Why?"

"Inspector Lane said, when you did, there would be messages for you," Eyrie answered from the sofa where she had huddled in the corner and drawn her legs up.

Dante turned the phone on, and there they were. It looked as though Lane had been sending him a message every few hours. The gist of each was: call right now. About to call Lane, the detective beat him to it. "Mr. Skorna?" Charles asked.

"He killed my mother."

"Your sisters told you."

"You need to send EMTs to a basement squat across from Chin's Review: there's someone there who knows about Caspar and a friend of his who went down into the Komodo."

"What? The Komodo — what's this business got to do with the Komodo?" Dante put the phone on speaker.

"Something to do with this thing called the Komodo Voice, but I don't know what it's about. If this other guy is anything like Caspar, then they're both barking mad."

"Komodo Voice? First, I've heard of it, but there's someone in a squat across from the Review that knows more?" Charles asked.

"Says so, but he's in bad shape. Doesn't look to have lost a lot of blood, but he's been knocked around. Get someone there fast before he goes into shock."

"I'm sending a car for you; we need to find out what's going on with Caspar and whether..." Dante interrupted the inspector.

"There's a Quetzal connection?"

"Yes."

"There's something in the Komodo; I don't know what, but according to this fellow I talked to, it is getting ready to come out." Dante set the phone on the coffee table and sat next to Eyrie, taking her in his arms.

"Coming out?" Charles had turned the phone on speaker as well, and in the background, Dante could hear several voices speaking at once.

"I heard from other homeless, something's been going on in the Komodo for a long time. Whatever that is, things are about to get ugly."

"I'm certain we can handle anything the homeless can throw at us." Charles did not sound certain of this.

"From what I can gather, the homeless are leaving Bornler as fast as they can. A number have gone to the south-side, the north-side, and a few to the west-side. Those up to it have left the city. If what I've heard is accurate, city workers won't go down into the Komodo without an armed escort; even then, they will not go deep into the sewers for fear of what's down there."

"That's..." Charles did not finish the thought. "We need to talk, understand?"

"Yes, inspector — I'll be waiting for the car." Dante ended the call and rocked Eyrie in his arms. She was weeping again. Juanita had turned back from the window, leaning against this.

"Dante," he looked up, "what's going on?" He shrugged, looking at the knitting left on their father's chair.

10

DOWN WE GO

"This is it?" Anbessa looked about the street; there were no other occupied buildings. Occupied? The neighborhood was derelict as any Pollack had seen in Bornler. There was an abandoned strip mall at the end of the street, not large at perhaps six stories. The rest of the street was small family run factories closed a quarter-century before. However, the factory they were in front of was three stories high with another two stories on the office block to the left. The top floor of this was lit; there were security details at either end of the street and another at the reinforced entrance.

"Seems so." Reina stepped back, hands on her hips, craning her neck to take in the top floor. Each was patted down; from Reina, they took an automatic, a knife, and a pair of brass knuckles. Pollack, Anbessa, and Ava were not armed. That was not true. The others had left their weapons in the truck. Since learning of Juan's connections with the sketchy and mysterious investors (meaning cartel), they had been cautious. It was true the investors and Juan could not move against the zemmoans. The rational argument said this much, but these were career criminals, so it was uncertain reason played a role.

"There's an elevator," the first guard said, "at the end of this corridor." The hallway was indifferently lit. Every second or third ceiling light was flickering. The concrete walls were painted an olive green; the floor was scored bare concrete. At the end of the hallway was a freight elevator with an accordion door. The group stepped in.

"This is a good idea?" Reina stared at the florescent bulb on the wall to her left; the twin was dead, its tip blackened.

"If we are going to do this," Ava said, speaking to no one in particular, "we will need help."

"We could have gone to Harold. I know he wants to lock you up again, but I'm sure we can convince him working with us would be better than working against us," Pollack said.

"Our next stop." Ava shifted from one foot to the next, testing the stability of the car.

"You can't be serious?" Pollock had turned from the doors, staring at Ava. Smiling, she shifted her weight, and the car rattled. Anbessa and Reina reached for the walls. Ava giggled.

"The thing must be safe if he uses it daily."

"If Juan," Pollack began, "works for who we think, safety may not be an overriding concern."

"Overriding? I believe his backers placed him here for a reason," Reina said.

"That would be?" The car came to a stop.

"Hello," Juan called from the center of an open concept condo. Behind him was a good-sized kitchen; to the right of this was a workout area; there was a small loft that looked to be a bedroom. The washroom was to their right, and to their left was an ad hoc living room. Bookshelves lined the free space on the walls, though there were few books on these. The zemmoans had never figured Juan as much of a reader — not much of a thinker either. True, the two often went together but not always. Even the least of the zemmoans, there was a debate about who this was, recognized thinking and books did not always share the same space.

"Juan," Pollack said, stepping from the elevator and from behind Reina, hand raised, "you've a beautiful place here."

"The neighborhood's shit, but the digs are nice." The zemmoans had made it a point of pride, though not honor, to avoid inquiring into the personal lives of clubbers. It was not a simple matter of being rude, though most zemmoans were this; it was that, in Zemmoa, they existed in a space outside reality — social and physical. The point for most zemmoans was to leave reality behind. With Ava, she brought along her pain, manifesting in sex, drink, and drugs. Reality was not more than a psychopathology away. Most acknowledged this when pressed, but no one at Zemmoa pushed.

"Yes," Ava drawled, stepping out and twirling around to take in the room. In another few minutes, Juan had everyone seated with a drink. They talked for the next several minutes before working up to why they had come. The request for the meeting had been unusual, but since the murder of Quetzal, unusual had become normal. Not that any of the zemmoans, or Juan, had much use for or experience with normal. All at the meeting were damaged in their own ways. Not all trauma was visible, except the wasted appearance of Ava, but everyone carried a psychic weight.

"So," Juan brought them to the point of the meeting, "you have something you need — something to tell me?"

"Need, not tell," Ava said.

"What is it?" Juan growing cautious.

"Still uncertain about this idea of yours, Pollack," Reina complained.

"What idea is that?" Juan asked.

"It is," Ava began, "in all of our interests to find out who did for Quetzal, no?"

"Quetzal's death has gone far beyond your idea of *interests*. There are rumors the death is being felt in the prime minister's cabinet." The zemmoans looked one from the other.

"Best none of us inquire how you know that." Pollock finished his whiskey, and Juan gave him another.

"Isn't it enough we've guaranteed Reina's alibi?" Juan sat after topping off the drinks.

"Thank you for that." Reina raised her glass, swallowing half of this.

"But there is more?"

"This will interest your investors," Ava said.

"Spit it out, Ava." Juan rubbed the side of his face and yawned.

"We want to find out who killed Quetzal," the young woman said, stopping Juan's glass as he was about to swallow. The glass lowered, and Juan looked from one zemmoan to the next. Slapping his knee, he laughed.

"You can't be serious...you are?" Pushing from the sofa across from Ava, he stepped around the group and came up from the other side, finishing his drink.

"You lot have trouble finding the toilet or, when you can do this, deciding which of them you identify with." Juan switched to mezcal.

"We feel," Pollack began, "there is no choice. The police don't seem all that interested."

Juan interrupted, "Are you insane? This has reached the PM's cabinet and is all over the media. The police are shaking down pretty much everyone in Bornler."

"But what are they accomplishing?" Ava asked.

"It's one thing to investigate," Juan responded, "and another to bring charges. You've got your alibi, Reina. Let it go...or are they still looking at you?"

"They aren't, and I'm not sure how I feel about this foolishness — it's Ava and Pollack here who want to chase down rooftop ghosts." There had been speculation in several publications about who, if anyone, was on the roof with Quetzal. This had only increased with the leaking of the coroner's report.

"Still, you want to go poking around in Bornler with all this Komodo nonsense kicking up?" Juan asked.

"The Komodo?" Pollack leaned forward. There had been rumors about a Komodo connection. Most of these rumors were from the street, spread by the non-institutionalized homeless, and all involved the Komodo Voice. Juan filled them in on the latest rumors and the fact the CID was now looking into a Komodo angle. This because of information brought back by Dante Skorna after he had been looking for a former friend, now suspected of killing his mother and abducting his younger sister. None of this information Juan could verify, and the zemmoans tore into it.

"Then talk to your brother. Can't think of a pie he hasn't a finger in," Juan continued.

"So," Ava pressed, "you will not kick our request upstairs?"

"I'll do that — there's no choice now if you're serious."

"We are," Pollack said. "Wish we weren't, but I believe we are."

"Your enthusiasm doesn't inspire." Juan took a mouthful of mezcal.

"The sooner we find out who's behind this, the sooner we can all return to our lives, the sooner the police will leave Zemmoa and Bornler alone." Ava tapped a nail on the glass coffee table. Juan noticed the nail lacquer was chipped.

"But you're looking into something that is more dangerous than anything else I can think of that's happened over the last thirty years," Juan said.

"So, you will pass it along: we'll need a little help with Intelligence." Ava leaned back.

"More than a little." The joke fell flat. "Yes, I will, but you should expect nothing. Rather, the best outcome for you would be silence."

"Any word?" Sernof asked. Harold dropped his briefcase on the foyer table, loosened his tie, and unbuttoned the collar. "No, I take it?"

"She won't be found until she wants to be — it has always been that way with Ava."

"What of those zemmoans?" Sernof balanced her belly in both hands, arching her back. She was going on nine months and had been complaining about Ava for the last six weeks. *What kind of life could the babies have with an aunt like Ava running around? Who knows what she might do to the children in one of her fits?* Sernof would not talk about her addictions, would not discuss the problems with their father, did not care about anything but how the family appeared.

Harold was sympathetic. It was important to give the child, and those Sernof promised would follow, the best chance.

With a manic-depressive running free through the capital, this would not be possible. People were already talking — those she considered her equals, those that could damage her husband's future prospects. When Sernof let her imagination fly, she would see him in a cabinet post or as the PM. Each day that woman was free was one more her husband might fail to achieve even a riding seat. She was aware how filthy the business of politics was and did not care. Sernof would manage the home; Harold would deal with money, power, and politics. It was a division of labor they had agreed upon before marriage.

Ava was a complication that Harold had failed to mention. At the time of their engagement, Ava could still pass for a member of the Diez family and their class. Even before the wedding, though, there were warning signs, but Harold had promised to deal with his sister's indiscretions or passed them off as youthful folly. Sernof had been doubtful, but the Diez name still carried weight. If the name had not been enough, their wealth in-country and offshore convinced her the marriage a good idea. Now, though, Sernof was almost a mother, there was no longer any question but Ava had to be brought to heel. Harold had promised to do so for over a year. His last attempt was almost successful, but his baby sister again slipped her lead.

This time, she vanished, as had most of the zemmoans. Rolando, however, was still about. Sernof knew how to deal with men from the lower orders that wished to get ahead; they were easily manipulated through their lust for wealth, position, and power. Harold and Sernof knew enough about their sort to use them but never allow them to advance beyond a position they could control. The couple seldom spoke of this: when they did, it was in their bedroom where they had agreed to ban electronics. Sernof had decided early on, and Harold agreed, the bedroom was for four things: sleeping, sex, reading, and private discussions.

Since the pregnancy, there had been little enough of sex, but before Ava had gone off the rails, Sernof had agreed to oral satisfaction. When Ava slipped into what Sernof considered madness, even this was off the menu until her problem was solved. Though Sernof was uncertain if Harold was taking his pleasure elsewhere, it did not matter. She had the ring, name, and the right to torture him until he fixed the problem. Truth was she had not married him for love or sex but for all the Diez family could bring her. Though Sernof came from an old and distinguished family that could trace their roots back to two northern empires, the family had, over the last three generations, squandered its wealth, land, and name.

Sernof was determined to recover all three.

With Harold's help, she had wealth; with Harold's influence, she was reacquiring the land; with Harold's name, despite Ava's antics, she had reclaimed position. Inconceivable to her was the possibility Ava might destroy the name and, with the name, their wealth. Harold had political ambitions, one more reason Sernof had married him, and without the good name of his family, the career would not be possible. Without his family name, much of his influence would vanish. He could still leverage the cooperation of lesser ministers and independents, but access to the ruling and opposition parties would be closed. If this happened, her plans to reacquire the entirety of her family's wealth and land would be impossible.

She pushed her belly forward, hands cupping the bottom of this, making certain Harold knew what this conversation was about.

"Zemmoa's owners have secured Reina Noche's alibi," Harold said, picking up his briefcase. "Let's speak upstairs." Sernof's eyes widened, and she followed him up the marble staircase. In the bedroom, he tossed his briefcase on the vanity chair and sat on the end of the bed, hands on his knees and elbows akimbo. Leaning forward, he pulled his tie loose, wrapped this about his hand, dropping it on the bed. Pushing off this, he stepped over to Sernof, taking her by the shoulders.

"The CID suspect us?" Harold's eyes widened.

"No, of course not — what it means is the Quetzal investigation has been re-opened. The investigators will look at the zemmoans again and everyone connected to them. They may also broaden their interests. That's the word Inspector Lane used — *interests*."

"I don't understand what you mean," Sernof said.

"This investigation may open into political channels the PM's office will not like."

"Harry, you're not helping." Pulling free, she stepped to the far side of the room and sat on the divan; Sernof had been intending to slip into the couch but landed with a bang, injuring her coccyx. Not willing to surrender her poise, she tightened against the pain and stared at her husband.

"If they open into political channels directed at parliament," Sernof interrupted her husband.

"Why would the CID be interested in political connections?"

"Several members of parliament, including two members of the PM's cabinet, were regulars at Zemmoa." Harold kicked off his shoes, picked up the briefcase depositing the contents in the wall safe next to the vanity.

"I assume they will look at Ava." Sernof pressed her hands into her knees, and Harold could see the knuckles whiten.

"Yes, and there's a rumor they may look into me — because of the help I've given her and the zemmoans in the past." The color from his wife's coffee complexion drained.

"That cunt."

"Ava had not intended this to happen."

"I no longer care what she intended or how bad her childhood was; that creature is destroying our family. Get her under control or I'm gone."

"Sernof, please try to understand..."

"Understand, my ass...that's all I've heard since our marriage. You need to decide which is more important to you: your sister or your family," hands going once more to her belly.

"Isn't it archaic to plead your belly whenever things go wrong?" Harold removed his vest, folding this and laying it on the bed next to the tie.

"You had it too easy for too long..."

"Easy, you can't be…"

"Don't, not again with your father. No one cares about how distant he was, how many women he had, how he treated your mother. No one cares about any of that — least of all me." Sernof stood, with some difficulty, and pointed a finger at her husband. "You have name, wealth, property, and position. Neither of you have had to struggle with the loss of any of those. You expect what you've always had you will continue to have, and I can tell you all it takes is a single false step."

"Sernof, I understand what you're saying…"

"Harold — you are not listening. We are on the edge of a razor slide your sister is aiming to push us down. Ava's daddy issues and addictions have taken her to the point she wants to destroy everything it took your family generations to build." Harold jammed his fists into the front hip pockets of his pants and rocked back on his heels, staring at the floor. "Are you hearing me?" Sernof's voice softening, "Because if you still are refusing to see the choice you have, I can return to my family."

Harold looked up. Nodding, he turned and pulled his shirttails loose, unbuttoned the shirt, and dropped it into the hamper. As Harold turned to the washroom, Sernof rubbed her backside. It felt as though her tailbone had pierced the flesh. There was still a burning sensation, but the tissue was intact. From the bed, she picked up the tie and vest when there was a knock at the bedroom door. "Come."

"Madam?" the maid asked, a matronly woman in her mid-fifties.

"Yes?"

"There's someone at the door."

"We're not expecting anyone."

"It's Ms. Ava Diez, and she's brought friends."

Anbessa twisted her fingers together and started for the wet bar on the other side of the room. What looked like a butler stood by the door, but he probably had been a Marine a few years before. Big and mean, with a white scar running along the lower part of his right jaw. He was the sort Anbessa went for, but right now she was more afraid of ending up in an interrogation room at one of the many black sites she had heard of. "They've called the police," whispering in Ava's ear.

"Not Harry's style," Ava stood, making for the wet bar. The butler intercepted her.

"No, Ms. Diez — your brother does not want you drinking."

"I've been through hell. I need a drink," attempting to circle around him. He grabbed her about the waist.

"Enough, Ava." Pollack stepped over. Anbessa continued to look about the palatial room with its sculptures, oil paintings, and furnishings.

"We should go." Anbessa bolted up, turning for the door as it opened. Sernof, in a charcoal pantsuit and flats, stepped in.

"Trouble?" Sernof asked.

"No, madam," glancing at Ava.

"I see," stepping to the zemmoans on the sofa. Sernof sat in a French Colonial inspiration at the end of an overwrought coffee table.

"Harold will be down in a moment." Sernof crossed her legs, laced her fingers, steepling the forefingers, revealing pointed and lacquered nails. "Would you mind telling me why you have surfaced?"

"I want to speak to Harry, alone," Ava said.

"Harold will not be seeing you alone, again. You may as well tell me what you want. I'll be the one to decide what happens next." Pollack's hand slipped into his jacket beneath his left armpit. As the butler moved to intercept Pollack, Sernof raised a hand, and he stopped. "No need to dig a deeper hole. What is your name?"

"Pollack," Ava answered.

"Well, Pollack, pulling a weapon on a Diez will only get you dead faster." She motioned with her finger over her left shoulder.

The butler was holding an automatic pointed at his head. "Remove your hand." Pollack did as he was told. The door opened and Harold stepped in, the tableau pausing him, but in a beat he regained his composure and moved to his wife's chair. Standing behind this, he put a hand on her shoulder, and she touched hers to his. The symbolism was calculated, crude, and effective. Except for Ava, the zemmoans withered. They were not all, however, present — Pollack and Anbessa were the only ones still about, willing to follow Ava Diez. Rolando had been playing dodgeball with their attempts to contact him. He had even given up going to the office two days before to sidestep any pressure Ava and the zemmoans might wish to put on him.

"It is good of you to come home. We were all worrying something had happened to you."

"That latest attempt of yours deserves respect." Ava applauded with the tips of her fingers. "I suspect the choice of hospitals was not yours."

"It was mine," Sernof said.

"Personal experience, dear?" Before Sernof could react, Harold stepped around the chair and sat on the coffee table facing his sister. He placed his hands on her knees.

"Ava, you cannot keep on like this — have you seen yourself in a mirror?"

"Harry, how many times have we been over this? How many times have you made the argument, and how many times have I told you to go fuck yourself?" Harold struggled to suppress a grin. Lowering his head, he pushed up and stepped away.

"If you are not here for a reunion, or to return to care, why are you here?" Sernof leaned forward in the overwrought chair, placing her fingers over her knees.

"Ah, we come to it." Ava stood, slipping her hands into her khaki pants torn at the knees and threadbare. She was wearing a black tank top with what appeared to be thin streaks of oil paint staining the bottom of this. Her jacket was little better than the pants; most of what she wore, and had been wearing since escaping the hospital, was whatever she could beg, borrow, or steal. Without access to Harold's funds, she was without resources. It was the first time she was without the means of sustaining herself or her many habits. Ava had not yet dried out but was well on the way. What replaced the hunger for nullification was a hunger Sernof had already identified to her husband: an absolute negation.

If Ava was going down, she would take her family and perhaps the country with her. The oddity of the Quetzal incident and the broadening of the CID investigation, Juan's backers had come through with Intelligence, had given her weapons that could nuke the family. She was of half a mind to use it no matter what Harold agreed to. If it had not been for the toxic Sernof, she might have had a hard time deciding. Now, however, she was not only committed to pulling the trigger but had to resist the desire to burn the Diez family to the ground. If lucky, she might take the better part of the economic and political establishment with her.

It mattered little she would destroy her niece or nephew's best chance at a future. With the drying out came a clarity about herself and family she had not experienced before. Part of the woman was uncertain, but this was a byproduct of her withdrawal; it did not matter. What mattered was getting what she came for. Pollack may have begun this as a lark, but the idea of finding Quetzal's killer had taken root. First, she wanted to direct the investigative energies away from the zemmoans, what remained of them. Second, Ava needed to cause as much suffering for her family and their class as she could. Until she dried out, this had not quite occurred. Since Ava's last stay in hospital, a dull rage had been building. No longer constrained by the opioids and alcohol, there emerged a clarity of thought informed by a rage she had used drugs and alcohol to disguise.

"We want access to police Intelligence concerning Quetzal's murder," finishing, Ava grinned. Harold recognized in his sister, for the first time, their father.

"I don't have access to that data."

"If you chose to, Harold, all you would have to do is pick up a phone. The information would be on your desk by the end of the day."

"That would expose me..." Sernof cut Harold off.

"Expose our family to suspicion; that could ruin us." Ava shrugged, the sickening smile broadening. At the door, the maid stuck her head in.

"There is an Inspector Lane to see you, sir." Harold dropped his head, shook this, and went to the door.

"Don't let him in, Harold." From the back of her pants, Ava pulled a subcompact pistol, Pollack following her example.

"Put that away, you fool." Harold looked back from the door. "If you kill a CID inspector, that will be it for you and your zemmoans. I know you don't care about us, but think about those things that matter to you. Put it away." When both Ava and Pollack had put their weapons away, Harold followed the maid out.

"You come to see your brother with weapons?" Sernof asked.

"No, only when coming within range of you." Sernof smiled and looked away.

"Has everyone here met Inspector Lane?" Harold asked; Sernof rose, extending a hand.

"No, I'm afraid I have not," and Harold introduced them.

"I'm surprised to find..." but the inspector did not finish.

"My sister and friends are visiting," Harold said. The inspector appeared to want to say something but chose to push forward.

"This afternoon at Rolando Seifert's apartment, we found him hanging in the shower, an apparent suicide." Charles waited a beat for the news to sink in and for anyone guilty to expose themselves. No one did.

"What happened?" Reina asked.

"Suicide, it seems."

"But he was fine last we spoke," Reina continued.

"I thought you and Rolando had not spoken for some time?" Charles inquired.

"Yes, what I meant to say was he never seemed the type," and Reina sat.

11

MEET THE FAN

"Sorry about the mess. Last quarter, we got our budget cut again, and Admin's combined office and examination rooms into one." Dr. Urbina was leaning against the examination table, a bloody cover pulled up over a body. Sancho put a handkerchief to his nose and mouth.

"What's that smell?"

"Our disinfectant supplies are limited, and we are between cleaning staff. The company we used closed about a month ago, and we've been having trouble finding another. The coroner's office is the last considered during budget meetings. We've been forced to adapt until the city decides dealing with their dead is as important as dealing with politicians' raises."

"We understand, Natal." Charles turned to Sancho. "This is my new partner, First Sergeant Sancho Korn." Dr. Urbina held out a stubby hand with what appeared to be dried blood about the fingernails. Sancho hesitated before taking it. When the detective did, he exchanged hands, holding the handkerchief.

"You get used to the smell, detective."

"No, you don't," another said, stepping through the swinging doors. The springs were long since blown, so the left door slammed against the wall before swinging back.

"This is my assistant, Mirva Fibla." If the doctor was in his early sixties, Mirva was maybe in a rough early thirties. She had the requisite black hair and eyes, and her skin was coffee-colored and smooth. Above the right corner of her mouth was a large beauty mark. The lips were full, the lower one fatter and looser than the upper one. She was wearing heavy makeup, the lips a blood red, with dark eyeshadow that flicked to a point at the corners. Her nails were long and blunt, lacquered the same color as her lips, with paste gems arranged in the center of each.

Charles had known Natal Urbina going on five years. He had been married for about thirty-five years and had Mirva on the side since Charles had known him. How long they had been together Charles never cared to ask. There was a protocol involved, and he needed Natal's help from time to time. The inspector neither approved nor disapproved of the relationship. In a job where Charles was required to make everyone's business his, he jumped at the chance to distance himself from the choices others made that did not involve him. Charles could see Sancho was preparing a series of personal questions for the couple but stepped in to forestall a rift.

"You've finished the Rolando Seifert examination?"

"Yes, Mirva, where did you put that report?" Dr. Urbina asked.

"Behind you, beside the sink under the supply requests." Mirva had stepped to the other end of the examination room/office and was resting against the side of a counter next to an old computer. She had folded her arms over a substantial bosom and crossed her legs at the ankles. These were thick but the calves toned. She was wearing a knee length skirt beneath a worn lab coat; everything about the coroner's office was worn, old, and in need of replacement. Dr. Urbina had wanted to retire three years ago, but there were questions about whether his benefits could be paid. So he stayed on. Charles suspected Mirva was happy with this since, upon Urbina's retirement, her position became problematic. Also, when he retired, there was a question of whether the doctor would keep her.

Charles had trouble turning the detective off, and when he and Ramira socialized, he could not help deconstructing the relationships of their friends. Early in the marriage, Ramira found this interesting, but as the years passed and the repetitive decoding continued, she became bored. Charles suspected she did not understand there were only a few personalities and relationship types. He supposed there was a romantic lurking somewhere in the woman's deeper heart he had never sought nor wished to touch. Sometimes this annoyed him, and other times the mystery of Ramira's heart filled him with hope the unknowable remained in plain sight. In the beginning, Charles had attempted to explain the personality types, but her eyes became glassy whenever he began the conversation.

Ramira was tolerating his expression of the obscene but was not allowing it to penetrate. The glassy look was an expression Charles came to understand early in the relationship and knew enough about what that meant to avoid pushing. He had taken this glassy-eyed expression of his wife's into his professional life, and it had stood him in good stead. Whenever superiors got that look, he knew it was time to change tack; doing so, he had a better chance of getting whatever it was he was after. So the detective was always with him, but when the chance came to turn this off, Charles jumped at it. With Mirva and Natal, for reasons of self-interest and courtesy, he had long since turned the detective off. If he could stop Sancho from breaching the peace, Charles would.

Having retrieved a thinnish folder, the doctor leafed through the papers. Finished, Dr. Urbina passed the file to the inspector. "The results are inconclusive," the doctor said, as Charles examined the report. "He may have hung himself, but there were signs of sexual activity that had become rough. I'm uncertain this was consensual, but it's far from clear it was not. He could've been practicing erotic asphyxiation to increase the power of the orgasm, and it went wrong. Here his partner may have chosen discretion as the better part of valor." The doctor avoided gender specific pronouns, for there was no longer any certainty about orientation. Charles and Dr. Urbina had conversations about percentages, and if he were to play these, it would have been probable Seifert's partner had been a woman. Still, this was no longer certain. On top of this, Urbina had gone into the autopsy knowing Rolando Seifert was a zemmoan.

"You brought us down here for an inconclusive report?" Charles held up the folder.

"Look at the toxicology screen, he took a lot of drugs. At Seifert's law office, Rolando had to submit samples of hair, blood, and urine. It is unlikely he would have taken any kind of illicit drug and risked his future."

"Then why not tell me this over the phone — you suspect murder?" Charles said.

"No, I do not suspect murder. It is a possibility but only one of many. What I know about this case is that it has a Quetzal connection."

"So..." Sancho began.

"So, I don't want my voice, or Mirva's here, connected with anything concerning that case."

"I don't understand," Sancho continued. "Why would that matter?"

"Yes," Charles answered for the doctor, "you don't want your report becoming a political football, pulling you and Mirva into the mess." The doctor nodded, slipping his hands into the large, stretched pockets of the lab coat.

"If you come into any other information, Natal, please send me a text, and I will come over. However, if you want these meetings to be off book," the doctor looked up at this, "you'll want to have all future meetings outside of your office." Charles handed the folder back to the doctor.

"You mean..." Mirva spoke up.

"I'm uncertain," Charles answered, "but if anyone has a connection to the Quetzal investigation, monitoring is likely — at least in their offices."

"In our homes, too?" Mirva pushed off the counter.

"No, but I could be wrong." The meeting ended; when Charles and Sancho left, Dr. Urbina and Mirva were looking about. Sancho supposed they would spend the day tearing the room apart looking for nonexistent bugs. Charles was less certain, but then Charles was not a plant. Sancho maintained he was not either.

Since being partnered, this argument chased the two detectives. There was little chance either would believe the other's assertion, and Charles was coming to accept he would never be certain on which side of the argument Sancho stood — if he stood anywhere. There was good reason to believe he was as narcissistic as Charles. Sancho's career meant as much to him as what remained of Charles' did. What concerned them both was the need to wrap up the Quetzal affair before more damage occurred to their collective careers. Sancho had admitted to superiors grilling him over the lack of movement on the case; Charles received the same grilling from Captain Slank. There was no avoiding the inevitable: they either solved this case or put it off on someone they could make it stick to. Failing that, the pair would burn.

"Wait here," the young woman said, pointing to a hardwood bench. Charles had only been in parliament once before for a meeting with benefactors after first coming to the capital. He had taken meetings with other benefactors frequently throughout the years. These meetings, however, took place in back rooms. Sometimes the back offices of a law firm, other times the storage rooms of grocery stores, bars, and strip clubs. Charles knew the business of politics was filthy. Everyone knew this. Seeing it, though, brought home the knowledge of how filthy it was at a sensory level: smells, sounds, tastes, sights, and the slick touch of well-manicured, greasy hands.

Never had he attended cabinet level meetings.

The halls had marble floors, wood paneling, and portraits of politicians. All were criminals, real and assumed; many were twisted — sexually and morally; some were suspected of mass murder or outright convicted of it after dying in office. If political history is a story of power and depravity, it found its perfect expression on the walls of parliament. Here the obscene was meritorious, the depraved laudable, the insane the norm. In the years since arriving in the capital, Charles accepted what the country was and why this continued. The inspector remained sane and content, if within a problematic marriage, by keeping his distance from such places as parliament and police administration.

If the coroner's office had a stink about it, the place had the advantage of it being an honest bit of filth. Here behind the bespoke lounge suits, the cologne, perfume, subtle makeup, and perfect grammar, there was a metaphysic of rot: with the sweet top note and a harsh, angular, heart note. The creep factor was off the chart, and there was a voice in the back of the detective's mind screaming: run and do not stop for the ocean. Charles looked down the hallway in the opposite direction, in which the clack of the woman's pumps disappeared, and sighed. "We're in deep kaka, son."

"What?" Sancho asked, looking in the opposite direction.

"Deep doo-doo, up that creek without a paddle."

"I was told it was a simple briefing." Sancho pulled out his phone, opening a message. "Here," passing the phone to the inspector.

"From your keepers?"

"Superiors."

"They only sent you a text, no meeting, no explanation?" Charles returned the phone.

"No, why?"

"We're here for a cabinet level briefing. I'm an inspector and you're a first sergeant — our rank never takes meetings at this level. Not even captains take such meetings. If there was a crisis, maybe the chief of police."

"There's a crisis?"

"Not that I've heard, but that doesn't mean much."

"Wouldn't it have been on the news or social media?"

"Not if expected and the government got there first."

"We're the government."

"We're window-dressing."

"You're talking about the Intelligence departments?" Sancho pushed from the wooden bench, facing Charles.

"Maybe, but at this level, there are groups within groups." The office door opened.

Captain Daniel Slank stepped from the room. Charles rose and looked from the captain to the first sergeant then back again. "What?"

"I wanted a word before the briefing."

"What is it, Captain?" Sancho stepped next to Charles.

"Neither of you are ready for the level of shit you are about to step into. My recommendation is to listen, promise nothing, and take no position."

"Who's in there?" Sancho asked.

"For now, the ministers of justice and defense."

"This is a criminal investigation — what's the defense minister doing here?" Charles stepped aside, looking down the hall.

"Don't, Charles, it's too late for that. You two need to tighten your girdles and deal with the shit that's coming your way." Daniel reached forward, taking Charles by the arm. Sancho smiled, and the captain saw this. "If you had any sense, Sancho, you would be as frightened as Charles. In there, one misstep could destroy your career or end in a prison term. None of us here, and none at HQ, qualify for meetings at this level. Do you hear me?" touching the first sergeant with the tip of his finger.

"Yes, sir," response perfunctory; lowering his finger, the captain shook his head.

"Follow me," stepping through the door.

"Ministers, I would like to introduce Inspector Charles Lane and First Sergeant Sancho Korn. Detectives, this is Minister of Defense Villa and Minister of Justice Bevin." The ministers looked up at the introduction but did not stand. Hunched over a small corner desk, the two had been examining a thick file. Beneath this was another.

"You've a colorful history, inspector." Minister Bevin took up the file, turning in the swivel chair. "From the provinces to the capital on the strength of a few cases. Do you sometimes feel out of your depth?"

"Every day."

"You do not inspire confidence," Minister Villa said.

"I'm an inspector, minister, not a politician." Charles did not hear the captain groan so much as sense it. The inspector was uncertain, but it seemed Minister Bevin smiled.

"I don't much care for your tone, inspector." Minister Bevin drummed the table with blunt, thick fingers. Minister Villa looked out the window then pulled out a pocket watch. Flipping the case open, he checked the time then put the timepiece back in his waistcoat.

"The PM's running a little late," looking up from the desk. Charles and Sancho exchanged glances with Captain Slank.

"Nothing was said about..." the captain began.

"The PM wants to meet those in charge of the investigation and to explain a few things that happened this morning." Minister Villa continued. The captain did not have time to question this before an inner door to their right opened and a retinue of ministers entered followed by the PM. Minister Bevin introduced the detectives.

"Bevin, have they been briefed?" the PM asked.

"No, Mr. Prime Minister."

"Why don't you do that."

"I'm uncertain, Mr. Prime Minister..."

"Just do it, Bevin."

"There has been a Komodo incident on the north-side."

"Komodo incident?" Charles interrupted.

"There have been," Bevin irritated at the interruption, "several events over the past eighteen months we can trace back to the Komodo. These incidents have ranged from assaults, robberies, kidnappings, murders, and mass murders. There was one incident where a local police station in Bornler was burned to the ground."

"That was an accident..." Sancho began but stopped when the captain elbowed him.

"We passed that off as an accident, but it was arson, originating near a Komodo access point. We sent a team down, and they disappeared. Two more followed: the first disappeared, and the second came back with odd stories; because of the trauma, we discounted the narrative," Minister Bevin said.

"Right, so what are we dealing with on the north-side?" Charles asked.

"The destruction of an apartment complex," Minister Villa said.

"By destruction, you mean…" Captain Slank began.

"Blown up."

"You're not talking about a gas explosion?" Charles continued.

"No, the military have examined the site; it was not an accident," Minister Bevin answered. Charles pushed his jacket back with both hands, slipping these into his hip pockets.

"I don't see how we can help with this."

"We need," the PM began, "to sort out this Quetzal mess in a hurry. If the Komodo is moving into an active phase, we need all distractions dealt with."

"You want we should stitch someone up?" Sancho asked. The room became still.

"What the first sergeant means," Captain Slank attempted to rescue the meeting, "is there are no suspects that make any sense."

"What do you mean?" the PM asked.

"There has been wild talk by a homeless man of the Komodo Voice — his injuries, or chronic alcoholism and drug abuse, may have impacted his mind. We have him in hospital and under guard." Captain Slank pulled out his phone, opening the Zavala file, passing this to the PM through one of his security detail.

"He looks half dead."

"He was more than that when the EMTs found him across from Chin's Review." Charles folded his arms over his chest and looked about the room. There was a stillness that a story like that should not have inspired.

"Komodo Voice." Bevin looked to the window.

"You've heard the Voice before?" Charles stepped deeper into the room, and security stiffened. The inspector took a half-step back.

"Yes," PM Hirvola answered for the minister.

"Have you heard the name Alchymist?" Charles continued. Each of the ministers exchanged glances but did not speak.

"We have a winner," Sancho said. The PM looked at the detective. Stepping up behind Charles and to the side, Sancho went on. "If you want us to sort this mess out, you need to give us something to work with. Have you heard of the Alchymist?"

"The name," Minister Villa answered, "is not unknown to us."

"What does that mean?" the captain unwilling to leave his men dangling.

"It means," Minister Bevin's tone arched, "there have been Intelligence reports concerning someone or something referred to as the Alchymist for the last year and a half of troubles with the Komodo."

"What are the sources of this Intelligence?" the captain continued.

"The same general source as your information about this Komodo Voice: the homeless." Minister Bevin pushed from the small table where he had been sitting, stepping toward the captain and his detectives. In his fifties, the minister was not tall, though not small either. His hair was short, iron gray, and slickered back. His eyes were black, small plugs in a fleshy face with a broken nose, thin lips, and a pointed chin, beneath which hung a small wattle. "You cannot share this information with anyone — on or off the force; this includes family and friends."

"You must understand," the PM pushed the point home, "we are struggling to maintain a government in the face of massive economic deprivation that has inspired many criminals to become revolutionaries. To date, none of these revolutions have been successful. However, the point here is important." Placing an elbow on the table, the PM pointed at the police officers. "If we have too many things going wrong at once, this could shift the balance of power toward the revolutionaries." Turning to look at Minister Villa, the PM continued. "There is a concern, if things get much worse, we may be ripe for another coup d'état." The PM stood along with Bevin. He was younger by almost ten years and fitter. With a few flecks of gray in his hair and a short, trimmed goatee, he was on the edge of an early middle-age. His face inspired trust, but there was a small, quiet point of emptiness in the eyes Charles had not noticed until the PM moved from behind the table.

"It is imperative we get the Quetzal incident out of the news, not only out of the cycle, but solved. Especially after the destruction of the north-side apartment complex. The longer the Quetzal incident continues to make news, the greater the chance people will make the connection between the apartment explosion and Quetzal's murder. It is uncertain this will occur, but it is a possibility the government needs dealt with." The PM slipped his hands into his pockets, staring at the floor. Daniel Slank cleared his throat.

"There is only so much the CID can do. Why not turn it over to one of the Intelligence departments?"

"Yes," Bevin tucked his thumbs into his waistcoat, "this is why we put you two together."

"We weren't partnered so he could destroy me?" Charles looked at the first sergeant then back to Bevin.

"No." The PM stepped back into the conversation. "With budget cuts, the departments have shifted toward the military."

"They are now underwriting many departments' operating costs," Minister Villa offered when the PM did not appear willing to clarify. "With the military in a position to remove the government and the Intelligence departments no longer under the control of parliament, we have had to become creative."

"Prime Minister, you might have told us this sooner. The pair of us almost killed each other," Charles said.

"Yes, we have been receiving updates of your progress — and your problems. These could not have worked out better for us. With the two of you at each other's throats, you diverted attention away from yourselves," the PM answered.

"What of now?" the captain asked.

"I don't..." Bevin began.

"Us being brought in like this, they'll know something's up," Charles broke in.

"The report will read you attended a meeting to debrief ministers Bevin and Villa on the Quetzal incident. When this does not go well, you two will find yourselves on probation," Bevin continued.

"What?" Sancho pushed forward; a security officer warned him off. "How can we do our job if we're on probation?"

"It is paramount we divert attention away from the two of you. By placing you on probation and reassigning the case to other CID detectives, we will free you from any interest from the departments. Also, this may be more important, you will have unlimited resources and manpower from a selection of our personal security details, still trusted, to investigate what is going on with Quetzal and the Komodo," the PM said.

"When this is over?" Charles asked.

"Yes," the captain jumped in, "their names will need to be cleared."

"If we're successful, the detectives will receive promotions and pay raises. A reward is also possible — if successful." Minister Bevin stepped over to the detectives as he spoke. "However, if you are unsuccessful…" the minister did not finish.

"You will ruin our careers?" Sancho wondered.

"If unsuccessful, ruined careers will be the least of everyone's problems." The PM turned back from the window. "Failure may trigger either a coup d'état or a revolution: hard to say which. My money is on the military moving in. Their last failed attempt continues to grate on many, and the distance between the military and parliament is becoming dangerous."

"There's the carrot, but where's the stick?" Charles asked the room.

"Stick?" Minister Bevin repeated.

"What happens if they don't do what you want?" the captain asked.

"If revolution or coup d'état is not enough of a stick, let me offer you this," the PM said. "There is not a police officer untouched by corruption. Are you following me?" The captain and detectives nodded. "We have enough on both of you not only to destroy your careers, but to make certain you go to prison. What, however, if you spoke up and told your story? Plenty of online media types wouldn't mind getting their hands on this dirt. That would not be advisable — if we," motioning to the security detail, "have to move against the pair of you, there may be an accident during your arrest. I hope it will not come to that. What is being offered here is a chance to save our country and to advance your own positions."

"Seems a fair offer," Sancho answered.

"Good." Minister Bevin held up a file. "These are the censure forms, already signed by the chief of police, who knows nothing of what we are doing here; you need only sign these, Captain Slank, and we can begin." The captain took the folder and turned to his detectives.

"Are you two certain of this? Once I sign the documents, you are in it up to your necks, and I will not be able to help you." Charles and Sancho exchanged looks, shrugging. Minister Bevin held out a pen, and the captain signed the orders of censure. Passing the folder back to the minister, the captain looked over the room. "Where will they be reassigned?"

"There is no reason to remove them from CID," Minister Bevin answered. "Put them on light administrative duties in another building, so no one will notice the pair are not at their desks. Whatever resources you need you will have if you contact me, and only me, at this number." The minister held out a small white card with a number scrawled in felt marker on one side. "This is the number of a burner phone, and I want you to use these phones to call me." The minister nodded to a member of the security detail, and he produced two phones. "Before the minutes run out on this, send me a text, and I will make sure new phones are sent to your dead drop." The detectives took the phones.

"What should I do?" the captain asked.

"Deflect," the PM said from behind the desk once more, "the most important thing you can do is to make certain everyone is convinced by the censure and reassignment. Beyond that, you should only have contact with the detectives in case of an emergency. Even then, the three of you should not appear together."

"Is there anything else?" the captain asked. Minister Bevan looked to the PM, who shook his head. In the paneled hallway, the detectives stared at one another. Charles wanted to throw up.

12

THE LABYRINTH

Awake again. How many cycles did this make? Seven...no, ten. Pushing up from the brick floor, Beatrice leaned back against a curved wall, also brick. She was in a vaulted room made of red brick; at the end of the room was what she had thought to be a large blackboard surrounded by an ornate frame and topped with a crown. Examining the board, it was not slate but a plaque with an effaced inscription. The crown was not a crown, either. Rather, this was a skeleton from the torso up with its arms spread out over half the distance of the upper plaque.

It was not a large chamber, but she would not have been able to reach the ceiling even standing on the shoulders of the fool. Beside and below the plaque was a short staircase with a tube metal railing with flakes of black paint still clinging to the rusted metal. The stairs, too, were a red brick, slick with the same secretion covering the walls. After arriving, Beatrice had run a hand over this. It was slimy to the touch, and her fingers smelt like a backed-up cistern. Rubbing these on her pants, the woman had stayed away from the walls as much as possible for the next two sleep cycles. Beatrice was alone for at least that number of cycles — her only method for marking time.

There was an antique chandelier hanging from the center of the vault, too high for her to grab, with electric fake flame bulbs in several of the sockets. One of these bulbs had flickered since she had first woken in the chamber or cyst; she was not sure which was the correct word. Unlike Father and Dante, she and her sisters (mother as well) were not readers. Except for herself, the others had been happy with their lot in life. Only she wished to be more. They all thought she was a spoiled brat. That much was true, but it was not the reason she wanted more. Beatrice was certain this desire for more came from their father. He had struggled all his life to improve their position.

Victor failed but through no fault of his own. The economy failed; the people working for him failed; their mother failed. Dante refused to remember the arguments their parents had over the new shop. He and her sisters refused to remember how anxious Lola had been about raising their status. Money she had been fine about; Lola always like spending whatever extra Father brought home. Putting this extra income back into the business appeared incomprehensible to her. Beatrice was certain Lola's preference for spending the money was her mother's attempt at keeping them where they were, with only enough to make it from one month to the next. She hated her mother for this: had always, would always.

If she was right, the always part was now past tense. When Caspar had carried her out, she saw what remained of their mother. The face appeared shoved-in, and one eye had already disappeared in swelling; Beatrice was certain she saw two or three of the old woman's teeth lying on her chin and breast. One arm was bent at an unnatural angle at mid-bicep. She was, however, not seeing well when Caspar carried her out. During the struggle, he had pushed the door in so hard the impact knocked her across the room, and she struck her head on the wall. Although she did not lose consciousness, the impact stunned her, and sparks of light popped on and off over her vision. Through this, she saw the big man grab her. The sensation of being lifted and carried was distant and insubstantial. When she thought back on this, it seemed as if she had been floating above his shoulder.

When she saw her mother, Beatrice was only recovering from the assault. It had been difficult to be certain whether what she saw was what she saw. Caspar, too, would not tell her whether her mother was alive. She suspected the fool did not understand and cared less. She did not learn this until he reappeared after two, or more, sleep cycles. For that amount of time, she had to deal with not knowing where she was or why. Soon enough, she decided Caspar had taken her into the Komodo. Though she had never ventured into the sewers, like some of her friends to have parties the police would not raid, she had gone over this many times. Beatrice could never bring herself to enter the Komodo. Over the course of her childhood, while being spoiled by her parents and siblings, Beatrice had been told stories about the Komodo and what lived within it. As an adult, she told herself she no longer believed these. However, as a child growing up with a fear of darkness and what lived in her closet, the anxiety never passed.

As an adult may keep a nightlight on, for emotional security, so Beatrice carried the stories of the Komodo with her. Imprinted on the oldest part of her brain and in the darkest corner of this where memory, imagination, and terror intersected, she had refused to enter even the least chambers of the Komodo. By way of defense, Beatrice argued shit and piss filled the tunnels and would team with disease. Although no germaphobe, most still accused her of fearing the Komodo. The truth was all feared the Komodo, and each of her friends was drunk and stoned when they entered the run-off canal. Nothing had happened to them the first three times they partied, and they had been loud. Beatrice had waited for them at the entrance of the canal for two hours each time, expecting them to run screaming and bloodied from the Komodo. The first three times nothing happened and, bored with waiting, she went home.

On the fourth occasion, Beatrice reckoned it was safe but could not bring herself to enter. She did, however, wait. After an hour, she screwed herself up and stepped in. Each carried a crude, sectional diagram of the sewer. Using her phone's light, Beatrice followed this in. Soon she did not need the map, instead following the sound of music and laughter. For fifteen minutes, she followed the laughter and music then both stopped. Returning to the diagram, Beatrice followed this for another couple of minutes before hearing the first screams. The screams rose and fell in an erratic wave of surges and regressions. Around two bends in the sewer, she heard splashes of water followed by several more.

Then the screaming returned.

This was somewhere between terror and the cathartic scream of a horror film — others followed. The screams shifted from giddy pleasure to sublime terror. On the first, Beatrice hesitated; on the second and third, she bolted. At the mouth of the run-off, she had not waited but ran for the highroad where she caught a taxi home. For the next few weeks, she had looked for her friends, and their families had called her mother, but nothing again was heard of them. Police reports had been filed; this meant nothing since the police had almost stopped investigating crime in Bornler — leaving the district to deal with its own. Beatrice told her mother the story of what had happened when it became impossible to remain silent. In her sleep, she spoke, and Lola had put enough together so she had to tell her mother.

With the story out, Lola had advised Beatrice not to speak of it to anyone — not even her brother. Dante had an overdeveloped sense of responsibility for the well-being of his sisters. They were all adults by this time, but he could not help treating them as children. There was a part of Beatrice that admired this quality, but the paternalism also led to him chasing her into places she did not wish to be rescued from. Sure, the north-side fiasco should never have happened. Still, it could have led to a short-term relationship that might have given her enough money to get out of the house. Beatrice had dreamed of nothing else. The dream had come true but not in the way she had suspected — even in the worst of her nightmares. And Beatrice had these all the time, concerning her future and place in the world.

The thought ended as the heavy metal door of the chamber scraped against the red brick. Caspar poked his head up above the stairway, behind the rusting metal balustrade. "You awake?" Every time he came in, Caspar saw she was, but each time it was the same question.

Stepping into the large chamber, vault reaching thirty feet above their heads, the slight, cowled figure knelt at the bottom of the staircase leading to a landing behind which was an iron door rusted about hinges and riveting. Before the door was a high-backed chair, wooden and weathered, with padded armrests of cracked leather. Its placement suggested the chair was a throne and the landing a dais. On this sat another figure in a fuller, longer cowl, with the hood thrown back. On his face, he wore a mask fastened by leather straps. The mask was not leather but appeared to be ceramic and black with almond eye slits and a thick lipped mouth with another slit. From each tear duct fell a single red tear; above each eye was an arched eyebrow painted white with flecks of black. On his hands, he wore leather gloves studded with metal spikes.

In his right hand, he held a staff tipped with a large clear stone, in the center of a silver disk, capturing the light from the half-dozen electric chandeliers illuminating the chamber. The figure at the base of the dais prostrated himself. "Alchymist, the complex has been destroyed, and they are reacting as you said." Alchymist stood and stepped down the long staircase; there was the clack of metal tipped soles beneath the foot-length robe. The figure at the bottom of the steps pushed up and pulled back his cowl. Perhaps in his late thirties with thinning hair and an aggressive widow's peak. The hair was fine, streaked with gray, and in need of a cut. His face was narrow and long, the eyes bloodshot bullets, the mouth a slit with no lips; he had a beard, which was sparse, flecked with gray, and as uncommitted as the hair on his head. The nose, humped and twisted, sat squat on a pocked face.

"Did I not tell you, Komodo, what would happen?" Alchymist stopped two-thirds of the way down the stairs and squatted.

"Yes, but they are moving against us now."

"The purpose of the gesture, but the government is too weak to move openly."

"But they are investigating."

"And will find nothing pointing them in our direction, unless you made a mistake?" Komodo rose, taking two steps toward the bottom of the stairs.

"There is nothing to connect the Komodo to the apartment complex, but I do not see the point in provoking their government."

"The point is to add another level of uncertainty. For generations, the economy has been stagnant; the military are hostile to the civilian government even if well-disposed to the PM. Industry and business, where they still exist, are hanging on by their fingernails; bandits and revolutionaries emerge and disappear with increasing rapidity. The South may now be in open revolt against the government. One or two more failures and the government will fall; the military will move against them, and in the chaos that follows the civil war, we will pick up the pieces."

"After all these years, our time is here?" Komodo asked.

"Perhaps, but we must move with care. If it is suspected the Komodo is moving against them, we may pull the people, government, and military together against us."

"We can defeat them: one or all."

"Confidence is dangerous, caution more so. We need to move now but with deliberation. The Komodo also needs to be certain our hand remains invisible in what follows. Do you understand, Komodo?"

"Yes, sir." Komodo went down on a knee, hands braced on the other. Alchymist motioned for him to rise with his left hand, the right holding the staff.

"The explosion damaged your exoskeleton?"

"It is being repaired."

"You are uninjured?"

"The armor did its job."

"Was it damaged?"

"It too is being repaired."

"How long will the repairs take?" Alchymist stepped from the stairs.

"A few days." Alchymist stepped further into the chamber and away from Komodo. The metal tipped staff rang in the hollow space. In the center of the chamber, beneath the largest of the chandeliers, Alchymist turned.

"It is good I have had a backup exoskeleton made for you. You will find it in the lab when you return." Komodo turned, his smile lipless. "Several enhancements have been made in strength and durability. The climbing claws also function as weapons. The exoskeleton is no larger than the previous one. I want it to fit within your robe. It has also been painted a flat black, improving camouflage while climbing."

"What of the old exoskeleton?" Komodo asked.

"I only want you to use the new device. The fewer that know of it, the fewer may speak of it."

"Few, even in the Komodo, have connected me to the device."

"Make certain it stays that way. If anyone were to connect Komodo and the Komodo Voice, much of the mystery will be lost. It is enough you are known as our chief technology officer." Alchymist had elevated the tinker to this level when he had found him scrounging a living through repairs in the Komodo. When he first found the little man, he was no more than a shell with skills that had gone unappreciated in the chaos of the Komodo. He was called, by many, Komodo as a joke. The Komodo was a place where the lost, the broken, and the helpless found retreat and a respite from the harsh life on the east-side.

Even Alchymist did not appreciate the little man's skills until he needed repairs made to a computer he had brought with him. All he had seen Komodo repair, until this time, were simple things: a cane, a cart, a small gas generator, and a few children's toys. After Komodo repaired the computer, however, he took a greater interest in him. Alchymist slowly wheedled out his life story. He had two PhD's in engineering and another in mathematics. Until the universities felt the full force of government retrenchment, he had been a lecturer in the departments of engineering and mathematics. Komodo had a family: a wife and two children. When he lost his situation, his wife took the children and moved back north to her parents' home.

When his wife and children left, he made little effort to keep his head above a rising tide of insolvency. First, he lost what money he had left to his wife. Following this, he lost the car on failing to keep up with the payments then the house. He sold what furniture his wife had not taken and moved to a small boardinghouse. For a while, he was successful repairing and trading electronics. As it became clear his wife would not return until his situation was restored, he took to drink. Komodo had attempted drugs, but these only left him feeling stupid, leaving the pain intact. However, alcohol killed the pain and self-loathing. He had never been much of a drinker, a bottle of wine and he was legless. Incapable of keeping spirits down, he never embraced the mystery and magic of mezcal. Where others had found a spiritual obliteration in the traditional alcohol, he spent an evening vomiting.

As the drink took hold, his business wavered then collapsed. No longer bringing in even this meager income, Komodo lost his room at the boardinghouse. Uncertain how long he would last on the streets, it was inevitable their brutality would drive him to the last place his kind could find safety: the Komodo. Alchymist was uncertain how long he had been in the sewers, but it could not have been over five years when he appeared. Komodo and others had attempted to find out who Alchymist was. These attempts were never successful, and as Alchymist's influence and power grew, it became taboo to question his origins. These faded in importance as it became clear Alchymist had come to help the Komodo.

Before Alchymist became the force behind the Komodo, there were those on the east-side who enjoyed hunting komodoans. These were beaten, raped, set on fire, or murdered. Sometimes all, in no particular order. It was after halting these attacks, Alchymist became a force in the Komodo. Before this, he had gathered to himself a following. One of the first of these was Komodo. After discovering his talent, Alchymist brought him an early version of the exoskeleton. It had been nowhere near as powerful as the one damaged in the apartment complex explosion, but it made Komodo a force those in Bornler were no longer prepared to challenge. Komodo, in turn, became a sycophant and bloody-minded psychopath. Once harnessed, he no longer was Komodo but the Komodo Voice. In the beginning, the Voice was only a rumor. The people of Bornler would find the remnants of his attacks but never a survivor. Only on the advice of Alchymist did he leave witnesses. Of these, some were injured and others mutilated: depending on their crimes against komodoans. Over time, he would leave some uninjured but with a threat.

The threat concerned more than injury or simple death. Not everyone took the threat to heart: those that did not found themselves on the receiving end of the climbing claws. Sometimes Komodo would take a finger and, on other occasions a hand, perhaps a foot. When pushed to extremes, he had strangled those that did not take the warning with their own gut. In the beginning, the harness and exoskeleton required a great deal of training; some deaths resulted from this; others were killed for fear of exposure. He always wore a robe with a hood, but in those early days, he had not seamlessly fused disguise and technology.

With care, Komodo and Alchymist developed a material that could withstand the strain of the exoskeleton. It took time and patience, but the problem was solved. That done, Komodo discovered a level of freedom and spiritual independence releasing him from the restraints of humanity. Not only a moral sensibility but an empathic one: Komodo discovered a distance from those he punished and those he protected. As his empathy and sympathy failed, he fell back on an abstraction of codes. If he had been a police officer or an officer of the court, this may have been understandable, perhaps inevitable. But Komodo and Alchymist were neither of these — they were vigilantes.

Komodo, in the beginning, dreamed of becoming a superhero, changing the face of the Komodo, the city, and the country. Soon it became plain he was not in it for what the country would applaud.

He did not understand what Alchymist was in it for; Komodo had no idea who Alchymist was, let alone what he wanted. When alone in the lab, where he also slept in an alcove, he knew Alchymist wanted something it was better not to think about. There had been too much violence and death for this to end well. Komodo, alone in his alcove, while attempting to sleep, hoped, dreamed, for a tragic end: perhaps a denouement stitched together from Homer and Shakespeare. He had loved both at college and continued to read them afterward.

Whenever the world became too much, Komodo retreated into these and their ambivalent understanding of human nature. He never felt capable of effecting change in the manner of Achilles or Macbeth. His lack of physical presence made this impossible, but he fed his spite upon those that kept him down: from colleagues to the east-side hunters. When Alchymist appeared and offered him the exoskeleton, it was a dream come true. Over time, Komodo mastered the exoskeleton and could control himself when doling out punishment to those who thought it sporting to pray upon the helpless. That done, he turned his attention to those colleagues, who still kept their positions. While taking out his revenge on these, Komodo was certain to make the deaths appear accidental or suicides.

A few he made disappear, but suspicion emerged around these, and Komodo decided a better way to deal with them was outright death or suicide. There had not been many colleagues he hated for taking credit for his work and getting the tenure that should have been his. However, enough were suspected of taking credit for Komodo's work it was a good thing he was thought dead. In the process of gaining control over the cloak and exoskeleton, then taking his revenge, Komodo lost much of the man he was. Perhaps, much of that had already disappeared when he lost his family and slipped onto the street with no one noticing.

Lost in his own history and the strange turns his life had taken, Komodo had not heard Alchymist call.

"Are you listening, Komodo?" Alchymist asked.

"Sir?"

"Some loose ends need tidying. Take that Skorna girl, for instance."

"Beatrice Skorna — she belongs to Caspar. He won't take it well if we kill her."

"She's safe down here, and the girl ties Caspar to us. Better we should keep her alive. However, this places Caspar in our debt, and we need to think about collecting on that." Alchymist turned from beneath the large chandelier and walked back to Komodo, staff tapping on the stone floor along with the metal plated soles of his boots.

"What were you thinking, sir?"

"Our associate needs to be certain of silence."

"You wish to use Caspar? Bit of a blunt instrument." Alchymist considered the observation, tapping the staff on the floor and spinning this between his fingers.

"There's no denying," Alchymist began, "Caspar has a tendency to be emotional. Still, he may be useful in dealing with dangling threads."

"What threads need clipping?"

"Zemmoans and the Skorna family."

"The zemmoans will not be a problem; the Skorna family, however, Caspar will not do. Killing the mother was an accident, and he feels bad about that — he does not show it, but her death has affected him. He was only attempting to rescue Beatrice. Lola, the mother, got in his way, and he lost control."

"You are certain he will not finish what he started?" Alchymist tucked the staff under an arm and placed a hand on Komodo's shoulder. The metal spikes on the gloves catching the light from the chandeliers.

"He considers Dante his only friend."

"From what I know of Dante Skorna, he's not the sort to take the murder of his mother well."

"Yes, and Caspar half-expects his friend to find him but isn't convinced Dante would come down here alone. I told him Dante would if he suspected Caspar is here."

"How did he answer?"

"He only wants to protect Beatrice and appears incapable of understanding his lust. Caspar, privately, might admit he loves her but would never admit to lust."

"If Dante," Alchymist continued, "were to come after Beatrice, what would Caspar do?"

"If convinced she was in no more danger, he may allow Dante to take her."

"What if Dante wanted Caspar's life for his mother's?" Komodo thought about this. Shaking his head, he folded his hands in front of his robe.

"Caspar feels considerable guilt for the old woman's death — because of this, he may allow Dante to kill him."

"May?"

"Hard to say, with certainty: if pushed to it, Caspar might defend himself, but I believe he loves Dante."

"What if I were to order him to do that — kill Dante?"

"He might turn on us, if he felt Beatrice was safe. Beatrice is the key: if we can convince Caspar that Beatrice may be in danger from Dante, we may have leverage to move the idiot against his friend."

"For now," Alchymist tapped a metal-plated shoe on the floor, "let's play it safe and send him against the zemmoans. If we hold off on Dante, the young Mr. Skorna may do the work for us."

"What have you heard of Dante?"

"Not more than you, but he seems the sort to need to prove to the world that he is every bit the man his father was. From what I've heard, he's far more than his father. Not better, but driven to protect his family. I suspect, deep down, he hates them."

"Deep down, we all do, but this does not alter our need to protect them."

Balancing the staff in one hand, Alchymist leaned back, adjusting the mask, and laughed. A staccato of barks bounced from the vaulted walls filling the chamber with laughter and the echo of this. As the last of the echoes faded, Alchymist turned to the greatest of his followers. "Sometimes I forget who you were."

"I am Komodo. I have no past."

"We all have a past. None of us care to be reminded of that because of where we are, but there is no denying the pull of our connections. Deny your past, deny who you are (what you were), and you only leave yourself unguarded against this. History will not be put out, locked away, or denied. Those that believe we have moved beyond the past end up being consumed by it."

13

—————

RAIN DOWN HELL UNTO ME

Dante broke through the door. Slamming this closed, he pressed his back against it. Reaching for the deadbolt, there was none. Feet hammered on the staircase below; there had been six homeless chasing him when he bolted from the last squat, but over two blocks, he picked up half a dozen more. Slipping the automatic back into its holster, he adjusted the backpack and from the side pouch pulled another clip — it was his last. He had three boxes of ammunition in the backpack but did not have time to reload. He was on the third floor of a ten-story abandoned warehouse in Winchell. The largest of the east-side districts, Winchell buttressed Bornler and kissed the southeast of the north-side.

Winchell had been harder hit than Bornler over the last decade; few shops remained and no industry to speak of. The outer eastern edge of the district opened onto abandoned subdivisions half-completed before the Great Collapse destroyed the east-side economy; beyond these was countryside. Those that could not escape to the south-side, or even Bornler, now lived in a district with only pirated power and little by way of plumbing. The city shut the water off when they abandoned the district. Water piracy continued, but in one of the last efforts to hold onto the Komodo, the city sent a force into the Winchell sewers to turn the water off at the source. The tactical squads accompanying the city workers suffered nearly fifty percent casualties. It was the last time the police department offered security for workers intending to go deep into the Komodo.

After the incident in Winchell, the only tactical teams sent into the sewers with city workers would be the Marines. Even these were loath to penetrate deep into the eastern elements of the Komodo. The civilian government, each time they wished to reassert control over parts of the Komodo, on the east-side, had to treat with the military. This meant either giving up more control over the Armed Forces or increasing their budget. In response, the government only sent workers into the periphery of the Komodo. Everywhere, problems with water and sewage had been increasing for the last half-decade. In the eastern and southern districts, water and sewage issues had been at crisis levels for a good ten years.

Dante, knowing the condition of the Komodo on the east-side, Winchell in particular, had investigated this district first. Bornler may have been a better choice, since this was where the Quetzal murder had taken place. Dante, however, thought this too obvious a point of departure; Winchell would be a better access point, this being cut off the longest. It had been years, though, since he had been last in Winchell. All he knew of the district was what he heard from clients at Mendelssohn's Ink: these few enough. When he got a customer from Winchell, Dante worked for barter.

His Intelligence of the district was problematic if not fictional. Scanning the empty floor with I-beam pillars dotting this and weathered hardwood floors, splintered and loose, he suspected what he knew of the district was next to nothing. Dante stepped onto the floor and crossed to the tall wire mesh windows facing north. Outside of these was a fire escape. Rusted, decayed, and missing several steps, it would not have been his first choice, if there had been a second. The windows, many with cracks and holes, were held intact by their embedded wire mesh.

Unlocking the first, next to the fire escape, he stepped out and threw the window closed as the interior door burst open. A collection of men, women, and children toppled over each other, blocking the door. Dressed in a variety of rags, they ranged in age from prepubescent to geriatric. The danger in the group was not from the weapons they carried or their physical presence, none had any training, but their numbers. He had emptied two clips into them and shot at least four. Two more replaced each he downed. What they hoped to get from him, he was not sure. His clothing was typical of Bornler, well-worn and patched — not worth killing over, nor dying for.

Dante assumed they were after the weapon, ammunition, and what currency he had been splashing about for answers concerning the best way into the Komodo and whether they had heard any news of Beatrice. Several times in Winchell, he had flashed his sister's picture but only a hard copy. He carried his phone but never pulled it out and left it off for fear of attracting attention. Dante even stashed the bike in an empty garage, securing this with a length of chain and a heavy padlock. However, he pulled the weapon when several in the last squat decided they wanted his clothes and shoes and to see what he had in the backpack.

Staring at the street below, there were more homeless down there. Dante's only choice was up, but on the roof, they would have him trapped. If he went down, with only one extra clip, he would not escape. Going up, he probably would not escape. Staying on the fire escape, he would not escape. Already, the mob was running toward the window. Dante had taken his first step up the fire escape when he heard several shots from the street. Looking down, the mob had broken and fanned out across the street. Two more of these went down before the others retreated as one gunman let loose on full-auto.

Two men, one on each side of the road, were walking down this, bullpup assault weapons tucked into their shoulders. Each wore a tactical vest; their shins and upper thighs protected with armor, but their heads were bare, except for safety glasses. The clamoring at the windows stopped and the mob stared down then ran. Dante had a choice; he could continue on to the roof or climb down. Neither of the men were from the east-side. They had to be government, what branch he had no idea. He suspected other military or the police — in Winchell, neither made any sense. With the mob dispersed, the two men waved him down; the first of these pulled a badge from beneath the tactical vest. "Police," Dante muttered.

He climbed down the fire escape.

"Dante Skorna," the first said.

"Inspector Lane?" Charles nodded.

"You remember Detective Korn?" The detectives had allowed the bullpup weapons to dangle from their straps attached to the tactical vests as they took Dante's hand.

"What are you doing in Winchell?" Lane swapped out the spent magazine for a new one.

"Beatrice."

"You're up here looking for your sister?"

"No one else seems to be." The two police officers exchanged glances.

"What was that about?" Sancho asked.

"I think they wanted my kit." Dropping his pack on the ground, he refilled the spent magazines.

"You have a license for that?" Sancho asked.

"You have," not looking up, "reason to be down here, dressed like that?"

"Dante, you cannot expect to find your sister with an automatic and a few questions." Charles squatted next to Dante, taking an empty magazine and loading this. Sancho continued to scan the street.

"Like I said, no one else is looking." Finished loading the magazine, he swapped this out for the half-spent one in the automatic.

"We are," the first sergeant said. Dante looked up at Sancho then over at Charles.

"That's true?"

"It appears," Charles began, "the business with Quetzal and your sister may fold into one another."

Finished loading the spent magazines, Dante replaced the ammunition in his backpack; standing, he threw this over his shoulder. "What's that mean?"

"For a long time, we were looking hard at a group of people from Zemmoa," Sancho answered.

"The zemmoans?"

"How did you..." Charles did not finish the question.

"Remember, I did that fullback tat on Quetzal. Often, one or more of his zemmoan friends would come along. More often than not, it was Reina."

"It looks like they are now being targeted." With a grunt, Charles pushed off his knees and arched his back then rubbed the shoulder that had braced the bullpup.

"They take getting used to," Dante said.

"You served?" Sancho asked.

"In the South." Dante stepped back, looking up and down the street.

"I don't care how much service you've seen or how ugly it got, this is no place for anyone armed with a simple automatic," Charles said.

"I've also got a knife; when that fails, I find harsh language does the trick." Charles tried not to smile.

"You should go back to your shop," Sancho continued.

"Nothing to go back to. I closed the shop up and sent my sisters off to stay with family friends — out of the city." This caught Charles' attention.

"You know where they took her, right? That's why you sent your sisters out of town."

"The Komodo is a big place, so I can't say where she is or even if she is there, but there's a good chance."

"You're going down with a pistol?" Sancho exchanged another look with Charles.

"The two of you are going down with urban assault weapons on your own?" Dante holstered his weapon.

"We are on a reconnaissance mission. If we find any hard evidence of Komodo activity, we call in reinforcements." Dante looked at Sancho; if there was a smile on his face, there was not one in his eyes.

"You and which armies?"

"What do you mean?" Charles asked.

"Everyone knows; the government will send no one into the Komodo without backup — even then they won't go deep. Here in Winchell, they've turned off the water and sealed the Komodo. No matter what happens, parliament will send no one into the sewers."

"Situations change," Sancho's voice hollow.

"What situation is that?"

"Dante, did you hear what happened on the north-side?" Charles adjusted his pack and from another leg pouch pulled two energy bars, offering Dante one.

"The apartment complex?"

"That's the situation."

"That was the Komodo?"

"We can't answer that," Sancho said.

"Come on, Sancho. We're all in the same crapper now."

"What crapper?" Dante asked.

"If you don't find your sister, she's dead. If we don't figure this out, it's our careers and maybe the country."

"You want I should sign-up? I'm not learning any creepy handshakes."

"Charles, you don't have the authority." Sancho stepped to the inspector, placing a hand on his shoulder.

"We are, more or less, looking for the same thing."

"Which is?"

"The best way in and out of Komodo — with some knowledge of what is going on down there and how best to leave with as much Intelligence as we can. In your case, you want to find your sister and get out," Charles said.

"If I get to kill Caspar, that might also be a good thing." Dante was eyeing the bullpup dangling from Charles' tactical vest. "Do I get one of those and a vest?"

"Certain you know how to use them?" Sancho asked.

"Better than the two of you — you tore up the better part of the street when all you needed to do was drop a few of the mob and the rest would have broken and run. As it is, you wasted a magazine or two when you needn't have used more than half of one." The detectives exchanged glances but appeared unconvinced. "Those idiots are desperate and terrified; all they want is to make it to the next day with some food and a little security. You challenge their lives and they will not give you any trouble."

"Didn't work so well for you," Sancho observed.

"I was one man with an automatic, and I made the mistake of running from the squat when I should've dropped three of their leaders. Won't make that mistake again."

"So," Charles drawled, "yes, you get a vest, a bullpup, and a nifty decoder ring."

"You can keep the ring."

"It's a communication device that no one else can listen in on," Sancho said.

"Oh, yes please, I'd like one of those — do they come in hot pink?" The detectives frowned. "Don't worry, when the shooting begins, you will be happy to have me along." Sancho did not seem convinced, and Charles did not appear to believe any of this would end well. Not just drafting Dante, but the whole Komodo business seemed on the fast track to perdition.

"We're down a block and a half," Charles said.

"Parked?" Sancho nodded, and Dante shook his head. "You will be lucky if the frame's left." This brought a smile to Sancho's face.

"State-of-the-art antitheft for an apocalyptic economy."

"What does that mean?"

"Means, whoever tries to mess with our SUV will not live to figure out why they shouldn't have."

"Your dick is that big?"

"Something the minister of justice snagged from the Army. They picked up one or two of these in China for a song. The Chinese needed what cash they could lay their hands on to deal with problems on their Western frontier." Dante had heard about the trouble the eastern Eurasian empire was having but had filed this away under information that would not help him feed his family.

An hour later, they were back in northern Bornler, and the detectives had been right, there were three bodies scattered about the sides and back of the SUV. It occurred to Dante, whatever these two were up to, it was about as deep and dark as the PM's cabinet. There had been speculation, online, for years about this and what they were up to. Most of the speculation was conspiracy crank material, but sometimes a site went up, only to be taken down, in which the material was almost believable. That the detectives were working for the office of the prime minister and cabinet members seemed almost inevitable, given the chaos since the Quetzal murder.

Still, it was not until he climbed into the plush interior of the SUV and rooted through its weapons locker that he understood how dangerous the situation had become. All of this appeared to be revolving around the Komodo. What it was the Komodo was responsible for was uncertain. Still, with the death of Quetzal, adduction of Beatrice, destruction of the apartment complex, and a restive east-side, it appeared they were hurtling toward the conclusion of a grand narrative.

"Where are we heading?" Dante stared out at the familiar neighborhoods winking by.

"I've received a text message from one of the last zemmoans known to still be around, maybe alive," Charles answered over a shoulder.

"Should I guess?"

"Ava Diez," Sancho said.

"Harold Diez's sister?" Charles admitted to this. "Didn't something happen to him?"

"What did you hear?" Charles shifted in his seat, looking back at Dante.

"Picked up a few rumors while looking for Beatrice; something happened in the family's Sonando estate."

"What happened?" Sancho asked, staring back through the rearview.

"Some kind of house invasion; everyone was killed. At the time, I thought it wishful thinking — news about what happened at my place had spread throughout Bornler, and I thought maybe they wanted the rich to get a taste." Charles shifted back in his seat, placing a hand on the dashboard.

"No, it happened. Harold and his pregnant wife were assassinated, along with their security detail and servants."

Dante let go with a long, low whistle. "That's got to be freaking more people out in Sonando than that business with the apartment complex."

"One more reason we're down here." Sancho took a sharp left.

"Until the Diez estate, the government, the office of the PM, had given us a certain amount of latitude in our investigation of the Quetzal murder and its connection to the Komodo. Even after the apartment complex was blown up, we were given a considerable amount of freedom to investigate what was going on down here. But after the assassination of the Diez family, we were told to solve the case or expose the Komodo." Charles checked the action on his side-arm.

"If you don't?" To Dante, this seemed the obvious next question.

"The conversation," Sancho picked up, "never got around to the stick — all we heard on the other end of the line was find out what's going on and find out *now*."

"We are around the corner here," Charles said to Sancho, who nodded. They pulled up next to an abandoned photocopy store — all the shops on the street appeared to have been abandoned years before. Many of the storefronts no longer had glass but were still safe behind their rollout cages.

"Nice and quiet for a late afternoon," Dante slipped across the seat next to the curb, "a good place for an ambush." He put on the tactical vest from the weapons locker and hooked his bullpup to this.

From the locker, he grabbed six magazines for himself and another six each for the detectives.

Dante brought up the rear of Charles and Sancho. Charles tested the accordion security door; it was unlocked. Sliding this back, the three men entered the shop and fanned out. "Ava," Charles called.

"Inspector Lane?"

"Yes."

"Are you alone?"

"I'm with my partner first sergeant Korn and Dante Skorna."

"Dante?" Ava's head poked out from the office door. "Dante, what are you doing here — with them?"

"Beatrice has been taken."

"Beatrice — where? By whom?"

"To the Komodo, by Caspar."

"Caspar, that huge idiot?" Dante nodded. "Why?"

"This is not why we're here." Sancho stepped in.

"There's no one else?" Charles peered around the woman's head into the office.

"I'm the only one that has not been kidnapped or killed."

"We know of Rolando, but the others?" Sancho lowered the weapon and stepped forward; Eva did not flinch, but her face tightened. Charles put a hand on his partner's shoulder, and Sancho took a half-step to the side.

"Come on out."

"Is it safe?"

"No, but it's not as dangerous as being on your own," Dante said.

"You three are working together?" Charles nodded, taking the young woman by the arm and leading her from behind the desk. "Pigs can fly."

"Tell us what happened," Dante said.

"Since the questionable death of Rolando," Charles continued.

"The zemmoan?" Ava nodded and began her story.

We decided, those of us that remained after the deaths of Rolando and Quetzal, there was no choice but to find out what was going on, on our own. When the CID, these two, motioning toward Charles and Sancho, *believed Reina had murdered Quetzal, they came after all of us. It freaked Harold out and that money grubbing whore he married; they hung us out to dry, though Harold still had enough sense of propriety or self-preservation to pack me off to a mental hospital north of the city. I escaped. By the time I got back and found my way to Zemmoa, the case against Reina was collapsing as those frightened of getting involved found the courage to come forward.*

Both Charles and Sancho disagreed with the assessment and made to correct the argument, but Dante waved them off.

After two or three of my sort, upper-class fops, came forward, the CID had no choice but to redirect their investigation into more reasonable areas. With their continued concern, it was only a matter of time before the CID, pushed by their keepers, would return to the easy fare of Zemmoa. You two may not have returned to us zemmoans, but you would have turned on any of the lower orders fed upon by the sons and daughters of the country's elites. Don't deny it; we've seen this happen too many times. Where was I, putting a hand to her head, pinching her eyes closed. *Yes, it was only a matter of time before the CID came sniffing around Zemmoa and Juan again, so we had to do something. With help from Juan's associates, we dug up enough information to satisfy us that something else was going on. When it became clear this was no simple matter of a tiff gone wrong, what remained of the zemmoans went to my brother, Harold.*

Harry didn't much care for our approach to the problem of inspiring him to help us. Before you ask, I threatened to air our family history. No one is more afraid of the facts than the rich. Much of our social position and perhaps all of our power are founded upon the narrative we feed the people. With my family, and other elites, the narrative is a lie and the truth far uglier. Family histories are dark and twisted. Though this may not always be true, it is more often the case than not. Having Harold on our side, or working for us, we had access to some of the best government and military Intelligence there is. With much complaining from Harold, information trickled in from government, department, and military sources, suggesting the problem was not that of a simple murder. Increasingly, the Komodo was mentioned then whole reports were devoted to the relationship of the Komodo to the murder of Quetzal and government problems.

As we pursued our interests in the Komodo and its relationship to the murder of Quetzal, we accessed data concerning other crimes and the attack on the police station in Bornler. We failed to notice, or believe, the government was tracking what reports were being accessed through Harold's requests and where these copies were being sent — the Sonando estate. There were no warnings given to Harold; there was no sign we were drawing any attention to ourselves. One day, however, what passed for a close friend of Harold's warned him he had come to the attention of the PM's personal security detail. Harold did not know who these people were, but they weren't attached to any of the State departments used to guard parliamentarians.

Harold had argued with me about whether to continue probing the connection between Quetzal and the Komodo. He was certain we were exposing ourselves to legal action; the fool, no less I, did not understand what we were getting ourselves into. The first sign that anything had gone wrong was when Reina disappeared. There was no warning we were being targeted. No one, that we saw, had been following us, nor were our devices being tracked. We had all put anti-tracking software on our phones and mobile devices; these detected nothing. I know, I know there's no reason retail software should pick up serious spyware — I know that now. New life lesson, and it only cost me all my friends and asshole brother, along with the bitch he married.

Reina's disappearance was only a foreshadowing of what was to come in the next days. Pollack was killed by an out-of-control delivery van whose driver was drunk. Anbessa was the victim of a mugging that went too far; she died in a northern hospital after being admitted. So there we have it. Reina is missing; Pollack, Anbessa, and Rolando are dead. By this point, I got the message and made for Harold's place. Perhaps, one reason I managed not to get caught or killed was that I had stopped living with Reina in the secret apartment in back of Chin's Review. She had been too difficult to live with, or I had been too much trouble for her. But I took off, moving from squat to squat in Bornler and the southern part of the north-side. It had been easy enough, since I had known many artists from Zemmoa, living in reduced circumstances.

Building on this network, I have been able to move about undetected. I was also using burner phones and dumping these after every few calls. Whatever the reason, I stayed ahead of whoever was looking for me — I suspect it was the Komodo, but it could well have been the government. I know — how could the government be working with the Komodo? It is far from clear the government and the Komodo are colluding, but it would explain why everyone I know involved in investigating the Quetzal/Komodo connection is missing or dead. Although, it is only Reina that is missing — which suggests the police have not turned up her body. She isn't in the apartment we shared in back of Chin's Review; she isn't in any of the doss houses I've known her to use in the past.

I suppose it is possible Reina is still alive, but I'm not putting money on it.

As Ava's story ended, the detectives looked at one another and out the broken windows of the copy shop. "Did you come across any information about how best to get into the Komodo…"

"And out," Sancho finished for Charles.

"The manhole behind Chin's Review."

"You can't be serious?" Dante sputtered.

"Right where it all started."

"Are you certain you've not gotten hold of some bad data?" Sancho asked.

"I've gotten a hold of a lot of bad stuff in my life — drugs, drink, men, women, and things that don't know what to call themselves. So there is no way to be certain whether what I've learned from Harold's sources is good or not, but it's all I have. Also, here's the important point, I'm coming with you."

"The hell you…" Charles began.

"I'm coming with you, or I'm following." There was a pause before Dante spoke.

"Are you coming for Reina?"

"Yes." Ava shifted, slipping her hands into her pockets and eyeing the men. "Do I get one of those?" pointing at Dante's automatic on the left side of the vest behind the bullpup.

Half an hour later, the group was standing in back of Chin's Review over an open manhole cover. Charles was on the burner asking Captain Slank to pick up Ramira and get her out of town. That done, the four stared down into the Komodo. "Second thoughts, anyone?" Sancho asked. No one answered. Charles had gone down first, and he had not reached the third rung, head still above ground, when a low chuckle filled the alley and a shadow disengaged from the darkness.

14

MERRY SQUALOR

"Anyone get the number of that bus?" Dante rolled over and vomited. No one answered, and he shifted onto his back, staring up at a vaulted red brick ceiling. Running his hands over the floor, it appeared to be the same brick. Clearing his throat, Dante spat a plug into the corner. His mouth was hard and thick with stomach acid. Taking a breath, releasing this, then taking another, less painful, Dante rolled toward the center of the room and pushed himself up. For a beat, vertigo gripped the back of his skull. Reaching for this, Dante had to steady himself to avoid collapsing.

That done, he tested the injury above the neck; there was a goose egg there. Pulling his fingers away, dried blood dappled these. "Okay, bad but you had worse. Remember the time…"

"Nobody cares about your great adventures in the South."

"Bea, you okay sweet-pea?" squinting against the cell's low-light.

"She's not here — next-door, across the hall." Dante looked over his shoulder. It was Ava. Pushing to a sitting position, he crossed his legs, looking about. Ava was sitting against the back wall; across from him were Sancho and Charles. Sancho appeared to be unconscious, and Charles was dabbing a cut on his upper left forehead near the hairline.

Falling back on his training, Dante looked at the bright side. They may have all been in a medieval sewer cell, but they were alive and together, and he had located Beatrice. "Any idea," Dante spoke to the room, "how we got here? All I remember is laughter and this floor." He drew his fingers over the slick surface of the brick and sniffed these. Bad idea. Wiping his hands on his pants, he waited.

"I believe the Komodo Voice took us," Charles began, "what the guards are calling Komodo."

"As in the sewers?"

"I suppose," Ava answered.

"Any news about Reina?" Laughter came from across the hall.

"She's dead," Ava said.

"How do you know?" Dante pushed up; for a beat, he thought he would collapse.

"The guard said she was," Ava answered.

"None of you," Beatrice called from across the hall, "know what's going on here, do you?"

"Mom's dead."

"That's on you for bringing that freak into our lives."

"Caspar?"

"He's joined them and came for me because of Mom's beatings and for locking me away. Caspar thought he was saving me — still thinks he is... Can you believe that?" Dante supposed he could. As bad as Caspar was, his heart had been in the right place. No matter the reasoning, Dante would still kill him.

"Yes," Dante called back.

"What do we do now?" Sancho asked from the other side of the cell where he had rolled onto his back and was examining an injury above his right ear.

"Let's start by testing that door." Dante was staring at the short stairway with the iron balustrade beyond which was an iron door with large rivets. There was no window in the door, but there was a flap for food trays, saving jailers the trouble of having to open the door and risk being attacked. Tottering toward this, Dante had to stop two or three times to check his balance and prevent himself from blacking out. He had taken off his belt and was jamming the prong from the buckle so hard into his palm this bled. The idea was to use pain to remain conscious.

"We've already tried it; the thing would withstand a direct nuclear hit," Ava said.

"What is it with you zemmoans — the only way you can communicate is through hyperbole?" Dante took his first steps toward the door, holding the slick metal balustrade. Flecks of paint still clung to this, but as he held onto the railing, these flaked away in his hands along with layers of rust. Pulling his hands away, Dante dusted one against the other. This, at least, was new. *What did this mean? Whatever it was down here, whoever was down here, had not been so for long. There were the castoffs using the place for generations, but whoever built things up did so in the last few years.*

Ava was right, the door was solid, and nothing short of military grade explosives would open it. Yet the lock took a simple skeleton key. Whoever had put money into repairing the Komodo had not updated security. That was interesting. *Can you work with that?* Maybe he could, if the jailers made the right mistakes, and they were not too far from the nearest open manhole. Dante was certain, if whoever was running the show had a little sense, they would have locked down all manholes, key to security. Even if city workers were unwilling to enter the Komodo without security, there was still the chance the government might decide now was a good time for some proactive behavior.

What this new behavior would be Dante could only guess but supposed it would involve several tactical teams. The upside for the defenders was a simple one: no heavy ordnance would get through the tunnels beyond the runoff canals. Even heavy caliber weapons would be difficult to maneuver through the tunnels. They might still be used, but their effectiveness would be questionable. Then there was the issue of RPGs, hand grenades, and SAMs — not unless they wanted to bring the sewer down on everyone. Marines and Special Forces were a half-mad lot, but even they had their limits now commitment to the state had evaporated.

For a long time, each was devoted to their own fiefdom. Mendelssohn's Ink was Dante's; with the Marines and Special Forces, it was their brothers; for Charles and Sancho, he assumed the police department; he knew not what for Ava, and with Beatrice, it was escape from Bornler and her family. Everyone had their patch of earth and their abstractions of faith they were not prepared to trade upon. Fair enough, but without the state, how did you keep even these — especially the military and police? The state was all that supported these institutions, gave them what validity they still possessed. Without the appearance of order offered by parliament, what was there for these men to hold onto? Dante supposed the military might become a force unto themselves led by a junta of officers; this might also be true of the police.

If this were so, it would no longer make them the military or police but a private Army populated by mercenaries. Without the state to pay them, they would have to earn their bread by some other means. Extortion seemed as good a strategy as any. Another reason to get out of town, but where would they go? If the country was coming apart, where could any of them go? Dante might abandon his sisters, almost wanted to forsake Beatrice, but where would he go? The military was no longer possible — he was not a mercenary. Dante had put that part of his life behind him and had no wish to return to it. Taking a breath, he leaned back from the door and looked over his shoulder.

"Waiting it is," and he tottered back to his place against the wall. "Any food or water?" Charles pointed to a bucket next to him. "Any good?"

"Had some a little while ago and haven't vomited yet, but it's rough."

"Well, beggars and all." Dante stepped across the chamber and knelt down, taking hold of the ladle. He was careful not to bend over, so as not to go face-first into the wall. Charles had been right; the water tasted like metal. "Delish."

"That's it?" Ava asked from the other end of the cell.

"Nothing to do for now," Dante used the wall to brace himself as he slid to a sitting position, "but wait to see who will be calling on us."

Charles had been dozing when the metal scraping woke him. He never seemed to get more than halfway asleep since first waking. It could have been the rich, deep, and redolent smell — the Komodo had its own peculiar scent. Decay would have been the shorthand, but there was something else behind this: hard, sharp, and metallic. Raising his head, he watched the door push in with the hard scrape of grit and stone. This was the first time it had been open since he woke in the cell. Until now, only food trays had come through the door.

The guards had not collected the bucket of waste since he woke; it was now two-thirds full, and they had moved it as far away as possible. Was that what they were here for? Two guards climbed the short staircase and stood before the balustrade, armed with automatics and bullpup assault rifles. They appeared to have minimal training in these. They knew how to hold the weapons, but Charles was uncertain they knew how to use them. Testing the theory did not seem a good idea. Beyond these two, there would be many others between them and the nearest exit.

Strained and indistinct voices came from the passage: two or more people were arguing. Charles recognized one voice as Beatrice's from when she and Dante had spoken. Since that time, three sleep cycles had passed, and the two worked at ignoring one another. The argument ended, and someone else entered the room behind the guards. There was a beat where they remained hidden, then a woman's head peered around the balustrade. "Hello." Charles tapped Sancho on the shoulder, curled up and sleeping, jacket pulled tight against the cooler air of the Komodo. Sancho pushed up on an arm and stared toward the door.

"Told you, didn't I?"

"Pay up if we make it out."

"You." Ava pushed up against the wall.

"You won't make it, so don't try."

"Came down here because I thought they took you." Ava dusted the grit and slime from her backside.

"Komodo took me long before and offered me a deal I couldn't resist."

"What kind of deal, Reina?" Sancho was standing beside Charles.

"Komodo and his keeper, Alchymist, gave me my life and allowed me to join — they also guaranteed your lives."

"Didn't work out so well for the zemmoans, did it?" Ava stepped forward next to Sancho, Charles, and Dante, who had joined the others.

"You had to come looking, didn't you? If you lot had left well enough alone, I could have convinced them you were no threat. But when you began looking into Quetzal's murder, there was nothing I could do."

Reina motioned to the guards and stepped back against the wall. They handcuffed each of their wrists behind their backs and led them from the cell. Reina was waiting outside against the far wall, next to another cell door. She was talking to whoever was inside. Charles recognized Beatrice's voice. "Don't beg," Dante called, being led down the hall.

"She wasn't begging for your life." Reina followed along as Ava emerged from the cell.

The group was escorted down one passage then another and another. It took them twenty minutes to find the new room. This was another high vaulted brick-lined chamber several times larger than the last. To Charles, it appeared a classic — right out of a 1930s horror movie. There were four metal operating tables from the same era and several more devices he could not identify. One may have been a Judas Cradle used for splitting one wide in places best not thought about. Lining the walls on each side of the chamber were manacles. There were tables, three of them, with instruments on them and covered by grimy cloths. There were three car batteries with cables;

behind the batteries were two medicine cabinets filled with small vials and hypodermics.

Tying the esthetic together were three of the largest any-things walking on two legs Charles had seen outside of documentaries. Both were wearing leather hoods with slits for eyes and mesh coverings over their mouths. The front and back flaps of the masks reached down to the middle of their backs and covered their chests. Neither wore shirts; their pants, perhaps denim and baggy, were black; boots laced up to their mid-calves. Arms folded over barrel chests, they waited. Ava and Dante were manacled to one wall and the detectives to the other. There was a desk at the far end of the room below a platform with a metal balustrade. On either end of the platform were metal doors and a large mirror, running the full length of the platform, looking down on the room.

"Someone watching?" Charles nodded to the mirrored wall when Ava looked at him.

"Not at the moment." She opened a large ledger and wrote with what appeared to be an expensive, antique fountain pen. Next to her was an ink blotter and a small vase with withered pink and cerise flowers. Someone's attempt to homey up the torture chamber. *Torture chamber — well, yeah, it had to be, didn't it?* Smiling to himself as the guards locked his manacles, Charles whistled "Nearer, My God, to Thee" — he was not sure where his memory of the hymn came from, but it seemed an appropriate choice. With the manacles fastened, the guards stopped and stared at the detective then looked to Reina.

"Enough, Inspector Lane." He finished the last bar; Reina turned back to her ledger and continue to scratch for another several minutes. With nothing else to do, Charles examined the room. There were four electric chandeliers, one in each corner of the large chamber, with one more, by far the largest, in the center hanging from the peak of the vault. None of the lights were flickering; the room seemed to be an important element in the political identity of the Komodo and was treated with something approximating reverence. The leather hooded men moved from one prisoner to the next, checking the manacles. Turning to his partner,

Charles could see Sancho was holding it together by a loose thread. Ava, for all her bluster, had gone a starker white than he had seen before.

Dante, chained beside Ava, appeared disinterested, as if roused from a deep sleep and told he was late for class. "Look here," Charles began, "Reina, what's all this business about you hooking up with Komodo?"

"*The* Komodo," she corrected.

"What's the difference..." Charles adjusted himself in his manacles.

"One's the state and one's an individual." The detective noticed how she had avoided assigning a sexual identity.

"I am corrected, thank you. So, what is all this business about you and *the* Komodo? Don't tell me it's about them getting their claws into you and threatening your life."

"Komodo caught me and threatened my life: you think about things when that happens. Most especially, you think about where you are in life and where you want to be. When these don't sync up, it's important to reassess what one wants of life."

"What did you want in life that was not syncing up?" Charles continued when Reina had returned to scratching in the ledger.

"Quetzal," more scratching.

"What about Quetzal," Dante stepped in, "was not syncing up for you?"

"Us — we weren't syncing," replacing the pen's cover.

"Come on," Charles prodded, "what are you talking about?"

"Quetzal," Reina took a breath, placing a hand on either side of the closed ledger, and continued, "through me over for his work — that wasn't selling."

"I knew you were pissed about that." Ava shook her head, and in doing so, the chains rattled.

"He didn't throw me over for you — though you wanted him to."

"No, Reina, I didn't want him for anything other than what he was giving me."

"You are a black hole — broken, twisted, and hungry. Nothing can fill a void like you." Reina pushed back from the table, the metal legs of the chair scraping along the brick floor.

"Oh, I'm not sure about that. A few have filled it adequately; for the rest, well, there are always sex toys." Charles, uncertain how to take Ava's rebuff, turned away, choking back a chuckle. Reina moved from behind the desk to a device near this. Standing about five feet high, there was atop the legs, of which there were four, a metal pyramid with tiny rivets holding the plates together. Above this, attached to the ceiling and the wall, were chains. On the ends of these were manacles: two for the wrists and two for the ankles. On either side of the pyramid device was a series of weights with hooks on the end. There was a dark stain on the floor beneath the device and what appeared to be gore and hair fixed to the peak and sides of the pyramid.

"In the spirit of competition, I was hoping you would step into the argument with as much thought as you put into everything else." Reina placed a hand on the lower platform of the device and ran a nail over the wooden surface. Taking her hand away, she examined the contents beneath her nail and flicked this away. "This is called…"

"A Judas Cradle." Reina frowned at the inspector.

"You know your history."

"I've seen sketches and documentaries about that." Charles motioned toward the cradle with his chin. "Were they ever used?"

"The Spanish Inquisition did, and there are records of it being used about Europe and the Americas."

"This," Dante began, "appears to have seen much service."

"The first time I saw Komodo lower someone on to this, I threw up — I had never seen anyone's bowels spill from their body, let alone from between their legs. Done right, this device is the most insidious form of torture I've read of or seen. Since hooking up with the Komodo, I've seen a great deal. There are other tortures more painful, but these depend on a level of empathy Ava, here, does not possess. She may not be violent, but this girl is a pure psychopath. How could she not be, with a father like hers? Harold survived his childhood and became a husband and father. He also became a successful businessman, and if Ava here had not shot her mouth off at the wrong time, he might have become a successful politician. Pity that, right?" Reina motioned to one guard and pointed at Ava.

With the leather hooded guards fastening Ava to the chains and raising her, naked, above the cradle, Reina had two others unchain Dante and tie him to a chair before the desk with two metal boxes at the foot of this. "You want to know what Beatrice was begging me for? If I break you into bits, she promised to join the Komodo."

"Beatrice and I," the guards unfastening Dante from the wall, "have had our problems, but that isn't who she is."

"Not who she was, but the last go-round with your mother changed her." Ava motioned to a guard by the door. He opened this, and Beatrice entered, followed by Caspar. Dante's erstwhile friend could not look him in the eye. Beatrice stopped near the middle of the room and folded her arms over her chest, while Caspar hung back, hands in his pockets, staring at the floor.

"Caspar, you are part of this?" Dante asked.

"He is." Beatrice turned to her side and placed a hand on his chest. "That bitch has had her way with me for the last time."

"I told you, Mother is dead — Caspar killed her."

"See sweetie, I told you." Caspar turned away and looked at the wall where the detectives hung.

"Here he is, Beatrice. This is what you want?" Reina asked.

"Those work, but not fast?" Beatrice stepped toward her brother.

"As fast or slow as you wish: we could crush every bone in his feet in less than half an hour. With a little more time, we could render the feet pulp. However, I'm certain you will want to spend a little bit longer paying your brother back or returning you to Lola."

"I want this to last as long as we can make it, maybe a bit each day. Can you do that?" Beatrice squatted before her brother and unlocked the metal boxes. One of the leather hoods placed each foot in its box.

"Ms. Skorna," Charles began, "please do not do this." Beatrice ignored him, but Reina stepped over to the officer and struck him with the back of her hand. Wincing, she grabbed this and turned away.

"Hurts, don't it?" Sancho asked. "You okay there, Charlie?" the inspector nodded. Beatrice looked back over her shoulder at Caspar, who had withdrawn to the door. On either side of this stood the two armed guards, the only ones with weapons.

"Don't run away, sweetie; we're only starting."

Reina, the pain in her hand subsiding, motioned Caspar back into the room. There followed a gurgling cry suffocated by what had to have been blood and surprise. Turning back to Dante and his sister, Reina saw the hooded guard was backing away from the siblings — a hand, then two, going to his throat. Even as he was turning toward Reina, Beatrice darted toward the tray of instruments and threw one of these at a guard holding the chain supporting Ava's left leg. Releasing this, Ava screamed as her other leg and two wrists took her full weight. The guard, now facing Reina, had a small knife sticking out of his throat; he dropped to his knees then to his side. A woofing grunt came from the door and Reina, backing up between the detectives and Ava, suspended above the Judas Cradle, turned.

One of the armed guards was already on the floor, and Caspar had the other by the throat. With a wrench, he broke the man's neck and grabbed his weapon. Beatrice was halfway across the chamber floor before the other guards reacted. The three holding Ava, suspended by as many chains, released these and were running for the platform behind the desk. Ava shrieked before connecting with the cradle's peak. Charles watched as the cradle pierced her spine, exiting her sternum. The woman's arms and legs flailed as her head lolled back and a long, black line of blood ran from the corner of her mouth up into her eye and over her forehead. If Ava was not dead, she would be soon. Both Charles and Sancho struggled against their chains.

Before the guards could reach Beatrice or Caspar, she had the assault weapon he was holding out for her. Turning, Beatrice sprayed the room. Reina reversed direction toward the platform. The rounds were flying all over the room. All three guards holding Ava were dead, and the second hooded torturer went down, shot in the face. As far as Charles was concerned, it was a miracle she had not wounded or killed her brother. Beatrice chased Reina with the weapons fire as she ran up the steps toward the platform. She continued to miss the zemmoan but blew the glass out, behind which was an empty room with chairs, a table, and desks. When Reina made it through the door, Beatrice gave it up and, with the magazine empty, dropped the weapon, running to her brother.

Freeing Dante from the boots, she undid the straps. Once loose, and finished hugging, he released Charles and Sancho. "I thought you had gone over," Dante said as Charles picked up an assault weapon, lying by the door, and found four magazines.

"I had — until they brought you in then, I don't know...after hearing about Mother, I couldn't."

"Glad to hear it, but how do we get out of here?" Dante continued.

"This one's still alive." Sancho waved the others over to a guard that had held Ava suspended above the cradle. While Charles and Sancho got what information they could about an escape route from the guard, Beatrice and Dante lifted Ava from the cradle. Laying her on the floor, Dante felt for a pulse but found none. Sitting back on his haunches, he looked to Beatrice and the detectives, shaking his head.

"Did you find a way out?" Beatrice stood, turning to the detectives.

"Yes," Sancho answered, looking back at the door. "It's the same way we came in, about ten minutes from here."

"Ten minutes through the Komodo, dressed like this?" Dante asked. Charles suggested he and Sancho dress in the leather hoods, and if stopped, they claim they are taking Dante, Caspar, and Beatrice for further interrogation. It worked. In ten minutes, they were climbing out of the Komodo in back of Chin's Review.

15

SUNSHINE LOLLIPOPS

CHARLES AND SANCHO squatted by the manhole, staring down into the flickering lights. Something happened to the power, and the lights began strobing when they were halfway to the Chin's Review exit. A dull, throbbing gong washed up out of the manhole, filling the alley. "I believe," Sancho scratched the side of his face, "our little party has been discovered." Caspar picked up the heavy manhole cover and dropped this in place. Even with the Komodo sealed, the gong thrummed the air.

"We've done it now," Charles said.

"What do you mean?" Dante pushed Beatrice behind him.

"They'll be coming," Charles answered.

"Before it was all rumor," Sancho continued, when it appeared the others did not understand. "Now we have survivors and witnesses."

"I don't see how that will change anyone's opinion about the Komodo," Dante said. Charles looked over, raising his eyebrows in question. "Think about it: you have a tattoo artist, his younger sister, a homeless man," motioning to Caspar, "and two censured detectives. You have been censured, correct?"

"Yes," Charles stepped over the manhole cover, "but so we could investigate what's been going on in Komodo. We've accomplished that."

"But what did you find out?" Beatrice stepped around her brother, taking him by the arm, the pair ignoring Caspar.

"Well, let's recap," Sancho continued, staring at the manhole cover. "We've been imprisoned, threatened with torture, and the Komodo Voice is no longer a myth."

"More than that," Beatrice picked up, "from what I've seen and heard, Komodo is not a super villain nor a demon. He is wearing, beneath that robe of his, a mechanical frame giving him extraordinary power and the ability to climb, jump, and tear people apart."

"You have seen the exoskeleton?" Charles stepped from the cover; doing so, Sancho stepped onto it.

"No, Caspar has," motioning to the giant.

"Komodo is a tiny man, very weak — but smart. No one in the Komodo, not even Alchymist, is as smart." Caspar edged away from Beatrice and Dante toward the dumpster. Police tape still fluttered in the wind at the end of the alley where the body of Quetzal had been found. Since Chin's Review had opened after the murder, it was necessary to remove the tape. Charles had known of a command level discussion about whether the Review should have reopened. The Review, though, had too many friends in municipal and federal governments not to be reopened. Because of this, the police tape was cut. Charles, with the support of Sancho, had lobbied against the use of the alley by actors, managers, and staff.

This had been unofficially successful; few working at the Review used the stage door any longer. Nor did they move alone through the streets. With the disappearance of Petr, none of the actors were prepared to risk their lives. The rumor was, Mala had either moved North, away from the capital and the troubles brewing in the South, or had left for one of the northern empires to be a technocrat's mistress. Sancho and Charles worked hard on the latter. It had been

Sancho's idea, and when brought to Captain Slank, he took it to the CID commander, who took it to the chief of police. All agreed, it was better if Mala was thought to have run away. Charles thought she had done so after the initial interviews, but when a patrol car went around to her apartment, she was gone. Even though her clothes and luggage were missing, Mala's bank account had not been touched; that was a red flag.

Charles had kept an eye on the account for any movement: there had been none. Mala did not have a lot of money, but it was enough for an actor not to leave behind. As far as her whereabouts were concerned, there was no record of her exiting the country. It was not unheard of for people to escape without the correct papers, but these were often criminals and political undesirables. As an actor, Mala was neither of these — as with most in her profession, she remained a marginal entity. But this did not mean she was a member of a group the government would like to see disappear. Actors were not writers: the latter the most undesirable in the arts community. Writers seemed to believe it a moral responsibility to demonize government and the instruments of government, whether they deserved this or not.

So writers were encouraged to seek their livelihood in fields of enterprise more acceptable or to find succor elsewhere — meaning the northern states capable of absorbing political and deep state abuse without risking collapse. At worst, these northern states would experience embarrassment. Here though, the state and the institutions of the state were too fragile to withstand continuous and provocative attacks.

"Zhenli, that was Zavala's friend who turned on him, *along with you*." Charles tilted his head back, staring up at Bill's massive, doughy frame.

"Look at me. You see what I am, what I have — nothing. Komodo told me I could be whatever I wanted, save whoever I wanted," looking toward Beatrice. Dante raised a protective arm before his sister, but she pushed this away and stepped forward.

"You only were trying to save me from Mother." Turning back to Dante, she put her hand on his upper arm, attempting to make him understand. It did not appear to Charles, Dante understood much beyond the fact Caspar had killed his mother. "Caspar was only trying to save me; I didn't know when he took me, and it was hard for me to understand what he was doing after I saw Mother. She didn't deserve that, no matter what she did, and she did a lot," voice cracking. "Caspar was there for me when you and the others only wanted to blame me for wanting a better life."

"We could go over this again and again. It will never change what you, or he, did," drawing the automatic Dante had taken from a guard. Beatrice placed her hand on top of the weapon and attempted to push his arm down. The arm did not move. Caspar did not raise his weapon to Dante, nor did he attempt to step away. Whatever was coming, Caspar appeared ready.

"We know what he did, and we know why he did it; Caspar was wrong, and Mother died because of it, but it won't help either of us now for you to kill him."

"It'll help me." Needing all three on his side, Charles thought better of stepping in front of Dante. They were far from the best witnesses, and it was true Sancho and he had been censured; however, they were the only evidence the detectives had to present the PM and his cabinet. Without them, there was no case. There would be no case, even with their testimony, unless he could convince the PM to send people into the Komodo.

"We can't ..." Sancho staggered back from the manhole cover, almost falling.

"What," Charles did not finish the thought as a thud came from inside the manhole cover.

"Komodo." Beatrice stepped back behind Dante. Caspar jumped on the cover and pressed his enormous weight down upon this. The first of the locks on the inside of the cover snapped with a brittle snick.

"Run," the giant called, kneeling on the manhole cover. Beatrice hesitated, but Dante drew her after him. Charles wavered longer than Sancho, who was already running after Dante and Beatrice, toward their truck, but knew there was no stopping Komodo if he burst from the manhole. What he had pieced together about Komodo was enough to let him know the exoskeleton would protect him from just about anything. If the robe was bulletproof, there was almost no hope of stopping him unless he got a clear shot through the hood's opening. Charles had not seen Komodo in action and only could guess how much space there would be for him to get a shot. Without that knowledge, he had no choice but to run after his partner and hope they had enough of a lead to get away.

Back at the SUV, Charles heard a loud rending, followed by a long, piteous shriek.

"Where is this place?" Dante stepped from the SUV.

"Winchell, by the north-side." Charles closed the door. They had pulled in to an ancient estate with a tall wrought iron fence with spiked tips, still intact though rusted. The grounds were overgrown with a garden that had generations ago gone to seed and was choked with weeds. Untended, the trees had grown wild and wide, providing shade and shelter from prying eyes. The gate was still strong, but the lock had long since been broken by looters. Sancho and Charles had placed a chain around this and fixed it with a heavy padlock. There had been an attempt to make the chain appear old, but the padlock was bright and shiny. Charles had argued the new lock invited attention, but Sancho solved the problem by setting two guard dogs loose on the grounds. After the first attempt at scaling the fence, no future assaults were made.

Neither detective was certain whether they were being watched, but it was a good chance the neighborhood had noted their presence. Because the detectives did not interfere with the life of the district, the district decided interfering with whoever they were would have cost more energy and suffering than was reasonable. Sancho seemed to believe the issue ended there; Charles was less certain. The hope had been the assignment would be short-lived.

"Yeah." Dante stepped from the ruined garage and looked over the chevron brick driveway with weeds peeking up between the buckled brick road. There were, on the inside of the gate, the remains of barrel fires common amongst the indigent populations of Bornler and Winchell and other districts. The south was not much better than the east-side in the north — though it would take longer for it to sink as low as Winchell. "No one will think to look for us here."

"Komodo will." Beatrice stepped out from behind Dante, knotting a hand in the lower part of his jacket and pulling close.

"No one knows about this place, not even the government." Sancho opened the back of the SUV and pulled out a duffel filled with what weapons they had not taken down into the Komodo. Slinging this over his shoulder, he turned left and walked around the front of the house. "We're this way."

"If you have had trouble in the district," Dante noticed the dogs at the far end of the yard on the inside of the fence, "it is certain the Komodo knows someone is here, someone that doesn't belong. With us in the wind, they'll be looking for anything that doesn't belong."

"Feel sorry for any fool that decides this might be an easy touch." Charles unlocked the padlocks, all three of them, holding the front door in place. Though the original lock had long since been knocked out and the door ripped open, the door itself was solid metal. Its value had not diminished with the years, but the padlocks, though sturdy, did not appear up to the job the original lock had been. On the inside, the detectives had installed four huge deadbolts.

"Why?" Beatrice asked as Sancho slipped the bolts home.

"This," Sancho jostled the duffel on his shoulder, "is only a sample of what we have inside."

"The government has given us a stipend that any in the CID or tactical squads would envy. Whoever is their quartermaster, they've access to the best military tech. *Whoever* means the Chinese war machine." The Chinese were one of the few northern empires that had been shaken by the collapse of the international system.

Collapse, Charles knew, was too extreme — contraction would have been better. Whatever the cause or definition, the Chinese were in trouble, with many of their provinces in open rebellion. This had led elements of the military and government, not controlled by the politburo, into the international arms market. On the second floor of the mansion, Charles had said the building had forty odd rooms, but most of these were sealed and uninhabitable. He led them into a large ballroom that was also doubling as sleeping quarters and kitchen for the two detectives.

Paneling covering the walls at one time had been white with gold filigree overlaying the ornate reliefs. Electric lights had been installed along the wall in the form of faux candles, and electric chandeliers ran from one end of the long room to the other. None of the lights worked, and there was no electricity in the building except for a small generator the detectives were using. At the end of the ballroom was a low stage with heavy velvet curtains hanging to the left and right. These were covered in dust and cobwebs. There were three chairs on the stage, ancient in appearance, facing one another. At one time, these would have been expensive, but were now little better than kindling. Charles warned Dante and Beatrice against using any of the original pieces of furniture.

The flooring was parquet in a labyrinthine, geometric design, dizzying to look at for extended periods. Though filthy, it appeared in good repair with only a few pieces missing. Inside the door, Charles and Sancho had set up their headquarters; here there were crates of weapons and ammunition. There also looked to be rocket powered grenades and surface-to-air missiles. Neither of the detectives knew what they would face when taking over the building and did not wish to share where they were with the ministers, so they took whatever was on offer. Sancho explained their reticence about trusting the PM or his cabinet, which made more than a little sense to Dante and Beatrice. Being Bornlerites, they had no trouble understanding distrust of the government. The only reason either of them trusted the detectives was because there was no choice. Neither could go back to Mendelssohn's Ink, and Beatrice had made it plain, no matter what happened, she would not return to the apartment.

Dante appeared to agree, but Charles was uncertain if this was out of consent or a desire to deal with one problem at a time.

When the group had finished discussing the weapons, they dug into a variety of MREs, meals ready to eat. They were all so hungry no one complained about the taste; still Charles felt he had to apologize for the food. With food in their bellies and each with their coffee, the group agreed the next step would be to contact Minister of Justice Bevin. Dante and Beatrice had been less enthusiastic about the idea, but with no other options, they surrendered. On their own, they would not make it, not after Caspar had brought them to the attention of Komodo and Zhenli. If Komodo did not know where they lived, Zhenli knew the studio well enough through Caspar. Going back there, they may as well turn themselves over to the Komodo.

The phone connected on the second ring. "Where are you?" Bevin sounded as though he was moving through an empty hall.

"Minister, I thought you didn't want to know." Charles held the phone out before him on speaker.

"Are you with Detective Korn?" Bevin's voice became less expansive, as though he had stepped into an office.

"And two Komodo survivors," Sancho answered.

"You brought two komodoans out of that pit?"

"One was already a prisoner, and the other was going down to look for her; we went along for the ride — then we were all captured. With a little help, we escaped and have some fun stories for the kids," Charles answered.

"Such as?" Minister Bevin asked, creaking back in an office chair.

"Komodo, the pseudonym for the Komodo Voice (or the other way round), is a man using a mechanical exoskeleton and what we assume to be a bulletproof robe." Silence followed Charles' description of Komodo and his toys.

"Inspector, I'm not sure we've made any progress. Demon wasn't good, but we could explain that away. A man with such tech is far less comforting. The possibility of technology like that in the hands of komodoans will be real enough, so dismissing it will not be easy. The people of Bornler and the east-side may talk about demons and whisper about retribution, but no one believes it. This people will believe — say *nothing*."

"We need to get someplace safe," Charles continued.

"I don't know where you are and no one else does — sounds safe."

"We stand out," Sancho stepped into the conversation, "like a sore thumb in Winchell. People in the district know someone is living in their midst that does not belong. It is only a matter of time before the Komodo learns of us. Once that happens, you'll have a firefight on your hands. Before the dust settles, a big chunk of Winchell will be on fire. Do you want that so soon after the apartment complex explosion?"

"Your point is well-made, first sergeant, but things here are delicate." Charles did not like the way Bevin said that.

"What do you mean, minister?" A pause followed, and the minister pushed out of his chair. A door closed in the minister's office then another. With another creak and woof of air, the minister was back.

"There have been several developments since you dropped off the map."

"We haven't been gone that long," Charles answered the silence.

"Things have been speeding up since the apartment explosion and," Minister Bevin shifted in the chair, voice dropping, "I am no longer certain which members of the cabinet are trustworthy."

"In what way?" Sancho's grip on the assault weapon he was cleaning tightened.

"Part of the problem appears to be political. PM Hirvola is considering a cabinet shuffle, and the ministers are anxious. There's more, however, than simple anxiety over cabinet posts."

There followed the sound of a glass being sat on a desk then ice being dropped into the glass, followed by the sound of something poured over this. The minister swallowed and sucked-in a sharp breath. "The PM and I have had conversations over the last twenty-four hours, concerning whether Deputy PM Shogun is working for us or the opposition. There has been some concern he may have connections with whatever is occurring in the Komodo."

"Do you mean," Dante pushed in over a question Charles was forming, "the Deputy PM may be Alchymist?"

"To whom am I speaking?" Minister Bevin asked.

"That was Dante Skorna," Charles said, motioning for Dante to remain silent. "He is a survivor and witness to what is occurring in the Komodo. Dante had been looking for an entrance to the Komodo when we found him. His sister, Beatrice Skorna, was abducted by a homeless man, and it appeared he took her to the Komodo. With few allies, we decided it prudent to team up — for all the good it did us."

"A connection is suspected," Minister Bevin continued. "There is no hard evidence, but rumors have surfaced about suspicious meetings and absences that cannot be accounted for by his security detail. Neither of these, in and of themselves, are proof. However, taken together, they are enough to support an investigation. Once completed, we will have a better idea of where his loyalties lie and whether sedition is involved."

"How long will that take?" Sancho did not need to be told; investigations of parliamentarians were long, involved, and corrupt. He needed to know where this placed them as far as actions by the PM and cabinet ministers were concerned.

"The timeframe will be longer than we have to act upon your evidence," Minister Bevin answered.

"We need to act upon this information now," Charles continued.

"You are certain the Komodo is preparing to move on the city?"

"We are certain of nothing, other than the Komodo is well-organized, well-armed, and bloody-minded." Charles sat the phone on a crate of grenades and stretched; a riffle of cracks ran up his spine.

"What is your recommendation, Inspector Lane?" There it was, Charles' career turned on his next words.

"The Komodo is responsible for assault, torture, murder, mass murder, and assassination. It now appears to be attempting to destabilize the national government and trigger a crisis of confidence. Perhaps, and here I am speculating, whoever Alchymist is may attempt to trigger another coup d'état or civil war. Whatever it is Alchymist is attempting to do, the outcome for the government and the country will not be good." Charles tapped his fingers on the automatic strapped to his tactical vest as he stepped toward the tall window next to the crates of ammunition and explosives.

"We've company," Charles called over a shoulder, ripping the velcro hammerlock from the automatic. "We need a decision, minister — it appears we will have to vacate our present location faster than I supposed." Dante, Beatrice, and Sancho all joined the inspector at the window; Beatrice strangled a cry and ran for an assault weapon. Taking this from her, Sancho demonstrated how to load a magazine, turn the safety on and off, and how to fire without breaking her shoulder. Minister Bevin vamped for a minute or two until the first shots were heard. "I need your answer now, minister, before we vacate the estate."

"There are security agents I know of that can be trusted; these are not large in number, but they're excellent at what they do. The Army may wish to support us once the threat is proven. Not all the Army and none of the upper echelons that have become politicized, but the bulk of the officer corps and select elements of enlisted soldiers will be open to protecting the country." Charles was uncertain who these people were or whether they could be trusted, but his back was against the wall.

"Minister," breaking the glass on the window and returning fire, "I don't care who they are or what their political agendas — as long as they can be counted on."

"I can put together several strike teams within the next two or three hours, but you will need to disengage from where you are now and go to ground. Worst case scenario, I will have the teams ready to go before morning. Can you hold on until then?" Minister Bevin poured himself another drink and tossed this back.

"We have a fallback position that no one knows about, except Sancho and me," Charles answered

"Where?"

"We're going to keep that on a need to know basis. When I'm finished with this call, I will turn the phone off, remove the battery and the SIM card. After we have moved, I will contact you on this phone." Between rounds, Charles examined the gate and the mob gathering beyond this. Two men were at the gate with bolt cutters; Sancho was about to pick them off when Charles stopped him. "Let them break the chain. If they don't, we'll have to unlock it. Whoever tries will not survive the effort. When they've open the gate," he looked over his shoulder at the crate of SAMs "have you read the instructions?" Sancho nodded.

"It will make one hell of an explosion. And if we want to use it to best effect, we should attempt to get as many of that mob close to the gate as we can. However, this will leave behind a big stink, and PM Hirvola won't be happy."

"Minister Bevin, you still there?"

"Yes, if there is no other way, you have my authorization."

"You heard the minister, Sancho — let them clog the gate then let her rip."

The explosion had been louder than any had expected, and the cloud that boiled up from the impact with dust and debris made it impossible to see what happened. As the cloud dissipated, there was a smallish crater in the road. Charles was satisfied they could bump their way through that in the SUV, but there were more bodies and parts of bodies than expected. "Okay, minister, we are out of here." Ending the call, he removed the battery and SIM card.

Dante was certain that had been the bloodiest thing he had seen since Ava was dropped on the Judas Cradle, though the number of bodies sprawled across and around the gate perhaps made it worse. Then there were the parts of bodies and those that had not been killed outright. He tried not to think about that, tried to remain focused for the sake of Beatrice. His sister had insisted upon coming with them. The inspector had offered to have her jailed for the duration but could not guarantee her safety at police HQ. All those that could be trusted amongst the police the detectives had called in to bolster the few the minister could gather for the assault. This included Captain Slank and a few others from the CID; there had been talk of those on the tactical teams and several patrol officers, but neither detective was certain of these.

For the past hour, Dante, Beatrice, and Sancho Korn had been waiting in a small northeast sporting goods shop that had been closed up after the destruction of the apartment complex. The owners had left no information with the local police when, or if, they would return. Detective Korn had chosen this as a fallback position when they had moved into the Winchell estate. If Detective Korn was to be believed, neither he nor Inspector Lane thought it would be necessary to retreat here. At the same time, neither had expected to end up imprisoned in the Komodo along with Dante, Beatrice, and Ava.

The SUV pulled into the parking lot in front of the store in a small strip mall across from a larger mall. Traffic in both had been all but nonexistent for the last several hours. But it was now close to nine in the evening. From what Dante had been able to tell, since the apartment complex destruction, there was little by way of traffic even during peak shopping hours. From behind the cash register, Dante watched as Detective Lane climbed out of the SUV and shouldered a small duffel. Unlocking the front door, Dante took the duffel from the detective. "More MREs."

"At this point, I'll take what I can get — and Beatrice is ready to try the mall across the street if we don't get something in her belly."

In the back room, Dante passed Beatrice two MREs and gave another to Sancho. As the group ate, Charles told them they would meet up with the strike team south of Sonando. Their contact was to be Captain Slank. It appeared, the captain had more friends and knew more people than either of the detectives had suspected. But they would not be ready until three or four in the morning. Charles argued there were questions of security that had to be addressed before they could gather all those necessary for the strike teams. There was also a problem with weapons, ammunition, and bits and pieces he was not certain about. To Dante, this suggested explosives, grenades, rocket powered grenades, and whatever explosives the soldiers could rustle up in the time they had without getting caught.

When they finished their meal, Charles had the group get as much sleep as they could before leaving.

16

ANOTHER RUNNER IS BORN

"This would not be my first choice, but Winchell is closed to us unless we want to fight our way in," Beatrice spoke, standing over the manhole cover. They were in the northeast section of the south-side close to its frontier with the east-side.

"What of Chin's Review?" Captain Slank edged around the group until next to Beatrice.

"Alchymist will know the entrance has been compromised," Charles began. "If I were him, I'd have collapsed the tunnel and all those in the area that might feed into the main passage. We could try it, captain, but I wouldn't like our odds — if we got in, it would be to lure us into an ambush."

"I'm not sure going in anywhere will be better than an ambush," an Army officer, wearing Special Forces patches, said.

"What do you mean, Captain Bradacz?" Daniel Slank asked.

"You are of the opinion," Captain Jed Bradacz turned to Charles, "the Komodo is waiting for us?"

"I would assume," Charles hesitated, "Alchymist and Komodo, if not others, are aware two detectives have escaped with witnesses. It would follow we would report what happened there. If Minister Bevin is correct, and there is a leak at the cabinet level and seditious behavior is suspected of at least one minister, then the Komodo will be aware something is coming its way. How aware and what pushback they are expecting I've no idea. However, the Komodo has remained an undetected threat for some time."

"I'm not sure," Captain Bradacz continued, "what any of that means. Do you suspect they will be waiting for us?"

"Yes," the inspector answered.

"Then does it matter where we go in? Won't they be waiting for us at all points of entry they consider vulnerable?" The captain had slipped another bandolier over his shoulder and was eyeing an RPG launcher. He had, already, a bandolier of grenades. Captain Bradacz was a big man, almost as tall as Caspar and in better shape, but Charles was not sure he had the same power or how good he would be when the fighting got ugly. Bradacz was Special Forces, and that said a lot, but he was not sure whether he had seen combat. With Dante, Charles knew he had seen combat and how he would react under fire. That Dante was prepared to go back said even more about his character — or lack of sanity.

"I can only tell you what I overheard and what Caspar told me when attempting to convince me he had come to save me from Mother." Beatrice was staggering under the weight of a tactical vest, bandoliers, assault weapon, and a heavy pack. She stayed upright, but it would not take much to tip her over.

"We are to believe this girl?" Captain Bradacz asked.

"I was down there. We were all down there and escaped — what were you doing?" The captain ignored Beatrice.

"Are we?" directing the question to Captain Slank, who looked to Charles.

"Of all of us here, she was held the longest and talked to her guards and the fellow that took her. If anyone has any idea how to get in and out, it would be her."

"Looks like I'm all you have." Beatrice tottered toward the vans the Army had brought. Charles had been expecting troop transports, maybe an armored personnel carrier or two. When they showed up in three panel vans, however, appearing to have been through the southern wars, he suspected either they were in worse shape than he thought, or the detectives were smarter than he gave them credit. It turned out the captain and his men were smarter. Showing up in a transport then poking about on the south-side, near the east-side frontier, looking for an access point to the Komodo was not the best of ideas. But three old vans were three more that could be overlooked.

The captain appeared neither happy nor put out by what Beatrice had to say. All he did was gather the strike teams and load them into the vans. The police remained as one unit, and Dante, along with Beatrice, joined them. There was no break between the military and paramilitary (police), but there was a distance in psychology and tactics both recognized. To reduce the likelihood of getting one another killed, they separated into units that would not trip one over the other. Charles and the police, along with Dante and Beatrice, took the last van and their SUV. Sancho rode with the police in the van while Charles rode with Dante and Beatrice in the SUV. It was recognized the police did not trust the Bornler civilians. From what Captain Bradacz had said, it appeared to Charles he did not trust the east-siders either.

Charles was uncertain whether the feeling was shared by the brother and sister but assumed it was. Given this, keeping them separate from military and police seemed the best choice. He did not want to bring them along. He recognized Beatrice had been there a long time, but he was uncertain how much she had been moved about. In her debriefing, it seemed she had moved about often — from cell, to an interrogation room, to what might have been a cafeteria. The Komodo had been attempting to win her over, and so she was treated with trust and occasional respect. But Alchymist and Komodo never trusted her, that was if Beatrice had been correct about her reception. Much of this had come about because Reina did not trust her.

The issue of Reina was a sore one for Dante, less so for Beatrice. Dante had been fond of Quetzal and the zemmoans, while Beatrice had held them in contempt. It was not clear why, but Charles suspected it had to do with them being privileged and wanting to live close up against Bornler — through the experience of Zemmoa. When it became clear to Dante that Reina had been responsible for the death of the zemmoans, he wanted revenge. As he realized Reina was responsible for the murder of Quetzal, with an assist from Zhenli, his anger spiked. Charles could see he hid it well, but Dante's dedication to busywork, checking and rechecking his equipment, had not fooled the inspector. No matter how professional, Dante would bear watching.

They drove for half an hour before Charles asked Beatrice to take the lead now they were near the entrance. Down by the river, there were large runoffs that came out of the Komodo and into the river. It was not a healthy arrangement, but unless they wanted the city flooded during the rainy season, there was no choice but to build these runoffs. The east-side near the south-side frontier was indistinguishable from the more affluent south. "Here — yes, this is it. Pull over." Beatrice hopped from the back seat as Charles pulled the SUV to the curb. She ran across the street flush against the river and stepped down a dirt path.

"Wait, Beatrice," Charles called. Holding onto a young tree, she leaned further down the path, looking to the entrance. Now the rainy season had passed, the river was only a quarter of its flood levels. Much of the riverbed was cracked mud, and from this came a thick unhealthy smell. It was not helped by the desultory trickle running from the Komodo. In ten minutes, they had loaded their packs, and several of the soldiers were carrying duffels. Dante had pulled Beatrice away from the river and got her back into her pack with her bandoliers, assault weapon, and an automatic strapped to the tactical vest. He had warned her about what was coming, but she reminded him of when he had been a recruit sent into the South to put down an insurrection. He could not wait to get into the fight; at the end of the first week, he could not wait to end his enlistment.

Charles followed Beatrice down; behind him came Sancho and then Dante. At the entrance to the Komodo, the group had stopped and waited for everyone to make it down the path. The smell from the Komodo was overpowering, and three of the soldiers tied bandannas over their faces. Charles did not believe this would help, but if it made them feel better, where was the harm? Once they had collected at the entrance, Captain Bradacz led the men, accompanied by Beatrice. By unanimous consent, it had been agreed to distribute most of her pack amongst the others. If they lost Beatrice, they lost what might be their best guide to the heart of the Komodo and Alchymist.

"This is the best way in?" Captain Bradacz asked Beatrice.

"You said it would not matter which way we took — the Komodo would be waiting for us." Beatrice skittered across the tunnel and behind Dante. The looks she had been receiving since the first death were enough to keep her as far from the military as possible. The CID officers and detectives were a little better, but that was because Charles and Sancho had been sure to tell them that it did not matter where they went in, resistance would be heavy.

"I'd not expected this." The captain loaded another grenade into the launcher. The explosion hit the Komodo troops dead center. When the smoke cleared, there were two left alive but so mutilated, there would be no fight coming from them for some time.

"You spoke with Minister Bevin, did you not?" Charles stood and shot two of the komodoans in the head; the third was moaning in the corner, missing the better part of its bowels, with no legs. All teams had been warned about husbanding their ammunition and were to resupply off komodoans where possible. Luckily, from what the captain could tell, the komodoans were using the same ammunition as the Army, and when he had time to examine their weapons, these were found to be Army issue. That had worried everyone. If the Army was involved, this meant there had been high level defections in the officer corps, or civilian oversight had siphoned off a good chunk of weapons, ammunition, explosives, and small ordnance.

"Yes, inspector, I did, but nothing concerning this level of resistance was mentioned."

"Captain Bradacz, I too spoke with Minister Bevin," Daniel Slank stepped in, "and he told me to expect serious resistance, but there was no way of knowing how strong it would be. Did he tell you something similar, or were you lied to?" Captain Bradacz did not reply; instead, he stepped over to the surviving komodoan and ended its suffering.

"We have four dead and three injured; two of the injured cannot be moved," a corpsman reported to the captain.

"What are we to do with our injured?" Captain Bradacz continued.

"Our mission is strategic," Daniel Slank answered.

"What does that mean?" Beatrice asked Dante.

"It means we have to leave the injured to the clemency of the enemy."

"Clemency? From komodoans?"

"Most of their troops, all the komodoans, will attempt to prevent our entry into the main cysts and chambers you have described," Charles answered Beatrice's question.

"We cannot sustain this level of losses much longer," Captain Bradacz said to no one in particular.

"If you would get your men under control," Daniel Slank stepped over, finger raised to the captain, "we would no longer experience such losses. My men have been on point since we entered the tunnels, and we've only suffered one minor injury. Yours are treating this like a training exercise — get them under control." The chamber, emptied of gunfire and explosions, went quiet.

Instead of waiting for Captain Bradacz to answer, Captain Slank took the lead, and the CID, along with Dante and Beatrice, followed. For the next two miles, there was no trouble. Noises could be heard coming from beyond their position and down adjacent tunnels, but they met no resistance. The captain, having recovered from the insult, suggested some komodoans may attempt to flank their position. After sending two teams to reconnoiter komodoan movements, they returned after fifteen minutes, having found no sign of this. "They're pulling us in," Captain Bradacz said.

"Seems reasonable," Daniel Slank answered.

"What are we going to do?" Dante stepped from the rear of the column, leaving Beatrice with Sancho.

"If we can get them all in one place, we may have a chance of breaking their back without bringing more attention to this operation than Minister Bevin would care for," Captain Bradacz said.

"I don't care how much attention…" Dante began.

"You should," Charles interrupted. "If the government is found to have let a revolutionary organization grow beneath the streets of the capital and undetected for years, maybe decades, the government could fall." Charles motioned toward Captain Bradacz with his eyes.

"Let's get on with this." Captain Bradacz stepped into the next cyst and, clearing that, moved down the tunnel. For the next twenty minutes, they proceeded in a general northeasterly direction, meeting no resistance and hearing no more from komodoans in adjacent tunnels. There was the occasional shuffle of feet and equipment coming from down the system, but this was reckoned to be further away. Amongst the teams, there had been brief discussions whether they were being pulled into an ambush. Most had decided they were but had agreed it was the only way to bring this to a decisive conclusion. The hope had been they would possess greater firepower in the form of RPGs and SAMs. That, in combination with their grenades and anti-personnel weapons, it was hoped, would give them the advantage.

"There is a large chamber up ahead, filled with chandeliers. I saw nothing," the soldier reported, "but it doesn't feel right. If they are waiting for us, it would be there."

"Were you seen?" Charles asked. The soldier shrugged.

"I saw no one, and I made certain no one saw me — which means I was seen. This is their territory. If they're any good, they will know I was there. These komodoans have managed to hide from the government and military for years — I assume they are good." There were three access points from their position on this side of the chamber and half a dozen on the other side that did not appear to be accessible except by crossing the chamber with the chandeliers.

"That'll be it." Captain Bradacz checked his weapon and let this dangle then pulled his RPG launcher around and loaded a grenade.

Captain Bradacz distributed his teams throughout the three tunnels, while the CID, along with Beatrice and Dante, remained in the tunnel they were in, which was believed to open onto the chamber's center. "How do you want to approach this?" the Special Forces Captain asked Slank.

"I should go first," Beatrice said.

"I don't think," Dante began.

"What is your reasoning?" Charles asked.

"I escaped. They hoped to turn me. I don't know why they thought it would be a good idea other than Caspar had wanted me — or had wanted to save me. I'm certain the whole business about saving me was an excuse to get his hands on me. He may not have known it, but that's what he wanted from me. Komodo will be upset with my getting away, but more upset with the fact I rejected the Komodo and Alchymist. He's a psychopath and a true believer — I committed the greatest of heresies. I turned from the chosen people."

"Komodo will want to kill you?" Captain Bradacz allowed the launcher to dangle.

"No." Dante stepped forward, but Beatrice held out a hand.

"Of all of us, Komodo and Alchymist will hate me the most. After the damage we did escaping, after killing their interrogators, those two, and others, will want me...you too but me in particular. I've learned not to underestimate lust in all its forms: sex, power, spirituality, and position." Beatrice tapped the RPG launcher and looked up at the captain. "Give me one of those and a couple more grenades." She shucked off her pack, reduced in size after the contents had been distributed amongst the other team members.

Beatrice took the launcher and the extra grenades — stepping into the chamber.

"Komodo," the woman called, and the walls of the chamber echoed, followed by a tinkle of glass from the chandeliers, "I'm here."

"Unless they are dumb as trees, this will not work." Dante edged toward the mouth of the tunnel. Meanwhile, Beatrice had stepped almost halfway into the chamber.

"Don't underestimate arrogance and revenge," Bradacz said.

"I'm not sure…" the words died on Charles's tongue with a rustle from the central tunnel on the far side of the chamber.

"You should not have come back, Beatrice." A woman stepped out from the shadow of the tunnel on the far side of the chamber at the top of the stairs.

"Reina?" Dante squinted up at the figure. She was wearing a heavy robe, the hood thrown back. The material was stiff, and as she moved, it caught the diffuse light of the chandeliers and shimmered with multiple colors. Though not bright, these colors were distinct, and a silver brocade stitching ran down the front of the robe.

"What is it with these robes?" Sancho stepped up behind Dante and Charles.

"Ritual," Dante answered.

"What?" Sancho stepped up.

"They want to all think, act, and be as one — costumes, like tattoos, identify them as members of a tribe."

"Quiet," Bradacz put a hand on Dante's shoulder, "something's happening."

"We would have let you disappear for a while back into Bornler … maybe longer than a while if you had shut up." At the top of the stairs, Reina unhooked her robe and dropped this on the platform. Beneath, she was wearing fatigues, same as the Special Forces. A grumble came from Captain Bradacz.

"Hello, have we met? I'm the Skorna that's never done what I'm told. You know my brother, right?" motioning to Dante.

Charles snatched at Dante as he moved by, but he shook the inspector's hand free and stepped out. When Reina's eyes shifted to Dante, Beatrice fired the RPG from her hip. The rocket power grenade missed Reina's head by what appeared inches and exploded within the tunnel but not before Komodo had jumped from this. Landing on the side of the steps, he toppled over these, only catching the edge with the claw of his exoskeleton. Screams and moans came from inside the tunnel. "That," Reina looked over her shoulder then back down at Beatrice, "was foolish — worse, it was wasteful."

"Next you will tell me we cannot win?"

"No, you may — but you shouldn't." Beatrice was loading another grenade when the first shots rang from the tunnels on top of the stairs to the woman's left. The rounds ricocheted off the stone floor, and the chamber rang with the exchange of weapons fire.

As the komodoans spilled from the tunnels on top of the staircase, Captain Bradacz stepped out, shouldering a SAM. Aiming this at the tunnel closest him, he let loose; the others watched as the chemtrail disappeared into the tunnel, and a thundering explosion followed. The mouth of this tunnel partially collapsed. From the other tunnels, the Special Forces stepped out with more SAMs. Vapor trails filled the chamber, and before the last one struck at the mouth of the tunnel, Alchymist flew from this. Komodo had drawn himself up from the edge of the step and covered Alchymist with his body, still encased in the exoskeleton and partly covered by the protective robe.

From the right side of his face, blood flowed from a scalp wound over an eye swelling shut. Grabbing a fold of the robe, he pulled this over himself only in time to prevent the concentrated fire of the Special Forces and CID from killing him and Alchymist. The pair backed away from the staircase and toward the one tunnel vomiting komodoans. Dante reached Beatrice and attempted to pull her out of the way as she was loading another grenade, her last. As he did so, Reina was running down the steps, her rifle on full auto. The surface of the chamber's floor sparked and twanged about them. As Dante pulled Beatrice to the side, a round sliced along the outer side of his thigh.

Dante did not go down but twisted to the side, favoring the leg, and continued to pull Beatrice with him. Doing so, Beatrice locked the grenade in place and pulled free of her brother, dropping to a knee. Reina caught the grenade in the chest and disappeared in a spray of blood, bone, and gore. What remained, as he pulled his sister from the center of the chamber, with fighting all about them, was a leg up to the mid-thigh. Everything else was bits and pieces. All about them, the fighting had closed, and the lack of training for the komodoans was taking its toll. Dante was lucky to have come down with the Special Forces and CID — both of which were well-trained. His training kicked in as soon as he stepped into the chamber, but being a brother, responsible for an out-of-control sister, he could not leave Beatrice to her rage.

Komodoan numbers were all that was working for them, for every one that went down, from the single open tunnel, two or three more replaced them. Still pulling Beatrice back, with no more grenades, she dropped the launcher and went to her assault weapon. Dante got her no further than the entrance to the tunnel before she broke free and ran after Komodo. Alchymist was hiding behind Komodo at the top of the stairs while he attempted to protect him with the robe and use the exoskeleton to fend off any Special Forces reaching the dais. He knocked three onto the stone floor below. The fighting continued back-and-forth as more komodoans emerged from the tunnel, until a lucky SAM collapsed this. One or two more komodoans emerged from the collapsed tunnel, but they were dealt with by the Special Forces.

With the last tunnel collapsed, what had been looking like a desperate bid to destroy the Komodo appeared almost possible. "Cease-fire," the shout came from the top of the stairway by the dais. Alchymist stepped from behind Komodo and threw back his cowl. At the bottom of the steps, two teams of Special Forces were climbing. But the komodoans had not been listening, and those on the chamber floor pressed the attack. It may have been the last round fired, it may not have; Dante would never be sure. The last one he heard, though, had caught Beatrice in the head, spinning her into his arms. Holding his sister by the shoulders, Dante shook her then he saw the exit wound — she was never getting up.

At the foot of the stairs, Special Forces ceased fire, waiting for Alchymist to make the next move. Captain Bradacz, who had been fighting in the center of the chamber, ordered the others to cease-fire.

Looking around to see who was alive, there were not half the number he had come into the Komodo with. Charles was alive, but he had been twice wounded and was helping Sancho back toward the relative safety of a tunnel. Captain Slank was near the mouth of the second tunnel, slumped against the wall; he was not moving. Sounds became distant and images crisper but blurred as Dante stood and swapped out the rifle's magazine.

Alchymist unbuttoned the top clasp of his robe and let this fall to the platform in the same way Reina had. Still wearing the mask, Alchymist unfastened the straps. Taking the mask in one hand, he dropped this on the stairs. The ceramic shattered in three pieces, and the silence in the chamber deepened, with only the hard breathing of the combatants to be heard. There were no gasps, no laughter, no shouts of disbelief. It had not been what anyone had been expecting, yet it had been what everyone had been expecting. All had decided they knew who Alchymist was, and if they did not know who Alchymist was, many professed to know what he was. The *what* was no longer valid, but the who was about to shake the foundations of the nation.

"I order you to lower your weapons."

"I am arresting you," Charles limped toward the stairs, "for murder, assassination, assault, and sedition." Alchymist took a step back and was in a half-turn when Charles continued. "Arran Hirvola, do not move." Not listening, the PM made for the partially collapsed tunnel. A single round took him in the lower right calf, and he stumbled forward, going down on hands and knees. The Special Forces teams were climbing the stairs. Before halfway up, the PM was on his feet, limping toward the tunnel. Dante stepped forward and prepared to fire.

"Don't," Charles shouted from the center of the chamber as he was disarming the few surviving komodoans. Dante did not listen, and the next round took the PM in the right shoulder. Screaming, he went down but was up almost at once. Dante slipped the weapon onto full auto.

Even as he fired, the PM staggered into the tunnel. As the Special

Forces teams reached the tunnel, they disappeared after him. There was silence then the tunnel rang with weapons fire. This lasted less than a minute. A wounded man exited the tunnel and shook his head: the PM had escaped. "I told you to stop," Charles said, taking Dante by the arm. He motioned toward his sister. "You cannot help her by killing the Prime Minister."

"He isn't the Prime Minister, not anymore — he's just another psychopath, and the Komodo is filled with those."

"Not like him." Captain Bradacz stepped over, a bandage around his face covering his left eye. "He exists in a class alone, and what we need to do to him will have to be public." A shriek came from the ceiling of the chamber — all turned to this. Komodo leapt from the ceiling onto the chandelier, which swung under the weight of his exoskeleton. "Take care of that sergeant," Captain Bradacz said.

The chandelier exploded when the SAM connected with Komodo. Chandelier and victim collapsed to the floor, crushing several other komodoans that had been rounded up. Examining the remains, the sergeant looked up and shook his head. "One less problem to deal with — now, for the PM and his cabinet."

"Minister Bevin and most of the cabinet cannot be responsible for the PM's treason," Charles, now leaning on Dante shoulder, said.

"This was an act of sedition, and until we can decide who was and who was not responsible for it, the entire political class must be treated as an enemy of the state." Captain Bradacz turned and walked away.

17
<hr>

ANOTHER COUP D'ÉTAT

FOR THE NEXT HALF-HOUR, Special Forces cleared the partially collapsed tunnel then spent another half-hour killing off what few of the PM's followers remained. With the flight of Arran Hirvola, the rest of the komodoans lost heart and faded into the deeper, darker pits, tunnels, chambers, and cysts of the Komodo. Charles and Dante were of the opinion they would not hear from the komodoans now the head had been cut off and the arms lay broken on the chamber floor amid the shattered remnants of the exoskeleton. Captain Bradacz was less certain and had the surrounding tunnels mined. "If the captain," Charles meant Daniel Slank, "were still alive, he would not be inclined to blow up tunnels below streets whose load bearing walls are questionable."

"The streets are supported by these walls?" Dante asked.

"Unless we get engineers down here, I have no way of knowing, nor does Bradacz. However, I'm no longer certain the military cares how much damage they do."

"Why?" Dante squatted next to his sister, wrapping her head in a shirt. "If they collapse the streets, won't they be doing more damage to the infrastructure, causing more panic than that madman running around up there?"

"I'm wondering how much of this was the PM and how much military manipulation." Charles folded the young woman's arms over her pelvis and straightened her legs.

"But Bradacz was surprised by everything he saw down here — he may have seen an opportunity when he recognized Hirvola, but before that, it was all shock and awe."

"There was no way the military would've allowed that amount of weaponry and ammunition simply to disappear. Someone, high up, had to know about the theft. Since there were no investigations, I assume they knew where the arms and ammunition were going," Charles laid a hand on the young woman's upper chest, reciting a silent prayer.

"But maybe not what was being done with them," Dante continued the prayer.

"Maybe not, but they would've investigated where the weapons were going and who was transporting them — as you know, the military is particular about its inventory. Perhaps because their tech is all about mayhem."

"Technology?" Dante pushed from his sister's body.

"Yes, that exoskeleton may have been manipulated by Komodo, enhanced perhaps, but there is no way that little man," gesturing toward Komodo's body, "developed the technology down here. I'm not saying he wasn't brilliant, but he would not have the resources and the labs down here necessary to develop such a device. Even if he did, there wasn't the industrial capacity here, nor, I suppose, in the country."

"Perhaps." Dante stepped past the detective to the remnants of the exoskeleton, but a Special Forces sergeant warned him off. "Maybe," turning away from the soldier, "it wasn't made here or the city...maybe not even the country. It had to be made somewhere," Dante's voice trailed off, and he stared down at Beatrice.

"They've cleared the tunnel." Charles motioned with his chin, hands in his pocket and assault weapon dangling from his vest. Another Special Forces lieutenant was waving at the men on the floor to join them. From nearby tunnels came a series of explosions. The

Army had decided not to take any chances and destroyed much of the surrounding area to seal the chamber off from any komodoans attempting to return and reclaim what bodies remained. Dante threw Beatrice over her shoulder and pulled his automatic. Charles looked over at the body of Sancho Korn. "The department will want to take care of the bodies."

"Not Beatrice, our family will take care of her."

"I wasn't speaking of your sister," looking over the bodies of the dead CID detectives. Not one had made it through. "This will take a great deal of explaining."

"To who? If you are right, the new power will not be a civilian government or the police, maybe not even the Intelligence departments." Dante adjusted Beatrice on his shoulder and stepped toward the staircase. Charles followed.

"Command will still want to know what Captain Slank and the rest of us were doing down here with Special Forces, without alerting them." Charles stopped. "Somebody had to be in on it with the PM." Dante turned, looking over the bodies.

"You know who?"

"No, but the military will find out. Until then, I will play it a little fast and loose — if I can get Captain Bradacz to go along." Dante shrugged and turned back to the staircase.

There was an hour in which Dante, Charles, and the rest of the Special Forces had to pick their way through the fallen tunnel roofs. Some of which were exposed to daylight, and large collections of bodies that had resisted the final push, or had nowhere else to go now the PM was dead. "How many of them, do you suppose, knew who Hirvola was?" Dante asked.

"With the PM's reliance upon ritual and disguise, none," Charles said, kicking more rubble out of the way and dancing back as several chunks of ceiling gave way, exposing more of the city. "We better get moving. It's only a matter of time before the rest of these tunnels give way and buildings collapse." The two men picked up their step; as they proceeded to the last of the tunnels, they heard a deep rumble in the direction of the central chamber. A whoosh of hot air and a thick billow of dust washed over them.

"The substratum is giving way," Charles observed, picking up his pace.

"The chamber, at least," Dante spoke through a handkerchief. In silence, the two men proceeded the rest of the way to a central workstation where a steep, spiral staircase wound up the wall. At the top of this, Dante saw the first of the EMTs, accompanied by firemen. The EMTs placed Beatrice on a stretcher. After examining the wound, they looked up. "I know."

"We have to take her to the hospital."

"My sister is dead. There's nothing to be done."

"She needs to be pronounced dead and a death certificate issued." Dante looked to Charles, who shrugged.

"I'm taking her," stepping toward Beatrice's body. The male EMT attempted to block his way.

Dante drew his automatic and placed it between the EMT's eyes. "Step aside."

"Better do it, son. This one, he killed three dozen people easy." The EMT looked from the inspector to Dante then turned away.

"Thanks, in Bornler we're used to doing things for ourselves."

"This isn't over. The PM is still out there." A thundering rumble came from behind and they turned. For the first time, the men realized they were in Sonando, and the rumbling was coming from parliament. It must have been standing over, or close by, the central chamber because half the building was disappearing in a shattering collapse of stone, girders, and glass. There had been no explosion; this was gravity doing its work. It appeared the House of Commons had collapsed into the Komodo, along with much of the administration.

"I'm not leaving Beatrice. They'll take her." Dante motioned to the EMTs.

"Over here," Charles spoke over his shoulder, heading toward a patrol car. Flashing his ID, the inspector demanded the keys. Dante placed Beatrice in the backseat and covered her with a blanket. Charles, meanwhile, had commandeered more weapons, magazines, and two bandoliers of grenades.

"Where are we going?" Dante climbed into the passenger seat.

"If you were a PM on the run, where would you go?"

"He wouldn't be that thick, would he?" The car wound through gaps in the road that opened into the tunnels below, and they swung east then south looking for solid roads. Finding these, Charles followed them as close to parliament as he could. The front of the building and east-wing were gone. To sneak up on parliament, he had to use the back streets. The building would have been under guard at all times, but with the collapse, the guards had either abandoned their posts or been killed.

It had taken the two men a half-hour to reach the building, but even so, survivors continued to stagger from the wreckage. Dante recognized two ministers. Covered in brick dust, sweat, and blood, the two men looked like any other survivors would, if in better suits. Charles stopped both, not to help, but to inquire if they had seen the PM. They had not, but before the building collapsed, there had been a disturbance on the PM's floor. Before anyone could arrive to tell them what happened, the building collapsed, and it was everyone for themselves.

Charles stood at the edge of what had once been a ministerial coffee shop and stared down into the ruins. Broken water pipes were fountaining gray-white into a pit that had swallowed a good half of parliament. Broken sewage pipes mixed their contents in with this, and the stench filled the ruins. There were, along the edges of the pit, survivors: injured, maimed, and dying. Of these, a few were attempting to climb up over the broken pieces of building, road, and sewer. Several had seen Charles and Dante, or others that had not fallen in, and mutely waved for help. "Emergency services will be here soon." Charles turned from the ruins and poured himself a cup of coffee. It was burnt, with the distinct aftertaste of brick dust.

"We need to hurry before Hirvola gets away." Dante opened the door and stepped into the main corridor.

"Don't be in such a rush. We may not get another chance to enjoy a good cup of coffee." Charles sipped at his.

"Smells burnt." Dante leaned back in from the hall.

"It is, but it's coffee, and this may be my last one for a while." Dante leaned on the doorjamb, folding his arms, and waited for the inspector. In the distance were the sounds of emergency vehicles, so many, and moving in a variety of directions, Dante was not sure when they would arrive — and if they did, how many there would be. "This will take days to clean up." Dante tapped the wood jam with the heel of his boot.

"Days? This," waving toward the ruined face of the building, "will take years — if ever."

"What do you mean?" stepping into the room and next to the coffee bar behind which the inspector leaned next to an espresso machine.

"You heard Captain Bradacz."

"Talk, that's all. He's angry about what happened. As for the rest of it — I don't know...things sort themselves out." Finishing his coffee, Charles sat the cup next to the espresso machine, grabbed three pound bags of beans, stuffing these into his backpack. From this, he took two magazines, jamming them into the large pockets of his fatigue jacket, and stepped back to the torn edge of the building. The flooring creaked, and more ceiling tiles collapsed from the floor below, tumbling into the ragged sinkhole and over the people.

"Not this time, but you know that."

"One problem at a time." Dante checked the magazine from his rifle, feeling for the extras in his fatigue jacket. Over this, he adjusted the tactical vest.

"I would agree, but these problems are falling one on top of another." Charles twisted from side to side, loosening his back.

"What do you propose we do — the first I understand is the PM; we've gotta kill him. The second, you're fretting over what the Army will do — but I don't see what anyone can do until they act."

"They've been doing it for some time: playing the PM off the Komodo, letting things get worse until they had the necessary explosion. And we may have provided it."

"We only did what we had to do." Dante stepped into the hall. "Come on. Let's get this over with. That done, you can go back to saving your country."

"Your country, too." Charles followed Dante.

"Those of us in Bornler and the east-side haven't thought of it as our country for as long as I can remember. You can rant about justice, and I can understand, wearing that badge, how you would think that way, but we haven't seen justice in a couple generations. Whoever sits in the PM's office, whether it be a junta or a politico elected by the rich and powerful, it will not matter. Perhaps one could be worse than the other, but there's no way to know which will be which. And to be honest, if that is happening, I doubt anyone on the east-side or south-side would notice the difference. Sonando, west-side, and maybe the north-side, could have their pretty lives fucked up. Us? No one gives a flying-fuck about us. So, keep your justice and do what you wish with it."

Not answering, Charles turned left down the hall then up a flight of marble stairs. The floors, wood paneling, portraiture, and everything else was the same — except the building had been torn in half. "Where are we going?" Dante asked.

"The PM's offices are on the third floor. It's where I expect to find him if he's come back."

"Where else would he go?" Dante knocked dust and mud from his boots as he stomped up behind the inspector.

"Out of the country, at least the city, if he's any sense...but Hirvola's mad."

"Maybe."

"Maybe?" Charles turned, two steps ahead of Dante.

"He was playing some long odds, and he lost. Don't see how that makes him crazy — maybe desperate, maybe unhinged...I'm just not sure crazy's one of them. But then, from my perspective, you're all loopy." The inspector chuckled. He was about to reply when there was a tearing rend from the next floor, and a woman screamed. Charles was on the landing in two strides then running up the last flight. Dante did not know what was going on but kept up with the inspector. At the top of the last flight, he threw himself against the wall next to the corridor.

"What is it?"

"Ramira, it will be all right — stay calm." Charles ignored Dante's question. Remaining on the stairs, Dante slipped to the balustrade. Lying on his belly, keeping the weapon before him, he edged his head forward. Before he could see what was going on, the hallway exploded with light weapons fire. Charles dove for the other side of the corridor, still not firing. There was a roar and the sound of tearing paneling and cracking marble. A man shouted, and a scream followed, trailing off into a feminine shriek. Dante threw himself across the corridor, sliding against the paneling a few feet behind Charles.

There was another series of explosions, not the rending of parliament collapsing into the Komodo sinkhole, but military explosives. The hallway was filled with the smell of high explosive and the dust from the stone torn up by the blasts. Something was moving inside the explosive cloud. Large and clumsy, it ambled away from them. As the dust settled and the cloud dissipated, it became clear what he was looking at. "But we destroyed..." The words died in Dante's mouth as the thing turned.

"He must've had one of his own." There followed another scream from the other end of the hall, not one, but two blending into one.

A body flew from the thin cloud and struck the marble floor to their right. It was not a body but two parts of one. The man's head was turned to Dante and Charles. Once, then twice, the eyes blinked and the mouth worked up and down, but no sound emerged. With one last stretch of the jaw, the mouth ceased moving and the eyes emptied. "Prime Minister?" Charles said.

"Charles, help," the woman shouted. This was followed by a shriek.

"Mr. Prime Minister, please let her go." A thumping mass stepped into view. A robe covered most of the skeleton, and the hood was pulled forward, so Dante could only see his nose and lower chin. From beneath the robe, two clawed feet dug into the marble flooring.

"Back away, inspector." The PM held Ramira out before him, a claw gripping her under the right arm. It appeared the arm was dislocated; each time the monster moved, she whimpered. Her face was raked, the eyes swollen closed, and her nose sat at an unnatural angle with a bump along the bridge. Ramira's lower lip was split; from this, a trail of blood had dried.

"Please, Prime Minister, let my wife go."

"Back away, inspector; when I'm out of the building, I will release her." The PM shook the woman, now only half-conscious.

The Special Forces had arrived and were filling the hall behind the PM. Small arms fire began, and this harmlessly struck the robe covering the exoskeleton. However, when the PM shifted and Ramira's legs flopped beyond the protection of the robe, several rounds took her in the lower legs and knees. Her left knee was blown off, and much of the tissue and sinew was taken with this, so her lower left leg remained connected by a thin strip of flesh. Ramira must have lost consciousness for she did not react. Thick arterial blood pumped from the torn limb. Captain Bradacz stepped forward and threw a grenade before disappearing back behind the PM. The grenade rolled in back of the PM and exploded. This staggered the exoskeleton, and the arm holding Ramira drooped; as the mechanism took a step forward, its claw foot caught her on the other leg.

The PM stumbled forward and overbalanced. Crashing, the exoskeleton landed on the woman's back. Several more grenades rolled around the PM and Ramira. Charles bolted for his wife, but Dante tackled him and rolled toward the staircase. As they tumbled down the first steps, the grenades exploded. Small arms fire followed the explosions, and the tramping of boots could be heard. Charles threw Dante off and clambered back up the steps. Before Dante could make it up these, there were more screams. Throwing himself across the hallway, he slammed against the far wall. In the smoke and debris, he could see the outline of the PM, in his exoskeleton, throwing bodies up and down the hallway.

"Charles...don't..." Before Dante could finish the thought, the inspector had slid to a halt before the PM and grabbed his wife by the collar of her jacket. The monster turned on the inspector and was reaching for him when someone stepped from the office the PM had exited. Charles, with a firm grip on his wife, pulled her from beneath the PM's claws. He had not dragged her more than half a foot when he stopped and looked down. Dante could see the problem. Ramira's body ended below her chest. The inspector knelt over what remained of his wife, staring at the shattered torso. Doing so, the PM was reaching for him when Dante fired at the robe's center mass. The PM did not stagger back but pulled up to his full height in the exoskeleton, which may have been close to seven feet.

The light weapons fire had done no more to the PM than had that of the Special Forces. Though he was favoring his right leg and arm — the grenades may have damaged these. The fire had distracted the PM from what had emerged from the office.

"Arran," the voice called. Dante could not place the voice, but it called again. "Arran, it's over."

"Minister Bevin," Dante took two steps toward Charles, "stay back." At the sound of Dante's voice, the PM wavered.

"This was never going to work. If you had told me at the beginning, I could've shown you why it wouldn't," Bevin said.

"There was no choice. The military have been strangling the country for decades. It was only a matter of time." The PM took a step toward the minister. Before the PM could finish the thought, there was a single shot. Dante thought the minister had been attempting to distract the PM so he could get Charles and run forward.

Taking the inspector under the arms, Dante lifted him in a swinging motion, throwing the two of them down the hallway. The

PM did not turn to the two men. Dante, covering the inspector, rolled further away.

Minister Bevin was standing before the robed figure, a shotgun tucked into his shoulder. Pumping this, he fired again then again and once more. Still, the creature did not move. Dante looked downed at Charles, who was not moving. He feared he had been injured or killed by the PM, but he had not. Charles stared past Dante at the ceiling but did not appear to see this or anything else.

Dante climbed off the inspector and approached the PM, weapon raised. "Prime Minister." No response then a faint tremor ran through the exoskeleton. The left arm of the creature rose, and the claw reached toward the minister, who fired another round into the hooded face of the PM. Then the claw-tipped arm froze as the minister took a step back, and a violent tremor ran through the mechanism. The exoskeleton's feet curled in, digging deep into the marbled flooring, and gravity took hold. The PM and the exoskeleton collapsed forward, landing with a crash, splitting the marble floor. Dust and debris blew out from beneath the fallen mechanism as Dante circled around behind the PM. "He's dead." Minister Bevin squatted over the hooded head of the politician and pulled this back. The PM's face had been reduced to a bloody pulp.

"Drop the weapon," Captain Bradacz said. Dante looked up, thinking the captain was speaking to him, but his weapon was pointed at the minister. Still holding the shotgun in his one hand, Minister Bevin released this. Doing so, two other Special Forces officers ran forward and dragged him into the office. "Thank you for your help, Mr. Skorna. We'll take it from here."

"You were right, Charles." Dante squatted next to the inspector, who was now sitting, staring at the two halves of his wife.

"What?"

"Charles, you in there?" Dante snapped his fingers before the man's face. Charles pushed Dante's hand away.

"I'm here."

"Best we be somewhere else for the time being," he picked the inspector up under the arm, and the two men struggled down the steps. Out back of parliament, the Army was everywhere. There were tanks, armored personnel carriers, and heavy trucks with mounted weapons lining the road. Some ministers were in handcuffs; others were standing to the side, circled by soldiers. "Believe you have your revolution."

"No, only another coup d'état."

PLEASE LEAVE A REVIEW!

If you enjoyed this book, it would be tremendous if you were able to leave a review on Amazon.

Reviews help bring my books to the attention of other readers who may enjoy them.

Thank you!

MORE BOOKS FROM DAVID S. WELLHAUSER

People of the Gate
Skull Island
The Sinister Yogi
The Taklamakan Skull
Darrow House
Dream of Empires Past
The Lunatic Parade
The Bureau of Unexplained Deaths
The Mad Bodhisattva
Blasphemies in the Wasteland
For Love of Monsters
Dr. Chum & the Taoist Terror
The Firingee's Pit
Come Fly the Black
The Wall
Dragon Bone Hill
Beluga Fay
Apocalypse Culture
End Times, Inc.
Fortuna's Bastard
When Dogs Could Talk
The Dog Particle
The Seurat Construct

Follow the link below for info on all my books

ABOUT THE AUTHOR

David S. Wellhauser, over the years, has lived and worked in many countries and traveled in many others. Presently he is an Assistant Professor, in the College of Liberal Arts, at Keimyung University, Daegu, The Republic of Korea.

Mr. Wellhauser has lived in East Asia for many years.

Author of genre mash-ups, gritty Fantasy, Satire, Black Comedy, Crime, Science Fiction, Horror, Mystery, Action, Adventure, Pulp, Noir, Apocalyptic, Post-Apocalyptic, Literary & Dystopian Fiction.

All things dark & twisted find a home in the pages of his books

David has an M.A. (English Literature from The University of Guelph, Canada)

CONTACT INFORMATION

Author Page
https://www.davidswellhauser.com/

Email
cryptobarker@gmail.com